THE NEW WIFE

Also by JP Delaney

The Girl Before
Believe Me
The Perfect Wife
Playing Nice
My Darling Daughter

THE
NEW
WIFE

JP DELANEY

QUERCUS

This edition first published in Great Britain in 2023 by

QUERCUS

Quercus Editions Ltd
Carmelite House
50 Victoria Embankment
London EC4Y 0DZ

An Hachette UK company

A CIP catalogue record for this book is available
from the British Library

HB ISBN 978 1 52943 039 4
TPB ISBN 978 1 52943 040 0
EBOOK ISBN 978 1 52943 042 4

Excerpt from 'When you are old' by W.B. Yeats, first published
in *The Countess Kathleen and Various Legends and Lyrics*, T. Fisher Unwin, 1892.

10 9 8 7 6 5 4 3 2 1

Typeset by CC Book Production
Printed and bound in Great Britain by Clays Ltd, Elcograf S.p.A.

Papers used by Quercus are from well-managed forests and other responsible sources.

THE NEW WIFE

In rural parts of Mallorca, you still come across clusters of carob trees surrounded by high nets, open to the sky. These are *es trampes,* the songbird traps. The farmers coat the branches with sticky lime; when migrating thrushes and other small birds land on them, they get stuck in the lime and, after a few hours of struggle, die from exhaustion, ready to be plucked off the branches next morning.

Roze told me once that they do something similar in Albania. But there, she said, they use 'mist nets' – so called because the mesh is so fine, the birds can't see it; or, if they do, they mistake it for harmless floating spiders' threads. But the aim is similar: to entangle the bird before it fully realises what's going on, so that its increasing struggle to free itself is the very thing that eventually kills it.

The glue and the net. Two different ways of hunting. But, in both cases, the prey doesn't even realise it's being hunted, until it's much too late.

ONE

Let's start with the Old Bastard's death, then, since that's where it all began. Or, to be more precise, with Jess's phone call to me about the Old Bastard's death.

'You sitting down?' she asked when I picked up.

'In bed. That count?'

'Jesus. I've been up for hours.'

I could hear her moving around, folding laundry as she spoke, the phone muffled against her shoulder. 'Your choice to have children,' I said smugly.

'Says the happy singleton. Anyway, I don't know if this is commiserations or congratulations, but I've got some news. Brace yourself. Dad's dead.'

It took me a moment to get my head around that. 'Wow . . . What happened?'

'He collapsed, apparently. Making a bonfire.'

'Not drunk?'

'Hmm.' There was a pause while Jess considered that possibility. 'Probably making a bonfire while drunk,' she conceded.

'Who told you?'

'The wife called me. Ruensa.' She pronounced the name with a roll on the R.

I pushed myself upright. Despite everything, it seemed wrong to be talking about my father's death lying down. 'Was she upset?'

'Well, it happened almost a week ago – my number was stored in his phone, and she didn't have his passcode, so it took her a while to track down my contact details. But it was pretty grim, from what I gather – the ambulance couldn't get up the track from the village, so they had to carry the defibrillator up, then stretcher him down. He was pronounced dead on arrival at Son Llatzer.'

'That must have been horrible.' A thought struck me. 'Should we go out for the funeral? Did she say when it is?'

'It's already happened. You know what they're like there – they never leave it more than a day or two. She was very apologetic about that. I told her we were sad to miss it, but we quite understood.' Jess's voice was dry.

'Are you?'

'Sad to miss it? No. Apart from anything else, that would be a bit awkward, wouldn't it? Meeting your father's third wife for the first time at his funeral.'

Neither of us had been invited to the wedding – a civil ceremony in Palma, just over a year before. We hadn't even known he was in a serious relationship. In any case, I doubted either of us would have wanted to go. We'd both lost patience with him a long time before that, and although he still phoned Jess at Christmas, I'd stopped returning his calls.

'We should write to her, though,' I said. 'I'll definitely write.'

'I guess. Hey, I suppose this means we're rich now.' Jess's voice was studiously casual.

'Technically. Christ, I never expected it to be so soon.'

'I don't suppose you'd want to live there?'

'At the finca?' I snorted. 'I'd rather saw off my hand with a rusty fish knife.'

'Me too.'

Silence. But even over the phone, I could tell what Jess was thinking. Our conversations were often like this – apparently jumping from point to point, seemingly inconsequential, but actually following some deeper train of thought. Children of divorced parents are often close, but children who also shared an upbringing like ours are even closer.

'So, we'll sell it – no point in trying to rent it out,' she said at last. 'What about the wife? D'you think she knows she doesn't get it?'

'Why would she want it? It's falling down. But yes, he must have told her.'

'You think? I mean, it's not the kind of thing that comes up in casual conversation, is it? "By the way, I'm such a failed drunken cheapskate, I couldn't give my first wife a divorce settlement, so my kids will inherit this house instead." Don't forget, he was a total coward, along with everything else.' Another pause. 'Either way, she'll probably have to be reminded.'

Now it was my turn to be silent. Because, much as I love her, there's a side to Jess I find hard and materialistic sometimes. It's a reaction to our childhood, I know. When your parents' lifestyle was so chaotic that sometimes the only foodstuff in the house was a plate of hash brownies; when going to school might be cancelled on a whim because there was a beach party happening in Deià; and when you never knew who was going to be turning up for breakfast until they ambled down the stairs, it was hardly surprising if you ended up craving convention and stability. And Jess had gone full tilt down that path, marrying a banker and putting her kids' names down for a private school.

'We should leave a decent interval, though,' I said, with what I hoped was enough finality to close the topic down. 'We wouldn't want her to feel rushed.'

'What about squatters' rights?' Jess went on as if I hadn't spoken. 'Did you look at that link?'

'I did, as it happens.' About a month before, she'd emailed me an article about squatters in Mallorca taking over empty holiday homes – the rightful owners were almost powerless to evict them, apparently, thanks to Spain's cumbersome civil legal system. At the time, I'd thought it slightly random of her, but perhaps she was making the connection with our father's house even then.

Or *our house*, as I supposed we'd have to start thinking of it.

'So the interval shouldn't be *too* decent, or she'll simply stay,' Jess continued. 'I think you should go out, pay your respects, and politely make sure she knows the house isn't hers at the same time.'

'Jesus, Jess!'

'What? You can offset your carbon emissions, or whatever it is you like to do. Besides, a break might do you good.'

'Oh? Why?' I said pointedly, but she wasn't going to rise to that.

'Mallorca's nice this time of year. The orange blossom will be out.'

'Yes. And the finca will stink of rotting oranges and maggoty unharvested olives. There'll be rats the size of foxes and pine martens the size of wolves.' I had a sudden mental image of the farmhouse the last time I'd seen it – half derelict, the roof gaping at one end, the window shutters falling off, the olive and orange groves a matted jungle of pampas grass, out-of-control oleander bushes and decomposing fruit. It was an imposing property, even a beautiful one – almost what Mallorquíns called a *possessió*, an agricultural estate, the equivalent of an English manor house – nestled high up in the mountains, but it had been empty for several decades before our parents moved in, and many of the repairs that were needed simply never got done. To begin with, it didn't even have electricity; for years our father talked loftily about 'living off-grid', as if it was a trendy lifestyle choice instead of a state of perpetual misery brought about by lack of organisation or funds. Then tourism in the area took off and, for a time, he made a decent income selling his paintings. But with the money came, first, drugs, and then brandy, and while the drugs didn't seem to affect his output much, the brandy certainly did. By the time our mother – a gentle, dreamy soul who almost never stood up to him – finally saw sense and brought us back to England, he hadn't sold a painting in years.

'Well, why don't you ask the lawyer to explain the situation to her?' Jess was saying. 'Then, when you turn up, you can be all, "Hi, I'm your long-lost stepson," and "Sorry for your loss."'

'You have a heart of stone, you know that?'

'I'm not going to pretend I liked him. I'm certainly not going to pretend I loved him.' She was silent a moment. 'I told him I loved him once. I must have been about eleven. I said, "Pa, I love you so much." D'you know what he said back?'

'Nothing nice, I assume.'

'He said, "Oh, don't be so fucking bourgeois."'

I didn't reply. I was remembering when I'd tried something similar – although, in my case, I think it had been a clumsy hug I'd attempted. He'd recoiled and said witheringly, *Why're you acting like a fucking pansy?*

Anyone who thought hippies were all about peace, love and tolerance had never met Jimmy Hensen. Not that he *was* a hippy, exactly – more of a chaotic, dissolute, self-styled bohemian – but more than one person had assumed from his lifestyle and the people he surrounded himself with that he was, only to face a rude awakening when his caustic tongue proved otherwise.

'Anyway, that's another reason it has to be you,' Jess was saying. 'You're better at all that touchy-feely stuff than me.'

I sighed. That much was certainly true. 'What do we know about her? She's a t'ai chi teacher, right?'

'Keep up – that was the girlfriend before. This one's a domestic help. They met when she came to clean the house.'

'Dad had a *cleaner*?'

'Wonders never cease, right? Who knows, perhaps the place isn't quite as squalid as it used to be.'

'Um,' I said. 'The roof needed more than a clean, the last time I saw it.'

'Incidentally,' Jess said, 'I don't think the path of true love was exactly running smooth. I got some texts one night that looked like they were actually meant for her. He called her a bitch. And he was clearly drunk.'

'Oh, great.' The more I thought about it, the less I wanted anything to do with this. In fact, Jess's suggestion that we pass the whole thing on to Tomàs, the lawyer friend who'd drawn up the agreement between our parents in the first place, seemed to me a good solution. But my sister was clearly on a mission, and I knew from experience that now wasn't the time to raise objections.

'It'll be fine,' she was saying. 'And it's only right we meet her – one time, anyway. I told her one of us would go out this week to pay our respects, but I said it would most likely be you as I've got the kids.'

'Oh, thanks, sis. Thanks so much for that.' My previous remarks about Jess's heartlessness had been spoken mockingly, but now I felt genuine anger at the way she'd manipulated me into doing this.

'Do you want to get the house back or not? I just googled unrenovated fincas. They're like gold dust on Mallorca now – even derelict ones fetch around half a million euros. Think what you can do with your half of that. And it's not like we got anything from Mum's side.'

I was silent, but I couldn't help glancing around my room in the tiny flat I rented along with two other people. While it was just like Jess to keep tabs on how much our inheritance was worth, it was also true that selling the finca represented my only chance of getting on to the London property ladder. Our mother was dead, killed prematurely by cancer; but because she'd remarried, what little she'd had passed to her husband. When he died not long after, it turned out he'd left everything to his biological children. I'd been trying to save up for a deposit, but, given my mountain of student debt and maxed-out credit cards, it looked increasingly impossible.

It struck me that Jess and I were technically orphans now. Alone in the world, in a way we hadn't been while one parent was still alive. It was a strange, disorientating feeling.

'I'll go and say hello,' I said at last. 'See what her plans are. But I'll get Tomàs to do the legal stuff before I get there.'

'Coward,' Jess said, happy now she'd got her own way.

'How did she sound on the phone?' In other words, *What am I walking into?*

'Don't worry – she wasn't hysterical or anything. She was . . . sombre, obviously, but perfectly calm. I liked her, actually – she sounded a lot less new-agey than most of them. More down to earth.'

'I feel sorry for her. It's a shitty situation she's in.'

'Oh, come off it. She was married to the Old Bastard. She's probably already realised she's better off without him. Just like we are.' A pause. 'Well, not quite the same way we are, but you know what I mean.'

When I tell people I spent the first fifteen years of my life on Mallorca, they usually say it must have been idyllic. They might even have heard of some of the people my parents hung out with – rock musicians, writers, that dodgy aristocrat who had an affair with a minor member of the royal family. But the truth is, the golden age of free spirits embracing the simple lifestyle of Mediterranean peasants had been decades earlier, and the older ex-pats who liked to sound off about knowing Joan Miró or Robert Graves were usually, when you checked the timelines, spouting bullshit. In any case, the epicentre of the island's counterculture back then was the old fishing village of Deià, where Graves had lived, and by the time my parents arrived, even that was out of their price range. So they went further along the coast, to Cauzacs, a small village clinging to the side of a mountain by the sea. My father wanted to be up high, for the light, but it also meant he got our old finca for next to nothing. The land up there was rockier and less productive than the farms lower down, and the original plan to become self-sufficient had slowly dwindled, just like the terraces themselves as the mountain gradually reclaimed them. And, although we might have looked directly down on to the village, a stone's throw below us, getting there meant either a fifteen-minute drive or a thirty-minute walk along a steep, switchback track. Jess and I spent most of our time hanging out at our friends' houses – ex-pat kids like us, with nouns instead of names: Harmony, Rock, Saffron, Meadow; 'Jess' and 'Finn' aren't our birth names, needless to say – putting off the moment when we'd have to tackle the climb back up to the house. As a group, we felt different from the genuinely Mallorquín children in the village school, but there were enough of us to make a self-sufficient gang, and the other mothers never seemed to mind feeding us, even if was usually just *pa amb oli*, slightly stale bread rubbed with the flesh of a tomato, anointed with olive oil and perhaps a smear of sobrassada, soft Mallorquín sausage.

My father was charming, though. I realise that's something I haven't mentioned yet, my memories of him being mostly bound up with his shortcomings as a parent and husband. (I don't mean that he was unfaithful – like many of the so-called artistic types in Mallorca, my parents had an open marriage.) Women adored him, and he them, at least until he got bored of them. From somewhere he'd acquired a supply of dashikis, African embroidered smocks – I cringe now to think of the casual cultural appropriation – and even after his long mane of hair went white, he cut a handsome, imposing figure, standing at his easel or talking the talk at a Palma opening. He could even be good company when sober, with a childlike sense of fun. But he was so determined not to accept any boundaries for himself, he couldn't see that his children needed some. We didn't even have a consistent language – we spoke English at home, Catalan at school and Mallorquí in the café; something Jess, in particular, struggled with; for a while, she couldn't really hold a conversation in any language.

I only went back a couple of times. Wife number two clearly resented us, and my father was too self-centred to keep a relationship with us going. Our mother talked vaguely about maintaining our heritage, but the truth was, there had been nothing authentically Mallorquín about our lifestyle in the first place, and, after she met someone new, she wanted to erase that part of her life as much as we did. For me, the only legacies of those fifteen years were an EU passport, a slight tendency to stutter when reaching for the correct English word, and a piece of paper saying that, in lieu of our parents splitting the house fifty–fifty on their separation, my father would have the use of it for his lifetime and we'd get it when he died – a deal known as a *usufructo*, not uncommon in Spain, that had been drawn up by Tomàs, a lawyer friend of my mother's, when he heard the Old Bastard was refusing to give her a penny if she, and we, left him. I think Tomàs even had to pay for our flights.

And now I was going back. Despite what I'd just said to Jess, I couldn't help feeling a twinge of curiosity. Not about the OB's third wife – I already knew what she'd be like, my father's partners conforming to an unvarying type; she might be a cleaner, but she'd still be sun-weathered and into yoga and wellness and all the narcissistic pseudo-healthy crap the counterculture had somehow evolved into – but about the place. The finca was where it all went wrong, fifteen years ago, and now I was returning to reclaim it.

TWO

I didn't rush it, though. It was the following Saturday before I flew out. My commitments would have been easy to rearrange – I freelanced for a web-development company, who were happy for me to work remotely – but I wanted to give the wife some breathing space.

Widow, rather. Ruensa. I must start using that name, I reminded myself. Not 'the wife'.

I also wanted to give the lawyer time to speak to her. Despite what Jess had said, I had absolutely no intention of turning up on Ruensa's doorstep and pointing out that it was my doorstep now. That would not only be crass, it might provoke a confrontation, and I was hoping to avoid any excessive emotion, whether anger or grief.

Tomàs didn't think there'd be a problem. 'It's hardly unusual for a man who's remarried to have made provision for his children in his will, and this isn't so different,' he pointed out when I phoned him. 'I'll call her with my condolences and tactfully find out how much she knows.'

'Thanks, Tomàs.'

'But you should be prepared for the probate to take a while. The deed will have to be translated by a forensic translator and witnessed by the *apostille*, then the documents drawn up and signed, and the tax agency has to give approval for the sale . . . I estimate it'll be several months before things are settled.'

'Can you act for us? So we don't have to keep coming out?'

'Of course – that is, I can prepare papers giving me power of attorney, but you'll need to sign them in front of a Spanish notary. We can get the process started, though.' His voice softened. 'Besides, it will be good to see you. Come to the office and we'll have lunch and a proper catch-up, yes?'

'Of course.'

Tomàs was the nearest thing Jess and I had to an uncle. Our childhood had seen a dizzying succession of people coming to stay with my parents – friends, lovers, crashers, acolytes – some of whom stayed for weeks, some months. A few even settled for longer, making jam from our fruit trees to sell in local markets, or offering henna tattoos and the like, until my father informed them that he was bored of them and it was time to fuck off. When they went, some bothered to say goodbye to the kids who'd become attached to them, but many didn't. Tomàs had been one of the rare constants in our life – a cultured, urbane lawyer who hung around the Mallorca art scene because it amused him, but who also became a genuine friend to my mother. I assume they were lovers at some point, since almost everybody slept with everybody else, but he was also a sympathetic ear and a rare source of practical advice.

I was sure, then, that he'd be true to his word and handle the situation tactfully. Even so, I felt a stab of apprehension when, at the airport, waiting for my flight, I felt my phone ring and saw a Spanish number on the screen.

'*Hola?*' I answered cautiously.

A pleasant female voice said, 'Is that Finn?'

'It is, yes.'

'Finn, it's Ruensa – Jimmy's wife. Is now a good time?'

I looked at the clock. I still had forty minutes before boarding – another legacy of a chaotic childhood; Jess and I were always ridiculously early for things. 'Yes, certainly.'

'I got your number from your sister – I hope you don't mind. She said you were on your way to Mallorca.'

'That's right.' We were talking in English, which Ruensa spoke well, but her accent didn't seem Spanish. She might be German, I thought, or possibly Scandinavian.

'Then I hope you are intending to stay at Finca Síquia while you are here,' she said firmly, giving the house its formal name.

'Actually, I've booked a room—' I began.

'No, really, you mustn't even think of it. Jimmy would be outraged if he knew.' The idea that my father would have given a shit where I stayed was almost comical, but I let it pass. 'After all, it's your property, and even if it wasn't, we couldn't possibly let you go to a hotel.'

'That's very kind.' As I spoke, I was mentally processing the fact that she knew about the *usufructo*. There would be no need for a confrontation after all. Relief washed over me. Despite what Jess had said, I wasn't great with that kind of thing – just better than her, which wasn't saying much, and probably only because I was slightly more aware of other people's feelings than she was.

I added formally, 'And Ruensa – I should have said sooner, I'm so sorry for your loss.'

There was a pause. 'I miss him terribly,' she said simply. 'I know he wasn't the best father, and he felt terribly guilty about that – I was gently encouraging him to invite you out here, you know, and I think it was only his embarrassment that was still holding him back. It was his biggest regret, he often said. That, and how much he used to drink. Anyway, that's how I know how much it would have meant to him to have you stay here.'

Unseen by her, I raised my eyebrows – unless my father had undergone a full personality transplant, barely a single word of what she'd just said seemed likely, but it was hardly the time to say so. 'In that case, I'll certainly stay. But just for a few days – I need to sign some papers in Palma, then I'll be coming back to the UK.'

'Then it'll be nice to see something of you while you're here,' she said firmly. 'And we'll scatter your father's ashes together – I thought perhaps at the Torre del Verger, that spot he loved so much. It will be a pleasure to have some family to do that with.' She paused. 'To be perfectly honest, I'm trying to keep busy. So you'll have to put up with being made a fuss of.'

We exchanged some more pleasantries, then she rang off. I was left thinking about that reference to 'family'. Was she going to expect some kind of continuing relationship when all this was over? I hoped not. Apart from a distant cousin, Rachel, who lived as a recluse in Cornwall, Jess and I only had each other – well, Jess had her husband and children, but that was different – and that was the way we liked it.

But the situation with the house was settled, that was the main thing. Of course, we'd have to agree how long she could stay on for – I'd want to be as generous as possible, so at least until the legalities were sorted and the sale had been arranged – but presumably Tomàs could deal with that side of things, too.

Something else struck me. Ruensa had said, *We couldn't let you go to a hotel.* By 'we' she meant my father and her, presumably – the verbal slip of someone who hasn't yet made the transition back to 'I', even though one half of the partnership is dead.

I went and got a bad coffee from an airport café. Twenty minutes later, my flight had just been called, and I was joining the queue at the gate, when my phone rang again. This number, too, was prefaced by +34.

'Is that Mr Hensen?' a male voice asked when I answered.

'It is, yes.'

'Mr Hensen, this is Subinspector Parera from the Policía Nacional in Palma. My condolences on the loss of your father.'

'Thank you,' I said, wondering why the police would need to speak to me.

'Mr Hensen, we need to assess whether a formal investigation is necessary into your father's death. I will need to ask you some questions—'

'What do you mean, "formal investigation"?' I said, surprised.

'When someone has died in avoidable circumstances, the police are always involved,' the subinspector said smoothly. 'At this stage, we're simply gathering the information we need. Do you have ten minutes?'

I looked at the queue in front of me, now moving slowly towards the boarding desk. 'Not really – I'm about to get on a plane.'

There was a short pause. 'May I ask where you are flying to?'

'To Mallorca.'

'One moment.' I heard the phone muffle as he put his hand over it to speak to someone. 'Then perhaps you could come and see us in person,' he said when he came back. 'Would Monday morning be convenient? At eleven a.m.? We are located on the Carrer de Simó Ballester, in Palma.'

'I suppose so, yes.'

'Good. We'll see you then.' He rang off.

Avoidable circumstances. I had a dozen questions about that, too, but clearly I was going to have to wait until Monday to ask them. Jess had mentioned a defibrillator and something about the OB collapsing, so I'd assumed it was a heart attack. Perhaps by 'avoidable' the subinspector had simply meant 'drunk'? Ruensa had implied that Jimmy was drinking less – or, at any rate, trying to. But he'd be starting from a pretty high base. When we were kids, the pile of empty bottles behind the house was so high we named it 'Puig Veterano' – Mount Veterano, after the cheap local brandy.

I messaged Jess:

Spoke to Ruensa. I'm staying in the house – ! And the police want to talk to me about the OB's death.

There was no reply at first. Then, just as we were taxiing and I was about to switch my phone off, two messages pinged in, one after the other:

Re house – good! Possession 9/10ths of the law!
Re police – ha! Maybe the new wife killed him?

THREE

As the crow flies, Cauzacs is only about twenty-five miles from Palma airport – but not even a crow could fly over the Serra de Tramuntana, the mountain range which stretches across the northern coast of Mallorca like a thousand-metre-high wall of rock. Getting there involves a lengthy detour around Puig de Galatzó, the highest point on the western part of the island, which in turn means traversing a tiny coastal road that's Instagram-perfect but not for the faint-hearted, a precipitous series of hairpin bends and sheer drops wound tight between the mountains and the sea.

I'd hired a car, a little Renault Captur; it had four-wheel drive, but still felt terrifyingly tinny as I nursed it round the corners. Accelerate ... brake ... change gear ... turn. Occasionally I spotted a griffin vulture, drifting around the pale limestone crags above me; sometimes an oncoming coach or lorry forced me into the side of the road, or I had to tuck in behind a line of cyclists, ant-thin in their Lycra and streamlined helmets, as they whizzed downhill. Mostly, though, this northern side of the island seemed deserted, the only sign of life an occasional fishing boat on the sea far below. Of death, though, there were plenty of signs – the pine woods had been ravaged by forest fires in recent years, and for mile after mile, the trees had been reduced to endless blackened stumps the height of gravestones.

Cauzacs came into view some time before I reached it – a cluster of houses clinging to a distant cleft in the mountain. Below and above the village, ancient terraces were carved into the hillside for agriculture, so that the lower part of the mountain resembled a giant wedding cake. There was meant to be a tradition that every son added another level to those farmed by his father. Needless to say, it had been many generations since any owner of Finca Síquia had bothered to maintain its terraces, let alone add to them. Nor were they the only ones to have neglected the custom – I could see at least a dozen places where the wedding cake's layers had collapsed in huge spillages of stone and earth. There were more of these breaches than the last time I visited, just as there were more patches of blackened forest. The whole place had an air of gloomy decay to go with its mountainous grandeur.

Yet, in the village itself, nothing had changed. The same handful of small hotels that doubled, out of season, as cafés and bars. The same bakery, the same furtive white-and-ginger cats padding through the empty streets, the same thickset Mallorquín mastiff hurling itself at my tyres as I turned up Carrer de sa Síquia. To my left, a dusty snake whipped along the road. It was a horseshoe, over a metre long, but not venomous, unlike the smaller false smooth snakes we got on the finca – whenever she found one, Jess would get me to deal with it; she loathed snakes, and, for all that our parents bleated about living in harmony with nature, I think they did, too. I was amused, rather than alarmed, to note that this particular specimen was actually going faster than I was. Even in second gear, the little car was struggling with the gradient.

The road got steeper still. Visitors often doubted a car could get up it at all; more than one lily-livered hippy had chickened out halfway up – though, since they couldn't turn round, doing that meant they were effectively stuck. Half a mile out of the village, there was a junction where a rocky track headed into the pine trees. It looked picturesque, and passable enough; it was only after a short while that you realised you now had to deal with ridiculously tight bends, an impossible gradient, and a loose surface, all at once. But the knack was in knowing the terrain as much as anything else, and although the Renault slipped and skidded, I never actually went backwards.

And then the house came into view.

There's something about going back to the place where you grew up – some looping of space-time that goes on in your head. I felt so many contradictory emotions – familiarity, revulsion, homesickness, regret. But most of all, a sense of waste, for the needless harm that was done here.

To my surprise, I saw the roof had been mended. Jess's words came back to me: *Who knows, perhaps the place isn't quite as squalid as it used to be.* Last time I was here, the deterioration had looked terminal. But perhaps marriage number three had finally prompted my father to take the place in hand.

I got out of the car and headed for the door we always used, on the back veranda. If I'd been surprised by the roof, I was amazed by what I saw when I came around the corner. The views had always been incredible – the mountains stretching away to the east and west, a series of barren, rocky crags gleaming pale grey in the sunshine. But views were all there'd been, and the jungle that had once been the finca's fields had reached right up to the house. As a kid, I used to fancy that the ancient olive trees, their twisted trunks dumpy from earlier generations of hard pruning, were a legion of old women, frozen into statues by some magical enchantment; when the olive flies laid their eggs in the unharvested olives, it was as if they were buzzing around the women's unkempt hair.

But since my last visit, the place had been completely transformed. The scrub of pampas and oleander had been banished, the olives harvested, the new growth pared back. Where once there had been nothing but weeds, now there was neatly raked earth. The oranges, too, had been picked – all except the late-ripening navels, which were hanging fat and thick on the branches. The avocado bushes were pendulous with fruit, the figs had been pruned, the prickly pears uprooted. And, next to the house, the lemon tree glowed with healthy yellow fruit, so different from the diseased, overripe objects I recalled.

In the distance, I caught sight of a small tractor reversing up to an almond tree, a figure in blue overalls at the wheel. So the OB had even employed some help.

As I went along the veranda, there was a further surprise. In the days when he was still painting, my father had used the old olive press as a studio. Between it and the house was a *cisterna* – an ancient irrigation tank, perched right on the edge of the steep drop down to Cauzacs. When the temperature hit forty degrees, we children used to plunge our limbs in it for coolness, ignoring the fact that its black depths were teeming with warty Mallorquín toads. But all that had changed, too. The tank had been turned into a small but pretty swimming pool, complete with decking and infinity edge. The cement liner was painted a dazzling cerulean blue, and the water was clear and sparkling in the sunshine.

It wasn't just that it was so unlike my father to want a pool – he used to sneer at them as symbols of Mallorca's supposed deterioration from authentic artistic hideaway to mass tourist destination: *Look at those idiots. Why d'you need a pool when you've got the fucking sea?* It was the cost. Together, the pool, roof and tractor must have cost tens of thousands of euros. Where had he found that kind of money?

Oh, God. I groaned inwardly as I wondered if he'd married it – traded in his charm for an easy life with some rich widow.

But then I recalled Jess telling me that Ruensa was a cleaner. Why clean houses, if you were wealthy enough not to?

Anyway, I'd soon find out. 'Hello?' I called through the open door. '*Hola?*'

Silence.

I stepped inside. Here, too, everything had been transformed. To my left, in the high-ceilinged kitchen, the old butcher's blocks had been scrubbed and bleached, and the floorboards patched and sanded. The walls – once covered with my father's awful erotic frescos – had been painted sky blue, the ceiling ochre; it was a combination that probably shouldn't have worked, but did. From the wooden beam that ran the width of the room hung strings of dried ramallet tomatoes, the essential ingredient of *pa amb oli*. The whole thing looked like something out of a style magazine – everyone's dream of a chic and simple Mediterranean bolthole.

'Finn?' a woman's voice said.

I turned. She'd come down the stairs without me hearing, and was standing in the hall with an expectant smile. I had a brief impression of a slight, dark-haired woman in her early fifties – I'd been debating how to greet her, and had decided a hand clasp was probably appropriate for a first encounter, perhaps accompanied by a formal peck on both cheeks, but she immediately swept me up in a hug. It was only when she stepped back again, still beaming, that I got a proper look at her.

'You must be Ruensa—' I began.

'Please, call me Ru,' she interrupted. 'You're so like your father!'

I was surprised at that – I'd never been aware of any resemblance. 'I'm so sorry we're meeting in these circumstances.'

She waved my condolences away with a brusque, almost fierce gesture. Clearly, she didn't want to discuss that. 'You're here. That's the main thing. Welcome back to Finca Síquia!'

'I hardly recognise the place.'

She smiled proudly. 'You approve?'

'It's incredible.'

She looked around. 'Jimmy chose the colours, of course. His eye – amazing. But it was me who made him throw everything out. When I first saw it, this was a dump! But we got it sorted in the end.'

She was a bundle of energy – every sentence laden with emphasis and accompanied by fierce nods and smiles. She gave a sense of always being in motion – when she turned to gesture at the walls, she whirled like a ballerina; when she looked back at me again, her eyes widened, as if she'd chosen me to be the recipient of some great secret.

'It's so kind of you to have me,' I said. 'I really would have been fine at a hotel.'

Again, she waved the words away, screwing up her face at the very thought. 'I've put you in the *caseta* – the guest house. I hope that's all right.'

'The *caseta*? You mean the olive press?'

She saw my expression and smiled. 'Yes, but it isn't like you remember. Come and see.'

She led me outside, to my father's old studio, and pushed open the door. It had always been light in there, thanks to the big doors on the far side, but it had also been a mess, a jumble of rusting farm equipment and half-built canvases. Now, the opening where the big doors had once been was glazed, the stone walls were painted cream, and it had been transformed into an elegant, airy bedroom suite – there was an old four-poster with a simple canopy of white netting, a ceiling fan tucked high up in the beams above it, rugs, a wood-burning stove. Behind the bed, they'd kept the battered internal wall, but it had been sanded down and waxed to reveal the grain of the wood. Beyond it, I could see a stack of thick white towels. There must be a bathroom back there, too.

'Again, amazing,' I said, and meant it. 'Ru . . . I'm just full of admiration for what you've done here.'

She laughed – a low bubbling laugh that was almost a chuckle. 'We were going to open it on Airbnb this summer. The hiking here is incredible.' She gestured in the direction of the mountain. 'The trails go all the way to Esporles.'

I nodded. It actually made a lot of sense – the finca might be forty minutes from a decent beach, but the flipside was that it was very close to the mountain. When I was a kid, few tourists bothered with the GR221, the trail that followed the old smugglers' paths from one side of the island to the other, but I'd heard that, in recent years, hiking it had become quite popular. And, since most trail accommodation consisted of simple mountain refuges and cells in monasteries, the finca's lack of luxuries such as air conditioning shouldn't pose too much of a problem.

One wall of the *caseta* was dominated by a painting – I recognised my father's style, although I hadn't seen anything so good by him in decades. It was of Ruensa, sitting in an old leather armchair. Her head was turned towards the light, her chin propped on her slender fingers, staring out at Puig de Galatzó. But it was the figure standing next to her, looking directly at the viewer, that drew my eye. A young woman – tall, slender, her long hair tumbling around her shoulders, her eyes dark as olives.

'Who's that?' I asked.

Ruensa looked at the picture approvingly. 'Roze. My daughter.' She turned. 'Ah, Roze! Come and say hello.'

A tall, slim figure in blue overalls was passing the open door – the same figure, I realised, that I'd seen driving the tractor.

The young woman in the painting.

She stopped. 'You must be Finn. Hi. I won't shake your hand – I'm filthy, I need a shower.' She waved, then pushed her hair back from her forehead, which was damp with sweat. 'I'll say hello properly later.'

She was gone. But already, in that instant, something rather wonderful had happened.

FOUR

If I describe Roze, I don't want to give the impression that her
appearance was the only thing that drew me to her – that brutal
swipe-left, swipe-right objectification that has so trivialised
relationships for my generation. In fact, Roze wasn't even con-
ventionally photogenic – her features were almost childish, with
large lips and slightly chubby cheeks, a quality exacerbated that
first time I saw her by the absence of make-up, the shapeless
overalls and her unkempt hair. But, even on that brief encounter,
there was something about her – a wariness, a bruised quality. It
may sound ridiculous, but she reminded me of a pine marten I
once taught to come to me for food. And yes, perhaps it was also
seeing her for the first time in that place, with the finca looking
as it did – an idyll, a little paradise among the mountains. A part
of me was fourteen again, eager to lay my heart at the feet of any
girl who would have it.

Not that there was any question of laying my heart anywhere near Roze, of course. While I was certainly aware of how
attractive I found her, and the little jolt of pleasure her smile of
welcome had given me, I knew it would be deeply wrong, given

the circumstances, to behave in any way that could be construed as inappropriate. So I kept my voice formal and my expression blank as I called after her, 'Of course. See you later.'

'And I'm afraid I must also leave you, for a little while.' Ruensa was twirling a car key on her finger. 'I'm cooking *arròz brut*, but I forgot to get wine, and we need bread as well. I have to pop down to the village.' Again, I wondered at her accent – the slight push of her lips on 'pop', so that it came out 'pupp'. Her dark features didn't seem Scandinavian, either. Not Swedish, I decided. Greek, perhaps, or Turkish.

'I'll go,' I offered. 'I want to say hello to Alejandro, anyway.' Alejandro was one of my *quintos*, my year group from school – a true Mallorquín, he'd lived in Cauzacs all his life, and inherited the village café when his father retired.

Ruensa demurred, but I insisted, and, twenty minutes later, I'd unpacked my few things and was negotiating the track again in the other direction. I glanced at the clock on the dashboard. The café would just be reopening after its afternoon break. It would be good to see my old classmate, but even more interesting to find out what the village thought of the situation at Finca Síquia. They would certainly have an opinion – *xafardejar*, gossiping, was the Mallorquín national sport, and the Cauzacis quietly had their views on every incomer – and I was curious to find out what it was.

'The best thing that ever happened to him,' Alejandro said, pushing back his coffee cup. 'Your father might have been an idiot, but he knew a good opportunity when he saw one. Apparently, she said she'd only move in with him if he stopped drinking and cleaned himself up. Three months later, they were married.'

I nodded. 'The finca looks incredible.'

Alejandro gave me a sideways look. 'I expect you know where the money came from.'

'Vaguely,' I said, hoping he'd fill me in.

'People say it must have been a loan, given that she was cleaning houses before, and your father never had any cash.' He paused. 'The finca actually belongs to you and your sister, doesn't it?'

I nodded, not surprised that he knew about the terms of my parents' divorce. So we were inheriting a debt as well as a house. Or were we? My knowledge of Spanish law was sketchy, but I had a vague idea that a bank loan, if that was what it was, might have to be paid off at death. Another problem to be dealt with by Tomàs, perhaps.

'I heard they were planning to turn it into an agroturismo,' Alejandro added. 'Your father was going to give art lessons, she was going to cook . . . Everyone's doing it, these days.'

'And the daughter? What do people say about her?' I said it casually, but again Alejandro gave me a shrewd look.

'I don't think many people have set eyes on her. I hear she's a looker, though.'

'Not by your standards,' I said lightly. 'You're married to Aina. I heard you had another baby, by the way – congratulations.'

He smiled and went on, 'They've mostly kept to themselves since they moved in, the daughter in particular. It's always the

mother who comes to the village to buy bread. Miquel can probably tell you more.' He nodded at someone behind me.

I turned. A short, stocky man in a tattered sleeveless shirt was
standing at the bar, a cortado in front of him. I recognised him
as the farmer who worked the terraces below us.

While Alejandro served another customer, we exchanged
nods.

'Been a while,' Miquel said tersely.

'Four years.'

He grunted. 'Sorry about your father.'

I shrugged. 'Thanks.'

'Finn was asking about the women,' Alejandro called over.

'They've made a few improvements to the place,' I offered.
'About time, eh?'

Miquel turned his head and made the gesture of a man spitting,
although he didn't actually do it. 'They might be the first round
here, but they won't be the last.'

'First what?' I said, puzzled.

He gave me a surly look. 'Illegal immigrants.' He threw the
rest of his coffee down his throat, slapped some money on the
bar, and left.

Alejandro gave me an amused look. 'Some things never change,
do they? Including Miquel's sunny disposition.'

'What did he mean, about illegal immigrants?' I asked.

Alejandro shrugged. 'Beats me. We've had a few Moroccans and
Algerians landing here recently. They generally abandon their
inflatable boats on the south side, then disappear – the people
smugglers hook them up with gangmasters on the tomato farms.

But they're young men, mostly, looking for work. Nothing like your two.'

I nodded. Like everyone, I was aware of the number of migrants trying to get into Europe. I'd made donations to organisations working to improve conditions in the refugee camps on the Greek islands, where thousands of people were still living in shipping containers and tents. I'd clicked on petitions to stop the EU from getting other countries to do its dirty work, turning boats back before they ever reached Europe's borders, or forcing them to cross shipping channels at night, in lethal, overcrowded inflatables, to avoid Frontex's patrols. But, as Alejandro said, the number who came to Mallorca was tiny by comparison.

'What nationality are Roze and Ruensa?' I asked.

Alejandro shrugged. 'You know what it's like round here – people are from so many places, you don't even think about it. Not unless you're someone like Miquel.'

He went off to serve another customer. He was right, of course – what did it matter where they came from? But something made me get out my phone and tap 'Ruensa', 'Roze' and 'origin of names' into the browser. It took a few goes, because of the different ways 'Roze' might be spelled. Nor was I quite sure what it meant when I discovered that they were most likely not Swedish, nor Greek, nor Turkish. Ruensa and Roze were almost certainly Albanian.

FIVE

'Part of some organised crime gang, you mean.'

'Jesus, Jess – talk about jumping to conclusions.' *You're as bad as Miquel*, I wanted to say, although in fact Miquel might well be right – if they were Albanian, it was possible that Ruensa and Roze had been staying in Spain illegally, or at least on expired short-term visas – whereas Jess's prejudice was far more irrational.

I softened my tone. 'Look, people tend to connect the words *Albanian* and *crime* in their heads because of lazy media headlines. There must be literally millions of Albanians who are completely law-abiding.'

'True. But they're not generally the ones who leave Albania, are they?'

Exasperated, I shook my head, even though she couldn't see me. 'Honestly, Jess – if you'd actually met them, you'd realise how ridiculous that is. They're nothing like anyone's preconception of a migrant – they're charming and cultured and incredibly hard-working. They've completely transformed the place. Alejandro says Ruensa was the best thing that ever happened to the OB.'

'I'm sure. But the reverse is also true, don't forget. By marrying him, she got Spanish residency.'

I sighed. I was leaning against the car, at the point where the track to Finca Síquia joined the road. It was no longer the only place you could get a signal, as it had been fifteen years ago, but it was still the most private. 'Maybe you should come and meet them.'

Even as I said it, I was hoping she wouldn't – the idea of subjecting Ruensa and Roze to Jess's hostile cynicism filled me with dread.

'I told you – I can't leave the kids.' She thought for a moment. 'But it's great they've done the place up. It'll make it much easier to sell.'

'When it comes to that. But if there *is* a loan, we'll have to pay it back, don't forget.'

'Will we? Is that what Tomàs said?'

'I haven't spoken to him about it yet. But we obviously couldn't expect Ruensa to go on servicing a loan Dad took out to improve *our* property.'

'Hmm. I guess not.' Another silence. 'Which is interesting in itself, isn't it? She gets the OB to take out some kind of mortgage – which is probably illegal, by the way, since he didn't actually own it – *ostensibly* for the purposes of doing it up, and then, a short while later, he's dead. Has all the money been accounted for?'

'Sis, now you're really being paranoid. She knew all about the house situation, remember? That means she definitely had no motive to want him dead. Why put all that money and effort into doing the place up, then bump off the only thing that's keeping her there? It wouldn't make sense.'

'OK . . . but are we absolutely certain she knew about the house before Tomàs talked to her? Perhaps his phone call was the first she'd ever heard of the *usufructo*. Before that, she might have been assuming she'd inherit everything.'

'That wasn't how it sounded to me. Besides, they clearly adored each other—'

'Not true,' she interrupted. 'There were those texts I told you about, remember? What if, before they got married, she'd only seen sober OB – so drunk OB came as a total shock?'

I sighed. 'Again – that wasn't how it sounded. And it's unfair to judge a whole relationship on the basis of a couple of texts.'

There was a short silence.

'Even so, I think you should double-check with Tomàs about what she knew and when,' Jess said with finality. 'Preferably before you speak to the police, so you can tell them what he says. Have you told Ruensa that they want to talk to you?'

'No,' I admitted.

'Maybe keep it that way? I was joking when I messaged you before, but something about this whole set-up seems really off to me.'

SIX

Despite what she'd said about seeing me later, Roze wasn't around when I got back – as I was to discover later, she had a desk in her bedroom, where she worked on the remote-access degree she was doing. Instead, I found Ruensa in the kitchen, preparing *arròz brut*.

How to describe *arròz brut*? A soup, a stew, a paella – it's all of those and more, a dish that has as many recipes as there are cooks on the island. It's called 'dirty rice' because it used to be made with pig's blood, which turned the rice grey, but these days it's usually coloured with saffron, if you're being fancy, or tomatoes, if you're not. The mother in the village who mostly fed us, Julie Fincher, used vegetables from her garden, plus whatever meat was cheap at the butcher's that week – pork rib, rabbit, oxtail – or, if it had rained, she'd send us kids out to collect snails, and we'd spend the rest of the afternoon blanching and winkling out their insides. But the smell, somehow, was always the same: an aromatic melange of cinnamon, pimiento, cloves and garlic, the incense of my childhood.

Ruensa was using rabbit. She'd skinned it herself – the discarded fur and carcass were still lying by the sink.

She saw me looking at it. 'It gives me double pleasure to cook a rabbit at this time of year,' she observed. 'First, when they're young, they're even more tender, and second, it's one less mouth eating our vegetables.'

'You shoot them yourself?' I said, surprised.

She swept the bloody skin and carcass into a waste sack. 'Roze does. She has better eyes than me.'

I was surprised by that, too, although I said nothing. A memory came back to me – my father deciding that, as a boy, I was too soft, and hauling me out to shoot partridge. He'd been drunk, of course, and failed to hit a single one, while for my part, I'd been careful to aim wide.

I blinked, and the memory was gone. But, just for a moment, the finca seemed once again full of his presence. The household had always been coloured by his moods; his silences could be as fearsome as his rages, and even when he was upstairs, sleeping it off, we all tiptoed around, trying not to wake him.

While Ruenza prepared the vegetables – artichokes, broad beans and peas, which she told me proudly were all grown on the farm – I opened the wine I'd bought in the village. Then, since the pile of beans was a large one, I reached for a bowl and quietly started podding beside her.

Picking up on my introspective mood, Ruensa glanced at me. 'This must bring back memories, Finn.'

'Yes. But not of this particular kitchen. My mother . . . I'm not sure she'd have known one end of a bean from the other.'

'Well, there are many ways of being a good mother,' she said tactfully.

I didn't reply to that.

Eventually, she spoke again, her voice quiet. 'Has anyone told you yet how he died?'

I glanced at her, but her eyes were fixed on the artichoke she was now cutting the heart out of. 'Not really. Jess mentioned a defibrillator, so I assumed—'

'It wasn't a heart attack,' she interrupted. 'Not to begin with, anyway, although the doctors think his heart may have given out as well. He poisoned himself on a bonfire.'

I stopped what I was doing and stared at her. '*Poisoned* himself?'

She nodded. 'He'd been clearing the oleander – there was a great wall of it in among the fruit trees, some bushes that had got out of control. He wore gloves and a long shirt to cut it down, but when it came to burning it . . .' She shrugged angrily, and lifted one arm to dab at her eyes with her wrist.

I thought. Oleander was everywhere in Spain, and, while it was undeniably beautiful, every Spaniard also knew how deadly it was. Eating even a single leaf could be fatal, and there were many stories of people poisoning themselves, like the one about the Boy Scouts who'd used oleander twigs as barbecue skewers. Inhaling the smoke could be lethal, too. Was it really possible my father hadn't known that?

Ruensa looked at me desperately, her eyes glinting with tears. 'We don't have it where I come from. I didn't realise it wasn't safe.'

'Was he drunk?' I said quietly.

She gave a little snort of disgust. 'Apparently. I didn't know that either, not at first. He never told me when he was drinking.'

'Because he'd promised you he wouldn't,' I guessed.

She nodded. 'When we found him . . . I thought that was what it was. He'd fallen over, and his eyes . . . He couldn't focus. I thought he was *pissed*.' She gave the word a savage English pronunciation, and for a moment I heard the Old Bastard's voice in hers. 'So you see . . . it was my fault. I should have known. I should have called the ambulance sooner. I could have saved him.' She gave a great strangled gulp, and then suddenly her composure was gone and she was wailing, almost shrieking, all self-control abandoned as she turned away from me to hide her distress.

'Mama?'

It was Roze, coming into the kitchen. She'd changed from the overalls into a dress – I wondered if that was for my benefit, and felt flattered. She looked from her sobbing mother to me – not angrily, but with resignation, as if to say that what I was witnessing was not uncommon – then gently led her away.

When Roze came back, a few minutes later, she was carrying the knife Ruensa had been using. Without a word, she picked up where her mother had left off.

'Does that happen a lot?' I asked quietly.

She nodded. 'But not as much as it did. It's a different kind of sadness now. To begin with, she was in shock, and then there was the funeral to organise . . . It was after that when it really hit her he was gone. What it meant.'

'She mustn't blame herself.'

Roze glanced at me. 'Tell her that, would you? I think, coming from you, it would mean a lot.'

'Of course,' I said, pleased to be entrusted with this small responsibility. 'But I should tell you – my father and I weren't particularly close. To be perfectly honest, I didn't even like him all that much.'

'I know,' she said simply. 'But you're still his son. She was so happy you could come and be with us . . . It's almost like having a little bit of him, to console her.'

I felt a sudden stab of guilt at the realisation that, while Jess and I had been thinking only of how quickly we could cash in on our inheritance, my father's wife had been struggling with this crushing burden of grief. How mercenary we had been – were still being.

I resolved then and there that I must do nothing shameful. Jess would just have to lump it. This simply couldn't be rushed.

'It must be difficult for you, as well,' I suggested.

Roze looked at me – I got the sense she was trying to read me, to make a judgement about what sort of person I was.

'Yes,' she said simply. 'Not in the same way, of course. But he made Mama happy, and I was grateful to him for that. And the way he welcomed us both here – it made a huge difference. To our situation, I mean.'

I wondered what she meant by that, and was trying to frame a question that wouldn't sound too prying, when she turned back to the vegetables, and the moment was gone.

'How have you found living at Finca Síquia?' I asked instead.

Roze reached for the peas, deftly running her thumbnail along the seam of each pod to tip out the green pellets. I noticed that her nails were short and unpolished, her hands and fore-arms criss-crossed with scratches from working on the farm.

Although her attention remained fixed on what she was doing, she smiled as she answered. 'I think it's the best place in the world.'

'It didn't always seem that way to me,' I muttered.

'But then, it wasn't yours.' She realised what she'd said, and corrected herself. 'I mean, because you were a child and couldn't decide what to do with it. For me, it's been different. When I suggested we get a tractor and try to bring the farm back to life, your father backed me completely.'

'That was your idea?' I said, surprised. 'I'd assumed it was your mother's.'

She shook her head. 'Mama did the house – she's brilliant at it. But the outside is mostly me. And your father, of course – he helped with the fruit picking. We had a plan to be certified organic. Or even biodynamic. That would be a big draw to the kind of guests we want to attract.'

'I'm not really sure of the difference between the two,' I confessed.

'Organic still uses chemicals, but only ones that are naturally produced,' she explained. 'Biodynamic is a whole philosophy of improving the ecosystem – putting nutrients back into the ground so you don't need chemicals, farming in harmony with nature, creating solutions from within the farm itself.'

And shooting rabbits, I thought but didn't say. Hadn't I read somewhere that rabbits on Mallorca had recently been given protected status, because they'd already been hunted so much? How harmonious was that?

But then, I was hardly an expert.

Roze was still talking – this was clearly a passion of hers. 'To be certified as biodynamic, we'd need to set aside a certain percentage for biodiversity, and encourage natural predators rather than use pesticides, even organic ones. It's about treating the land as a living, breathing organism. There's so much possibility here. I want—' She stopped abruptly, and scooped the vegetables into the pot. When she spoke again, her voice was quiet. 'But of course, it's not for me to say. You may have other ideas.'

'My sister and I don't have any plans yet,' I lied. 'Really, we haven't thought about that side of it at all.'

Ruensa came back fifteen minutes later, by which time the vegetables, rabbit and rice were all in the pot, simmering. She was back to her former self, brisk and bubbly, and full of apologies for getting so emotional. 'I hate falling apart in front of people,' she exclaimed. 'Really, it's ridiculous.'

Of course I told her there was nothing to apologise for – grief was natural and she must express it when she felt it, not bottle it up. And I added gently that it was also natural to blame oneself when someone died, but that I knew my father wouldn't have blamed her in the slightest – he was never one to blame anybody, much less someone he loved, and I was certain he would have said his death was just a tragic accident brought on by – if anything – his own belief that he was invincible. More than that, he died in the place he loved, married to someone he clearly adored, and he would have had nothing but thanks for everything she had done for him.

Ruensa's eyes filled again, tears not of grief this time, but gratitude and relief, and my reward for these bullshit words of absolution was a quiet nod and a half-smile of thanks from her daughter.

SEVEN

Finn to Jess, 23:10:

Sis, the more I think about this, the less OK it feels to chuck them out of their home Xx

Jess to Finn, 23:14:

Huh? Why? Tempted to just say grow a pair but you clearly have your reasons x

Finn to Jess, 23:16:

It's the amount of work they've put into the place. They had a plan – a low-impact biodynamic agroturismo. I think it could have worked Xx

Jess to Finn, 23:17:

BIODYNAMIC? Since when did you buy that crap???

Finn to Jess, 23:25:

I don't – but enough people do buy it to make it viable as a tourist proposition. Maybe we just let them rent it from us? Xx

Jess to Finn, 23:26:

With what? That's really naive. Besides, I need this dosh. School fees don't grow on trees x

Finn to Jess, 23:28:

Well, be prepared to be patient

Jess to Finn, 23:28:

Oh? ETA?

Finn to Jess, 23:30:

I can't see them wanting to leave any time soon, if I'm honest

Jess to Finn, 23:32:

MY POINT EXACTLY. They're going to have to be eased out eventually, so the sooner you tactfully start the process, the sooner it'll be done x

Finn to Jess, 23:40:

Just doesn't feel right. Why should we get everything and they get nothing at all? When – let's face it – they loved him and we didn't?

Jess to Finn, 23:44:

PRECISELY why. Recompense for all the years of no running water, broken promises and drunken verbal abuse. I need to go to sleep now xx

Finn to Jess, 23:48:

Ruensa cried over me earlier

Jess to Finn, 23:51:

Bet you hated that (probably why she did it)

Finn to Jess, 23:51:

Don't be so cynical. Turns out they adored each other

Jess to Finn, 23:52:

Did they though? Forwarding those texts I told you about. Stay safe. And resolute, please. Night xx

Jimmy to Jess, 21 February, 04:29:

>>*If you will not be a WIFE to me then what isthe point?*

Jimmy to Jess, 21 February, 04:30:

>>*You get EVRYTHING and I get 0*

Jimmy to Jess, 21 February, 04:30:

>>*bitch*

Jimmy to Jess, 21 February, 04:31:

>>*sorry too much*

Jimmy to Jess, 21 February, 04:31:

>>*brandy*

EIGHT

I woke early. Across the valley, cockerels were bragging to each other in the half-light. As the sky brightened, dogs joined in, their barking gradually subsumed into the rich, almost orchestral soundtrack of a Mallorquín morning: distant goat bells, braying donkeys, the occasional deep quack close by that sounded like a duck, but which, I knew, was actually a frog. When I was young, those sounds would have been supplemented from about six onwards by the rasp of generators, but it seemed everyone had mains electricity these days. At seven, the church bells in the village started.

I lay in bed, wrestling with my thoughts. Not over the texts Jess had forwarded – after the build-up she'd given them, if anything they'd been an anticlimax. All they showed was that the OB was drinking again, and Ruensa had already said as much. My real worry was that Jess was being so inflexible. I was determined not to make Ruensa and Roze feel pressured to move out, but I couldn't think of any alternative. Jess was almost certainly right that they wouldn't be able to afford a market rent – places like the finca, now it was done up, cost thousands of euros a week; tens of thousands, in high season. And then there were the transfer taxes Tomàs had explained we'd be liable for, and the loan that had reportedly paid for the improvements . . . How could those debts ever be paid off, unless the finca was sold?

Most of all, though, I would have loved to have thought up a solution and taken it to Roze with a flourish, like a gift; to see those solemn dark eyes light up with gratitude and relief. I wanted her to understand that I was a decent, moral person – yet how could she possibly think that, when my actions were effectively lumped in with Jess's? When I told her what our real plans were, she was going to be devastated. Not to mention homeless, and quite possibly stateless, too.

I hadn't been the one to bring up their immigration status, the previous night – I'd wanted to keep our first meal together casual, rather than look as if I was interrogating them. It was Ruensa herself who'd raised it.

'Of course, you know your father saved us from being deported,' she said matter-of-factly, as she cleared the plates.

I feigned surprise. 'Oh?'

'We're from Albania, which isn't part of the EU. But it isn't recognised as being dangerous enough to meet the usual tests for refugee status. Even though parts of the country are effectively run by criminals now, and if you get on the wrong side of them, nobody can keep you from being killed.' Her eyes met Roze's over the table. 'We had no choice but to leave everything and get out.'

I saw Roze give a slight nod, as if to reassure her mother she was right.

'What happened?' I said. 'If you don't mind my asking.'

'We came up against someone very powerful,' Ruensa said quietly. 'It was made clear that, if we didn't do what he wanted, we'd be in serious danger.'

Again, she glanced at her daughter, and I wondered if what the powerful person wanted had been Roze.

'We couldn't go to the people smugglers – they'd have taken us straight to the same man we were trying to get away from,' she continued. 'So we decided to get on a flight, then claim asylum. At the time, Spain had a reputation for treating refugees fairly. We took the first Iberia flight we could, and by chance it came here, to Mallorca. And in some ways it *is* better than in other countries. Six months after you've applied for asylum, you're allowed to work, which isn't the case everywhere. The catch is, non-EU qualifications aren't recognised here, and, even if they were, there aren't many jobs for college professors who don't speak Catalan very well. Particularly when the person hiring finds out you're Albanian.' She gave a wry shrug. 'We're not very popular in the rest of Europe, I've discovered.'

'You're a professor?' I echoed.

She nodded. 'I used to be. But here, I became a cleaner. Which was fine – at least I was doing something. I'd have gone mad sitting around, living on handouts.'

I glanced at Roze. 'What about you, Roze? What did you do, before?'

She hesitated. 'I was doing a post-grad. An MBA.'

'And now?'

'I'm still doing it, but online. And before I came to the finca, I did bar work in Magaluf, on the Strip.'

'That must have been grim.' Magaluf was the main destination in Mallorca for cheap package holidays and stag weekends, and the Strip – the unofficial nickname for Punta Ballena – was its throbbing, neon epicentre: a heaving mass of sunburnt teenagers, bikini-clad bar touts and bouncers in stab vests.

She shrugged. 'It was all right. But nothing like what I do here now, on the farm.'

'And then our asylum applications were rejected,' Ruensa went on. 'We hadn't realised, but to claim asylum, it isn't enough to be in fear for your life. Unless the danger is directed at a whole group, like your religion or ethnicity, it doesn't count. We appealed, but that was mostly just to buy time.' She was silent a moment. 'Then I met your father. It was at an art exhibition, in Palma. He told me he'd got this house in the hills he wanted to renovate . . . I took one look at the place and fell in love with it. Like a sleeping beauty, waiting for someone to hack through the bushes.' She smiled at the memory. 'It all started from there.'

So the house had been the lure the OB had used, I realised. He'd never shown any sign of wanting to do it up before. I felt a surge of anger towards him, for leaving this unresolved mess behind.

But even through my anger, I suddenly realised what Ruensa had said. *Fell in love with it.*

Not *him.*

But presumably that had come later.

Getting out of bed, I went to the wooden shutters that kept the sunlight from streaming through the big studio windows. I started to open them, then stopped.

On the far side of the pool, Ruenza and Roze were doing yoga. Roze's dark hair was tied back with a scrunchie. She was wearing black leggings and a loose tank top, but you could see from her movements how lithe and wiry she was. Both women performed the routine with synchronised fluidity – it was clearly a well-established ritual. Like the walls of the house behind them, they were washed with buttercup-coloured light from the morning sun. It was an image tailor-made for an Airbnb page: *Finca Síquia before breakfast.*

I watched for a few moments, then turned away, a little ashamed of my voyeurism. I gave it another five minutes, then emerged. By then, they were nowhere to be seen.

NINE

I found them in the kitchen, still in their yoga leggings, talking in Albanian. When they saw me, they stopped.

'Forgive us, Finn – we should stick to English,' Ruensa said with a smile. 'What would you like for breakfast?'

I said I could easily get my own, but she insisted, and once again – remembering how she'd said she liked to keep busy – I allowed her to ply me with food. Roze ate too, a plate piled high with omelette, avocado and slices of salchichón. I was amazed how much she put away, given how little there was of her, but then I remembered that she was doing manual work all day. Besides, the food was delicious. The eggs came from the old hippy woman up the hill whose cockerel I'd heard that morning, Ruensa told me, and the salchichón was from a family butcher in Sóller.

Ruensa leant against the stove with a coffee and watched us. 'Do you have a girlfriend, Finn?' she asked conversationally.

'Mama,' Roze groaned. 'You can't ask that.' She gave me a look, as if to apologise for her mother's directness.

I shook my head, smiling. 'That's all right. Actually, I don't, not right now. I just broke up with someone.'

'Why? What went wrong?'

'*Mama!*'

I said slowly, 'I think I probably wanted more from the relationship than she did.'

Ruensa nodded thoughtfully. 'You know, Jimmy told me something of your childhood here. He made it sound beautiful, but I think perhaps it wasn't always so easy. When the adults behave like children, sometimes the children have to become the adults.'

'Mama's subject is psychology,' Roze said, with a roll of her eyes. 'I'm afraid you're going to get a lot of this.'

'He also told us you used to tame the rats,' Ruensa added.

I shook my head. 'Not rats. Almond-eaters – they're rodents, but more like gerbils or hamsters. I used to find their nests and take one of the babies as a pet. But I never had a proper cage, so they always ended up escaping. And I had a pine marten once – I found her as a kit, with a broken leg, and taught her to come to me for food. She lived in the house with us, for a while.'

Until my father tired of her one day and chased her out with a broom, I thought, but didn't say out loud.

Ruensa gave me a look – the same appraising gaze her daughter had directed at me the night before, when we were preparing vegetables. Then she smiled and nodded, as if something had just become very clear.

'Well, I'm sure you won't be single for long,' she said firmly. 'You have your father's good looks. He was a rascal, of course, but so charming.'

A rascal. It was not the word I would have used to describe him.

*

After breakfast, Roze announced she was going to look for asparagus, which my father had told her grew wild on the farm at this
time of year. I offered to show her the best places.

She looked surprised. 'You know where it grows?'

I nodded. 'You have to understand, we were almost feral.
Anything we could pick and eat, we did. I'll just get my shoes.'

When I came out of the guest house, she was waiting for me.
She'd pulled a couple of oranges from the nearest tree, and we
peeled them as we walked. They were still cool, the flesh sweet
and refreshing.

'These will need to be picked soon,' she said, glancing up at the
laden branches. 'Then the peaches, then the apricots, then the
figs. And so on, until we get to the olives and it all starts again.'

'Proper old-school Mallorquíns don't pick their olives,' I said.
'They let them fall to the ground and scoop them up. That's why
our oil's so strong – it's actually overripe. In most parts of the
EU, it wouldn't even be legal to sell it.'

'I didn't know that.'

I gestured at an olive tree. 'And the reason the branches are
pruned so high is that they used to plant wheat under them, as
a summer crop. Which is why wild asparagus is also known as
wheat asparagus – it usually grows round the edge of the field.
Yes, look – there's some.'

I knelt down by a thorny, prickly plant and carefully parted the
branches. In the centre were half a dozen thin sprouts.

'Ah!' Roze breathed. Crouching down next to me, she pulled
out a knife. As she sliced the shoots off, her bare arm brushed
mine. I was suddenly very aware of her closeness – I could see the

slight fuzz of dark hair on her forearms and smell the shampoo she'd used that morning.

She must have become aware of it, too, because her voice, when we stood up again, was a little formal. 'How come you know so much about farming, Finn?'

I shrugged. 'Most of my *quintos'* parents were farmers. And I hung out in my friends' houses a lot.'

'Finn?' she said quietly.

'Yes?'

She looked at me squarely. 'Have you come here to throw Mama and me out?'

'No!' I protested.

'Then why *have* you come?'

I hesitated. 'I have to deal with some legal stuff. To do with my father's probate and so on.'

'Before you can throw us out.'

I started to protest again, and she stopped me.

'No – it's all right. I mean . . . the finca is yours; of course you must do what you want with it. It would just be good to know what your plans are, when you have some. But please – when you're ready to tell us, speak to me, not Mama. She's fragile enough at the moment, and I think being told she'll have to find somewhere else to live so soon will be devastating for her.'

'I understand,' I said. And then, because I felt bad not telling her more, I added, 'My sister – Jess – thinks she needs the money from selling up. For school fees.'

'I thought schools in England were free.'

'Some of them are,' I admitted.

Roze nodded. 'And you? What would you spend the money on?'

'Well . . . I share a small rented flat. In London.' I nodded at the fields around us – the house, framed by fruit and olive trees, with the sea far below in the distance, the sunlit mountains at our back. 'It's nothing like this . . . but if we did sell, my half would probably buy me a flat quite like the one I'm in now.'

She frowned. 'So you wouldn't actually gain anything? You'd move from one flat to another?'

'Yes . . . but it would be mine.'

'Oh, I see.'

We were both silent.

'Mama and I used to live in an apartment,' she added. 'In Gjirokaster, near the university.'

'What happened to it?'

'After we left, she got a friend to sell it for her. We had to give the friend a commission, so we only got four million lek for it – about forty thousand euros. But that's what paid for the improvements here.'

'Oh . . .' I said. 'So there wasn't a loan?'

'A loan?' She frowned. 'Not so far as I'm aware. And I wrote the business plan, so I think I'd know.'

'Right . . . And the money your mother put in . . .' I paused, unsure how to phrase this. 'Was it a gift, or was there some kind of legal arrangement?'

Roze looked at me steadily. 'Mama's old fashioned. After she married your father, she'd have thought anything that was hers was his as well.'

She didn't say, *and vice versa*, but the words hung in the air, unspoken.

'Of course. We'll have to find a way . . .' I stopped, suddenly aware of the need not to make promises I might not be able to keep. 'I mean, clearly, all that will have to be taken into account. I don't know exactly how yet . . . It's not like I can just write you a cheque, not before probate's settled, anyway.'

'It's very kind of you to think of us at all. Given that we don't even know each other.' Was there a hint of sarcasm in her voice? No, I decided, I was imagining it.

'Roze, look . . .' I took a deep breath. 'This is a difficult situation, isn't it? For all of us. But I want to do the right thing, I really do.'

She nodded. 'I know. And I think you will, Finn. Whatever that is.'

TEN

We picked asparagus for another twenty minutes. Even though it was only March, the sun was hot – or perhaps I was simply unused to it, after an English winter. I'd forgotten, too, just how sharp wild asparagus thorns could be. Neither of us had thought to bring gloves, and our arms were soon covered in scratches. I noticed how Roze didn't seem to mind. Even when a particularly sharp spine dragged across her forearm, she only muttered a mild '*uff*' under her breath.

'Let me see that?' I asked.

She held out her arm. The soft skin above her wrist had laddered like a stocking, and a few beads of blood, tiny as currants, fattened along the length of the scratch. There were half a dozen other scratches, too – the older ones I'd noticed the night before. Some had dried blood in them.

'We should get that washed,' I said. 'These spines can be infectious.'

'Oh, I'll be fine.' She pulled her arm away.

I looked at our haul of asparagus. 'Even so, we've probably got enough. Shall we head back?'

She nodded, and we walked back towards the house. As we passed the swimming pool, I said, 'Would it be all right if I used this?'

'Of course. But it's not heated. The water will be cold for a month or so yet.'

'I don't mind.'

She gave me a mischievous glance, and for a moment I thought she was about to say something else. Instead, she said, 'We got your father some swimming shorts, though I don't think he ever used them. I'll see if Mama knows where they are.'

Inside the house, we met Ruensa, coming downstairs with a pile of clothing in her arms. Roze explained what I needed and Ruensa said immediately, 'I've got them here.'

The clothes she was holding were all my father's, I saw. It seemed very soon to be sorting them – he'd only been dead a couple of weeks. But then, she'd said she needed to keep busy, and I could see how the same restless energy that had transformed the house would make it hard to put off any task that needed to be done.

'Here,' she said, handing me the pile. 'This is everything I thought worth keeping. I've washed and ironed them, of course.'

'Oh,' I began. I was about to say that I didn't want any of the OB's things, and certainly not his clothes, but then I saw Roze's expression, and read the message in her dark eyes.

'Thanks so much,' I said.

Ruensa beamed. 'I'm sure he would have liked to think of you having them.'

As I took the pile of clothes, I saw Roze give her mother a tiny nod. Of agreement with what she'd just said about my father? It seemed more meaningful than that, somehow. I wondered if it was about me – our conversation in the fields. Was Roze signalling that I was someone she approved of? That she thought we would ultimately be able to deal with this situation in a civilised way?

Or was it something more – some kind of go-ahead or acquiescence, the answer to a question I hadn't been privy to?

I took the clothes back to my room, then went for a swim. The water was cold, but no colder than the sea in England, and refreshing after the heat of the fields. I swam a couple of lengths underwater to immerse myself, and came up for air, gasping.

It took me a moment to realise that, immediately in front of me, there were two bare feet. Roze was standing on the decking.

'Mama forgot to give you this, Finn.' She put down a towel, then turned and walked away.

'Thanks.' I pushed the wet hair out of my eyes and watched her go. I wondered if she'd been watching me swim, just as I'd watched her doing yoga earlier, and, if so, for how long.

We ate lunch on the veranda – the asparagus, simply boiled and served with a little lemon juice, accompanied by slices of bread and oil. Then I went back to the guest house, from where, a little reluctantly, I called Jess. We hadn't actually spoken since Ruensa told me how the OB died – information that Jess was predictably horrified by.

'I don't believe there's a single person in Mallorca who doesn't know to be careful with oleander. And I find the fact that she's feeding you up deeply creepy.'

'She's not feeding me *up*, Jess. She's feeding me. There's a difference.'

'And she just happens to have selected the dishes of your childhood to do it with. Honestly, you can be so naive sometimes. She's messing with your mind, bro – trying to associate herself with all the happy afternoons at Julie Fincher's, in the hope of a nice fat pay-off. And that's another thing – she knows how to cook Mallorquín staples like *arròz brut*, but doesn't recognise the most poisonous shrub on the island? I just don't buy it.'

'Maybe the OB didn't like Albanian food, and she learnt the local recipes to please him.'

She sighed. 'Have you actually spoken to them yet about moving out?'

I thought for a moment. There'd been that conversation with Roze in the fields. 'I've mentioned it to the daughter.'

I tried to keep my voice neutral, but Jess knew me too well.

'How old is this daughter?' she said sharply.

'Mid-twenties, I'd say.'

A pause. 'Bear in mind she's technically your stepsister, won't you?'

'What's that supposed to mean?'

'You know.'

I didn't dignify that with a response. In any case, I'd just noticed a hoopoe bird bobbing about on the veranda, and I was wondering if it might be about to display its plumage.

Then I saw something else. At the far end of the orange grove, near the boundary with the hippy woman's property, there was a flash of reflected sunlight. A pair of binoculars, turning in the direction of the finca.

'Sorry,' I said to Jess, who was still talking. 'I think there's someone on our terraces. What did you say?'

'I said, let's not make this any more complicated than it already is.'

'Well – obviously,' I retorted, a little frostily. I could see who it was, now – a couple in their fifties, the woman clutching those absurd ski-pole sticks that are meant to signal serious hiking, as opposed to mere walking. The man had a map in a plastic pouch hanging from his neck. As I watched, he pulled a small notebook from his pocket and made a note. Birdwatchers.

There was a movement on the veranda. Roze was running along it in a low crouch. In one hand, she carried a small shotgun – I recognised my father's .410 – and, in the other, a backpack.

'I've got to go,' I said to Jess.

I went outside. Roze was already halfway across the orange grove.

'Roze!' I called urgently. 'Roze!'

She stopped and looked at me.

'It was a birdwatcher.' I gestured at the veranda. 'There was a hoopoe.'

She looked at the spot where the birdwatchers had been. 'Are you sure?'

'Certain.'

She scanned the area for a few seconds, then came back.

'Who did you think it was?' I asked as she passed me.

'We had some oranges stolen last week,' she said shortly.

I was left staring after her. A shotgun? To deal with someone helping themselves to a few oranges? It seemed unlikely. Besides, it hadn't looked to me as if she was going to accost someone. The gun, the packed bag – it looked much more as if Roze had been about to run away.

ELEVEN

The next day, after breakfast, I phoned the lawyer, Tomàs.

'Finn!' he said warmly. 'How nice to hear from you. Are you calling to arrange our lunch?'

'Partly. I'm actually coming into Palma this morning – the police want to talk to me. We could meet after that, if you're free?'

'Of course. Shall we say my office, at two? But I'm curious to know what the police might want with you.'

'I think it must be because of the circumstances of my father's death.' I explained about the oleander, and how Ruensa hadn't known it was dangerous. 'That's the other reason I'm calling, actually – Jess thinks the police might ask how much Ruensa and Roze actually knew about my father only having the house for his lifetime, and since it was you who spoke to them . . .'

'Ah. I see what she means. It was your father's widow I spoke to – Ruensa. And, yes, she knew all about the *usufructo*.'

'Right,' I said, relieved. It was ridiculous, but some of Jess's paranoia had been rubbing off on me, and it was good to know she'd been wrong. 'Did Ruensa say when my father told her? It was before they got married, I hope, so she knew what she was signing up for.'

'We didn't get into all that. I just expressed my condolences, and said presumably she was aware that possession of the house would now revert to your sister and you. And she said yes, she was. It was a very short call.'

'Hang on a minute,' I said, alarmed. 'So it was actually you who mentioned it, rather than her?'

'Well, yes. I could hardly wait to see if she brought it up. Why?'

I said slowly, 'Because I suppose it's theoretically possible that was the first time she'd heard of it, but she didn't want to say so and look as if he'd kept it from her.'

'She didn't sound at all surprised,' he assured me. 'She just asked if there were any papers to sign, and I said I'd be in touch again after I'd taken instructions from you. It was all very civilised. I'd be happy to say so to the police, if you need me to.'

'Thanks – I'll bear it in mind.' What Tomàs was saying made perfect sense. Of course Ruensa would have sounded surprised if the information about the house had come as a shock, so the fact that she hadn't was a pretty good indication she'd known all along.

But it didn't make it impossible. And if she'd been quick-witted enough to grasp the other implication immediately – that knowing about the *usufructo* absolved her and Roze of any obvious motive for murder, since it meant my father's death, far from making them rich, was going to make them both homeless and penniless – she might have also decided it was better to make it look as if it was something she'd always been aware of.

74

But no one was that quick-thinking, surely. Particularly when they were still reeling from the sudden death of their partner.

Something made me add, 'And Tomàs ... did you mention that I'd be coming out to Mallorca personally to deal with the paperwork?'

'I imagine I probably did. Why?'

'No reason.' One could overthink these things, I decided.

At eleven, I presented myself at the police headquarters in Palma, and was shown into an interview room where two men were waiting. Both wore the blue shirts of the Policía Nacional. The older of the two introduced himself as Detective Subinspector Parera, and his colleague as Detective Officer Castell.

Once Subinspector Parera had established that Jess and I hadn't had much contact with our father in recent years, he asked how well I knew Ruensa and Roze – or, as he called them, 'The señora and señorita from Albania.'

'I met them for the first time on Saturday,' I said.

Parera gave me a look. 'And do you have any concerns that you want to make us aware of?'

'What kind of concerns?'

He lifted his hands. 'As I understand it, your father knew this woman for only a few months before they were married. Sometimes, that kind of thing can cause difficulties in a family.'

'Not in this case.'

'So you have no suspicions that the marriage was in any way ... irregular?'

'*Irregular?*' I echoed.

'Sometimes migrants get married for reasons other than love.' The subinspector pulled a face, as if to say it was a wicked world. 'And sometimes those who marry them have other motives, too. But you have no concerns.'

'If you are suspicious of them purely because of their nationality,' I said hotly, 'that would be outrageous.'

The two policemen regarded me curiously.

'Were you invited to their wedding?' Officer Castell asked.

I shook my head. 'I told you – we weren't particularly close. It was just a simple town-hall affair, as I understand it.'

'And would you happen to know if their relations were that of a normal husband and wife?' Subinspector Parera paused. 'For example, whether they shared a bedroom . . . ?'

'So far as I'm aware, their marriage was extremely loving,' I said through gritted teeth. 'Though I haven't inspected the bed sheets to make sure.'

There was a short silence.

'We have established that a substantial amount of money passed through your father's bank account soon after the wedding took place,' Officer Castell said. 'Do you by any chance know the source of those funds?'

I almost laughed out loud. So that was what this was about – they thought my father might have accepted a pay-off in return for a marriage of convenience. 'I do, as it happens. It was from the sale of Ruensa's apartment in Albania. As for where it went, they were doing up the finca in order to rent out rooms.'

'Had they applied for a touristic rental licence?' Parera looked almost annoyed that there might be a simple explanation.

'I've no idea. But they used the money to repair the roof and put in a swimming pool – it's pretty self-evident those were their plans.'

Castell said, 'We've obtained a copy of your father's will from the registry. He left everything to his new wife, we understand.'

'Possibly, but he had almost nothing to leave. The house and land are already owned by my sister and me. My father only had a *usufructo* – a lifetime interest.'

The two policemen exchanged glances. Clearly, this was news to them.

'My father was an abusive, boorish drunk,' I added. 'He tried to clean himself up when he met Ruensa, but he failed. I can see why you're suspicious that a woman with as much to offer as she has would marry a man like him, but, honestly, I don't think there's anything sinister about it. Or, so far as I know, about his death.'

Subinspector Parera gave me a curt smile. 'I'm happy to hear it.'

'Unless, of course, there's something you're not telling me,' I added.

'We're awaiting more detailed toxicology reports – the samples have been frozen and sent to a specialist laboratory in Valencia,' Parera said. 'We will obviously inform the next of kin if they reveal anything further. Or if we have any more questions.' He nodded to indicate that the interview was over.

'And what will happen after that?' I asked as I stood up. 'Will they be able to stay in Spain?'

'Well, that is the fortunate thing,' the subinspector said. 'For his widow, anyway. Because Señora Hensen was married to a

Spanish citizen for exactly twelve months, she is now able to apply for continued residency on matrimonial grounds.'

'Except that my father wasn't a Spanish citizen,' I pointed out.

Subinspector Parera shuffled his papers together and slid a paperclip over them. 'You are mistaken, Señor Hensen. Your father applied for citizenship shortly before his marriage.' He nodded again. 'Thank you for coming in.'

'It just wasn't like him,' I said, baffled. 'My father would have hated having anything to do with something as official as an application for citizenship. He loathed all bureaucracy with a passion.'

Tomàs tucked his napkin into his shirt. 'People change – your father more than most, it seems. He was getting married, after all. It's a natural time to take stock. And, yes, it probably was prompted by a desire to make sure his wife would be looked after if he died before her. He couldn't leave her his house, but he could ensure that she had residency and, ultimately, Spanish citizenship. Why not? It's what I would have advised myself, if he'd been my client.' He sat back and regarded me steadily over the rim of his wine glass. 'And there was nothing else in what the police told you to arouse any suspicions?'

I shook my head. 'It was clearly a fishing expedition, prompted solely by Ruensa and Roze's nationality and their status as asylum seekers. It seems everyone wants to believe the worst of them.' I felt myself getting angry all over again on their behalf. Subinspector Parera's suspicions had almost bordered on racism. 'I've a good mind to make a formal complaint.'

'Prejudice is a terrible thing,' Tomàs agreed. 'But even so, it may not be a bad idea to take some simple precautions.'

I frowned. 'What do you mean?'

'While I don't have any reason to share your sister's wider concerns – or Subinspector Parera's, for that matter – Jess makes a good point, in one respect: this matter of them living at the finca with no formal agreement in place. I think I should draw up a simple waiver for them to sign, stating clearly that no tenancy has been established, and that they are staying there purely as a goodwill gesture during your father's probate. Once that's done, and I have power of attorney, you should be able to return to the UK and do the rest from there.'

I winced. 'Signing a legal document . . . Is that really necessary?'

'I hope not. But look at it this way: why would anybody object to signing such a waiver, if they accept the truth of what it contains?'

'It just looks a little . . . *untrusting* to ask them to.'

Tomàs looked at me steadily. 'As a lawyer, I can tell you that problems in families rarely arise because people have been clear and open with each other. They tend to occur precisely because people have relied on trust and assumption. And, as your sister has pointed out, we really know very little about them.'

TWELVE

I drove back to Finca Síquia in an uneasy mood. For perhaps the first time in my life, I was seeing up close how people's distrust of outsiders affected their perceptions of them. Increasingly, I felt it would be up to me to see that Ruensa and Roze were treated fairly.

Jess, had she been at the police interview, would undoubtedly have shown them those texts, and told them there was no cast-iron evidence that Ruensa had known she wouldn't inherit the house. Subinspector Parera might then have used that information to open an investigation. Which was ridiculous – but if he'd made Ruensa a formal suspect, that might in turn have impacted on her application for residency. And all because of the country where she happened to have been born.

There was also the problem of the money she'd put in. Tomàs, when I'd asked him, had frowned and said it was a grey area – although the actual phrase he'd used had been the more evocative Catalan expression, *una zona d'ombres*, a place of shadows.

'If she chose of her own free will to put her capital into improving the house and its surroundings – a house she apparently knew would never be hers – she has no claim on that money

81

now,' he explained. 'The tractor is different, as that's a possession rather than part of the house. Of course, you may decide you want to make some kind of ex-gratia payment in acknowledgment of her contribution, but, as your lawyer, I should emphasise that it would be purely discretionary and there is absolutely no obligation on your part . . . Do you suppose they kept receipts for the work done?'

'Knowing my father, it's highly unlikely. And it seems a bit petty to start demanding that kind of thing now.'

Tomàs nodded. 'Well, whatever you decide is appropriate, you may find it easier to deal with once you are back in the UK and no longer under the same roof. Or, of course, you could instruct me to do it.'

'She asked me to tell her to her face,' I found myself saying.

'Who? Ruensa?'

'No. Roze. And I said I would.'

Tomàs raised his eyebrows. 'Even so, you are under no obligation to. And again, it might be better to do it after they have signed something clarifying the situation, rather than before. Just in case it causes any awkwardness.'

As my car neared Finca Síquia, I found myself experiencing a mixture of emotions. On the one hand, there was no doubt that I should really tell Roze as soon as possible that the house definitely had to be sold – a conversation I was hardly looking forward to.

On the other hand, I felt my spirits lifting at the thought of seeing her again.

I would tell her the next day, I decided, so that I could enjoy a few more hours of her company before disappointing her. But Tomàs was right: first, I must mention this document he wanted them to sign.

I found them in the kitchen, frantically pulling saucepans and brushes out of cupboards.

'What's going on?' I asked.

'Oh, Finn.' Ruensa stood up, clutching a dustpan. 'Thank goodness. Roze has scorpions in her room.'

'A whole family of them,' Roze confirmed.

'I would have squashed them with a broom, but Roze wants to try to move them somewhere else.'

'May I see?'

'Of course.'

Roze led the way upstairs, with Ruensa bringing up the rear. She had the room Jess used to have, at the front of the house. But where Jess had had to make do with a tatty mattress on the floor, now there was a brass double bed in the middle of one wall, an old dressing table next to the open window, and a huge antique wardrobe against the wall opposite. Just like the downstairs rooms, the effect was sparse but somehow effortlessly stylish. And feminine, too. The dress Roze had worn on my first night was hanging up by the window, boogieing slightly in the breeze, and there were some popsocks and a bra draped over the bed.

'There,' Roze said, pointing to one corner.

I crouched down. Almost invisible against the cream-coloured floorboards, a small male scorpion – ghostly white, with crablike front pincers – was guarding his mate and four babies.

'They're Balearic scorpions,' I said. 'The venom does hurt a bit, but it isn't dangerous for most people. Would you like me to move them for you?'

'Please,' Roze said with a shudder.

I pointed at an empty shoebox. 'Pass me that, would you?'

Roze handed me the box. Putting it on its side, I gently shooed the smaller of the adult scorpions inside.

'If you start with the mother, the babies should follow, and then the male will follow his mate,' I explained.

We watched as the rest of the scorpions all did exactly as I had predicted. Roze looked suitably impressed. 'That's amazing!'

I stood up. 'I'll put them near an ant's nest. Then they'll have enough food not to need to come back.'

By the time I'd found a suitable spot and gone back inside, Roze and Ruensa were in the kitchen again. Ruensa was opening a bottle of wine.

'That was so brave of you, Finn!' she exclaimed.

I shrugged modestly. 'It's nothing, really. I got used to dealing with them as a kid. Though it's unusual to find them on the first floor – they don't usually get upstairs.'

'And your trip to Palma?' she asked. 'How was that?'

'Oh – it was fine, thank you.' Of course, they'd known I was seeing Tomàs, and that it was connected to the probate, but I hadn't told them I was also seeing the police. I decided to keep it that way for the time being. 'By the way, the lawyer is drawing up some papers for us to sign.'

'Of course,' Ruensa said, just as Roze said, 'What kind of papers?'

'Just to acknowledge that . . .' I stopped, unsure how to word this. 'That you're not actually the owners here.'

'That we're squatters, you mean.' Roze sounded angry.

'No,' I protested. 'He's just trying to—'

'Protect you. In case we refuse to leave. Like those scorpions just now.'

'Roze,' her mother said gently. 'If it helps Finn, of course we'll sign his papers.'

Roze stood up, her eyes blazing. 'I've got a better idea. We'll just go. Then we'll be out of his way.' She turned to me. '*You* can harvest the oranges. *You* can water the avocados. Or you can let it all fall down again, the way it was before we came.'

She strode out. I heard her feet on the stairs, then the sound of her bedroom door noisily closing.

I turned to Ruensa, a little taken aback by the sudden change in her daughter. 'I'm sorry. I probably didn't explain that very well.'

Ruensa gave a thin smile. 'She's been worrying about what will happen to us. Perhaps it really would be simplest if we left. I can still get work cleaning—'

'No!' I said. 'I won't hear of it. Please, Ruensa, this situation is complicated enough. We'll work it out, I promise. I'll go and speak to Roze.'

But when I knocked on Roze's door a few minutes later, there was no answer.

THIRTEEN

'I feel bad.'

'Why do you feel bad, bro?'

'I think I've offended the OB's wife. And her daughter.'

'Tell?'

'Tomàs is drawing up a document, as you suggested, to clarify that they don't have any actual rights to the house. I mentioned it to them, and . . . it didn't go down too well.'

Even over the phone, I could sense Jess's ears pricking up. 'Ah! So they *were* planning on staying.'

'No – not at all. Ruensa said straight away that she'd be happy to sign. But they both separately said it might be simpler if they just left.'

'Really?' Jess sounded surprised. 'Good work, bro. Job done.'

I sighed. 'Of course, I told them not to.'

'Why?'

'They were upset. Besides, there's a right way and a wrong way to do this.'

There was a pause while Jess considered this. 'So what's the right way?'

'Unfortunately, I haven't figured that out yet.'

Phone to my ear, I wandered over to where I'd hung up my father's clothes. Ruensa had even taken his wardrobe in hand, I'd discovered – in place of those awful African smocks, here were elegant linen shirts in shades of raspberry and sky blue; polos, shorts and chinos, all washed and neatly ironed.

I felt one of the shirts. The linen was thick and soft between my fingers. The beginnings of an idea began to form in my mind.

'When do you come back?' Jess asked.

I said slowly, 'Tomàs thinks I should stay out here.'

'Why?'

'Oh, you know – boots on the ground. If I'm here, I can keep a proper eye on things.'

'Well, he's right – particularly if they're being touchy. And you're really happy to?'

'Not *happy*, obviously. But I think it's probably the only way.'

'What about your things? You only packed for a few days, presumably.'

'I'll just have to wear some of the OB's clothes.' A phrase came back to me: *borrowed robes.*

'You'll cope. And, bro? Thanks. I owe you one. Love and kisses.' She rang off.

I wondered why I'd lied to her about Tomàs. It wasn't true that staying on Mallorca had been his suggestion – quite the reverse – and usually Jess and I were straight with each other, no matter how brutal the truth. But the fact was, I didn't want her speculating about my real motives for staying on at Finca Síquia.

FOURTEEN

That night, I dreamt of Roze – that she slipped into bed beside me, her body still damp from her shower, her limbs soft and urgent as she writhed against me. I woke up, gasping, and felt disappointment that it had only been a dream.

In the morning, I woke again, and wondered if I had really dreamt all that, or if the memory itself was some kind of mirage. I went and showered, and purged all thoughts of her under the running water.

Wrapping a towel round my waist, I crossed the room to open the shutters. On the other side of the swimming pool, mother and daughter were doing their morning yoga routine, as synchronised as a dance.

This time, I watched, unseen, until they'd finished.

Getting up, they rolled their mats and put them under their arms. As they walked away, I saw Roze give a brief, backwards glance in the direction of the guest house.

And so it begins, I thought.

In the kitchen, I found Roze on her own, eating sliced avocado and salchichón. I took another avocado from the bowl and sat down.

After a moment, she said quietly, 'I should apologise, Finn. What I said last night . . . I overreacted. It was rude of me.'

I shook my head. 'There's no need to apologise. It's a difficult time for you both. And of course you shouldn't sign anything you aren't happy with.'

'It isn't that we don't trust you – please don't think that. It's just . . .' She took a deep breath. 'I guess it isn't only Mama who'll be devastated to leave here. This last year . . . it's been like a fairy tale. I should have known it was too good to last.'

There was a short silence.

'When you ran away from those birdwatchers the other day,' I said curiously, 'who were you really frightened of?'

For a moment, I thought she was going to tell me it was none of my business. Then she said, 'Albanians.'

'What kind of Albanians?'

'Not the good kind.' She sighed. 'Mallorca's about as cut off from the big crime networks as you can get – that's why we thought we'd be safe here. But even on Mallorca, there are people smugglers, drug traffickers . . . Plenty of them would be very pleased to do a favour for the man we're hiding from.'

'I see.'

She nodded in the direction of the mountain. 'So my plan is that, if they ever find us, I'll go up there. Even a four-wheel drive can't get much higher than this. After that, it's just the old mule paths . . . I could go in any direction. Or simply stay up there until they gave up.'

'And your mother? Would she go too?'

Roze shook her head. 'We've talked about it. But she'd rather take her chances here. This place is so isolated . . . It's one reason we like it. But I guess that's all finished now.'

I took a breath. I knew I had to get this next bit over with. 'Look . . . Roze . . . I really can't see any alternative to selling. If it were just up to me . . . But my sister needs the money, and there'll be taxes that have to be paid as well. But I *can* drag the process out. Tomàs reckons it'll take months to get the probate sorted, and, until that's done and the *usufructo*'s officially extinguished, the house can't be sold in any case. If I do it as slowly as humanly possible, you'll be safe here, for a while at least – maybe even until the end of the year. And in the meantime, I'll try to persuade Jess that we should reimburse your mother for the cost of the pool and the roof. That way, at least you'll have something to live on, and some savings for the future too.'

'Thank you,' she said simply. She thought for a moment, then added, 'What about the tractor?'

'Tomàs said that, technically, it isn't part of the house, so it's yours.'

She smiled ruefully. 'A tractor without fields . . . But thank you, all the same. I'm sure you're being far more generous than you need to be.'

'It's the least I can do. I only wish there was more.'

'We might need to hire someone to help out on the farm. Even with your father lending a hand, it was sometimes too much for one person.'

'Well . . . since I'm here, why don't I help?'

She looked surprised. 'What about your job in London?'

'I'm freelance – I can cut down the time I spend on that. But you must treat me like you would any other farmhand. Just tell me what to do, and I'll do it.'

'I'd like that.' She smiled. 'Not the telling you what to do. Doing it together. It's hard work, and it's better when you have someone to share it with.'

I took a breath. 'There's something else you should know. I went to see the police yesterday, when I was in Palma – they'd asked me to call in. They wanted to talk about our parents' relationship – whether it was a real marriage, or if I was suspicious at all. Of course, I told them it was completely genuine. But they were clearly itching to find some pretext to open an investigation. They knew all about the money, for example, though not where it had come from – I put them right about that. And they mentioned that they were waiting on some specialised toxicology results. Their thinking seemed to be that, if the marriage was suspicious, then my father's death might be, too.'

Roze said nothing, but she suddenly looked thoughtful.

'That's another reason it's probably better if I stick around for a while. The police might go after two defenceless asylum seekers, but it'll be a different matter if the supposed victim's son is on hand to say loud and clear that they've got it all wrong. I've already told them it's a miracle my father lived as long as he did. And that I could tell from your mother's grief how happy they'd been together.'

'Again, thank you, Finn,' she said quietly. 'I think Jimmy would be very grateful if he knew. And proud, as well.'

I was silent a moment. 'I don't think my father was ever proud of me.'

Her eyes scrutinised my face. 'I can tell it was a complicated relationship. But he was always so good to me, let alone to Mama. I think perhaps we were lucky enough to meet him at a time when he'd been lonely, and really wanted to change. I'm just sorry you never got to meet the man we did.'

She reached out and put her hand on mine. I felt a jolt of pleasure – not just at the physical touch, but at the empathy behind it.

And grief, too – an unexpected pang of sadness, at the thought Roze might be right, and that, but for his sudden death, I could have come to Finca Síquia and met the man she and Ruensa had talked about.

Hugged him, even.

There were footsteps in the hallway. Without taking her hand away, Roze called, 'Mama?'

Ruensa came in. 'Yes?'

Roze said, 'Finn's going to drag out the sale of the house, so we can stay here as long as possible.'

She switched to Albanian and spoke a few more sentences very rapidly.

Ruensa turned to me. 'Thank you, Finn. We're very much in your debt.'

'It's me who should thank you,' I said. 'For making my father's final year so happy.'

She smiled sadly. 'Well, he made me happy too. We might have met late in life, but we loved each other very much.'

*

Did any of us speak a word that day that was true, I now wonder? Perhaps those few words that weren't in English might have been the cold, unvarnished truth – a brief instruction to the older woman on how she should respond. But as for the rest – how much of it was half-lies and evasions, snares in which to catch our prey? Each of us drawing the other in, trying to bind them with threads as fine as spiders' webs, even as we ourselves were being bound.

FIFTEEN

So began a new phase of my life at Finca Síquia. Every morning, after Ruensa and Roze had done their yoga and we'd eaten a fresh avocado or two for breakfast, Roze and I would head out through the orange groves on the little open-top tractor. There was only one seat, but there was room for a second person to stand behind it, balancing on the power hitch. It was a ridiculously exhilarating way to travel – childish and carefree, bumping along with the morning sun on your face, arms and legs braced against the ever-present risk that a rock or a hole in the ground would jolt you off.

That happened quite often, actually – standing pillion like that, there was almost nowhere for my hands to grab on to. After I'd gone sprawling for the third time, Roze suggested I grip her shoulders instead. We tried, but that meant I was pulling her backwards. Eventually she said, 'Oh, this is ridiculous. Put your arms round my waist.'

And so our first embrace was an entirely innocent one, my hands clasped around her slight body for purchase, my head turned sideways against her back, so close that every bump or sway of the tractor pressed her spine against my cheek. Even now, those are some of the memories I cherish most, when there was so much that we still didn't know about each other, and our growing intimacy was a kind of game, a secret all the more exciting for being unspoken.

There's no shortcut to harvesting oranges; unlike almonds, where you can nose the tractor up to the tree and bump them loose, an orange will bruise if it falls. We had long wooden ladders and stackable plastic crates, and we each had a canvas sack slung across our backs. And that was another game, too – seeing who could be first to fill their sack, run down the ladder and empty it into a crate – a game I was stupid to initiate, because Roze's sack was invariably full long before mine was. She was nimbler at climbing the ladders, more agile in reaching through the branches, defter in twisting the fruit free from the tree's grip. And, while I needed a short break after each sackful, she immediately bounded back up the rungs, as lithe as one of the wild goats that occasionally wandered into the orange grove to watch us. By mid-morning, unlike her, I was stiff and aching.

'You know why that is, Finn, don't you?' Roze called.

Through the branches, I saw her reach for another orange. This one, though, she pierced with her thumb, then put to her lips so she could squirt the juice straight into her mouth. I looked at the orange in my own hand and did the same.

'Why?' I said, when we'd both tossed our empty juice cartons to the ground.

'It's because I do Pilates every morning. It builds up your core. You should join us.'

'I think I'll give that one a miss, thanks.'

'Why? Isn't Pilates manly enough for you?'

'It's not that. Just that I had enough t'ai chi, crystal-waving and general hippy crap from my parents' guests to last me a lifetime.'

'OK . . . But Pilates isn't anything like that. It was developed for dancers, to stop them getting muscle injuries. Your father said it helped him a lot.'

'My *father* did Pilates?'

'Of course. How else do you think a man his age was able to help in the fields?'

So I started joining them before breakfast for what I now knew was not yoga, but Pilates. It was Ruensa, not Roze, who showed me what to do; back in Albania, she'd done an instructors' course, Roze told me, and had been going to give lessons as part of the agroturismo plan.

She went a little quiet after she said that. I could see that the death of her dream was still painful. But what could I do? I was already doing more than I should, drawing the process out as much as I dared.

Tomàs had sent the waiver documents by then, along with a list of all the other steps I had to take: *A full list and valuation of the fixtures and fittings, please, and it would be helpful to know if your father had any cash or other assets remaining in his bank accounts. I should also point out that I cannot advise your stepmother and her daughter on the suitability of this agreement for them, and, if they have any concerns, they should get their own advice.*

'Of course we don't need a lawyer,' Ruensa said when I relayed this. 'We can't afford one, and, besides, I trust Jimmy's son completely.'

And yet the documents still sat in the guest house, unsigned – somehow, I never got round to bringing them out. Time had stood still, and I was willing it to stay that way. I wanted to continue living purely in those moments of bright Mallorquín sunshine, my body slowly adjusting to the physical demands being made of it, my lungs full of mountain air that was heady with orange blossom – the Valencia and Canoneta trees were now in full bloom, and the slightest breeze sent their fragrance gusting across the farm.

My life in London seemed so grey and distant now, as if I had come out of some long hibernation or coma. A great calm descended on me. I worked, I ate, I slept. And at the centre of it all was Roze, and our growing ease in each other's company.

'Look at me,' I called to her one day as she came down her ladder. 'I'm going to show you my hidden talent.'

'I'm not sure I want to see that,' she said doubtfully. But she put down her sack and watched.

I had four oranges, two in each hand. I started with just the first two. 'One of the hippies who stayed here taught me this.' I got a rhythm going, then made it three before adding the fourth. 'They say if you learn young enough, you never forget.'

'Dancers have the same thing. It's called muscle memory.'

'Toss me another. Underarm, like we're playing catch.'

She did, and I added it to the ones I was already juggling. But I was overreaching, trying to impress, and within moments the whole thing had tumbled to the ground.

'Now you have to show me a hidden talent of yours,' I said as I picked the oranges up and added them to the crate.

She thought for a moment. 'Turn around. And close your eyes.'

I did as I was asked.

'My hidden talent,' she said, 'is that I'm very good at snowball fights.' An orange hit me, hard, on the back of my head.

'Ow!' I said, outraged, turning round. 'That actually *hurt*.'

Almost doubled up with laughter, she hurled another. I caught that one, and flung it back at her. She dodged behind the tractor and lobbed another at me, and suddenly we were like two seven-year-olds, grabbing fruit from the low branches as fast as we could and letting fly at each other, until eventually I cornered her at close range, my hand raised to throw—

'OK, OK, you win!' she spluttered. 'Don't – you'll hurt me.'

'Declare me the victor,' I ordered.

'You are the victor. For today, anyway.'

Were my feelings for her reciprocated? A cynic like Jess, if she could have seen us, would, I know, have said that Roze was simply trying to charm me; or even that she was working some longer, deeper game; one orchestrated by her mother, perhaps – the professor of psychology who was so interested in my childhood. But Jess was not there, and I was not a cynic. I was almost sure Roze felt the same way I did – oh, not to the same degree; my longing for her could be painful at times. But I was certain that she liked me – found me attractive, even; or at any rate, attractive enough to tease – and sensed that, in the right circumstances, there could be something more.

But, of course, these were not the right circumstances. The

farm was going to be sold from under her, and I was the one doing the selling. Perhaps, when all the legal stuff was sorted, in the interval before they actually left . . . But I tried not to let myself indulge even in that small fantasy.

When you pick an orange, the secret is not to pull. If you do, the fruit may not be fully ripe. Instead, you give it a small exploratory twist, and, if the orange is ready, it simply falls into your hand. We were neither of us ready, but we were ripening – ripening in that brilliant sunshine, as inexorably as every living thing around us.

SIXTEEN

It was Ruensa who decided we should scatter my father's ashes. What prompted the exact timing, I don't know; she simply announced one day that we'd do it that evening. So, after we'd finished work, we got dressed up – that is, I put on one of my father's linen shirts and a pair of his chinos, still sharply creased from being ironed by Ruensa, and Roze and Ruensa changed into dresses – and I drove the three of us up the coast to the Torre del Verger. The four of us, rather, because Ruensa had a small metal urn nestled in her lap. Occasionally, I glanced across and saw that she was stroking it.

I thought of how suspicious Jess had been before I'd come out to Mallorca. The police, too. How absurd those suspicions seemed now! There was absolutely no doubt that Ruensa was saying goodbye to someone she truly loved. I found myself imagining that it was my ashes in that urn, and that Roze was the one nestling it in her lap, perhaps after a lifetime together . . . It gave me a warm feeling, to picture such enduring devotion.

I glanced in the rear-view mirror. Roze was sitting in the back, her face turned to the window – she was watching the sea, flashing and glinting hundreds of feet below. Unseen, I kept my eyes on her, feasting on her profile, until a sharp intake of breath from Ruensa alerted me to an oncoming coach.

The stretch of coast from Cauzacs to Banyalbufar is the highest on the island, which is why, centuries ago, it was chosen as a vantage point for a watchtower. If the lookouts saw ships that might be invaders or pirates, they sent up a pillar of smoke that could be spotted by the next lookout, several miles away, and so on, all the way to the garrison at Sóller. The views from the cliffs were incredible, though that wasn't the reason my father went there. Any painting with the crumbling tower in it made a marketable souvenir, especially as he made the canvases the right size to fit in a tourist's suitcase. In a good week, he could churn out three or four, which kept him in brandy for a month.

Ruensa led us to a spot a little way off, to the side of the tower. 'This was where he proposed to me,' she said simply.

It was also where he used to put his easel, I thought, but kept that memory to myself.

'Because he loved to paint the view from here,' she added. 'It was very special to him.' She turned to me. 'Finn, would you like to say a few words?'

That threw me – I hadn't anticipated having to do that, and it would have been hard enough even with plenty of warning.

'Jimmy Hensen was many things to many people,' I said carefully. 'But he was always a man who forged his own path, a man of fearless personality and immense talents, someone who lived life to the full, and every day as if it were his last.' God, it was amazing how many of these clichéd phrases there were – they came to me quite fluently, an endless flow of bullshit. Warming to my theme, I went on, 'He was a wanderer, a creative whirlwind, a restless and inquisitive voyager, who nevertheless found in these mountains his spiritual home. And it was here that he finally found the love of his life, his inner peace and journey's end.' I lowered my voice and came to a solemn stop, to indicate that I was done.

I'd thought Ruensa might say something too, but she only nodded and unscrewed the lid of the urn. Then, with a dramatic flourish, she flung the contents upwards and outwards, towards the sea.

I think she must have meant to scatter them symbolically to the winds, as it were, taking her cue from my drivel about whirlwinds and voyages. But there was an actual wind that day, an onshore breeze, and it caught my father's ashes and threw them back at us. I opened my mouth to warn the others, but quickly closed it again as the cloud of ash hit me. I managed not to swallow any, but my lips were gritty with cinders.

'He always had a mind of his own,' I managed to say, when I'd wiped my mouth clean.

Roze laughed, and Ruensa smiled. Then she said quietly, 'If you'll both excuse me, I'd like a few minutes alone with him.'

'Of course,' I said. I looked at Roze. To my surprise, her own cheeks were shiny with tears. 'There's a path along the cliff. Shall we . . . ?'

She nodded, and took my arm as we walked, uncharacteristically silent. I was quiet too, reluctant to break the mood, or lose that arm.

'I expect you're wondering why I was crying,' she said eventually.

I communicated a shrug through our linked arms. 'It's a sad occasion.'

She shook her head. 'It's not just because of your father, though of course I'll miss him. It's because of what he meant – the life we thought we'd found here.' She hesitated. 'And I suppose I was thinking about my own father, too.'

I glanced at her, surprised. 'You haven't talked about him.'

'That's because it's not a good story.' She went to sit on a rock, staring out to sea, and I sat down next to her. 'He fought in the Albanian civil wars – he was a Kosovar, from an area the Serbs were trying to ethnically cleanse. There were atrocities on both sides . . . Mama said that, when he came back, he was different. You never knew when he was going to explode – he could be angry at the smallest thing. Even so, when he finally killed himself . . .' She stopped, then went on, 'He left a note. He said he knew he was a terrible husband and father, and that we'd be better off without him. But I never wanted him dead. I wanted him better.'

She wiped more tears away with her sleeve. 'So, you see . . . I do understand how you feel about Jimmy. But for me . . . Perhaps, in a way, I was looking for someone too, just like Mama was. A different kind of father figure, one who was actually facing up to his problems.'

She gave me a sideways glance. 'You know, you have some of his – what do you say? Manners? When you do something the same way?'

'Oh – mannerisms.' Her English was so good that it was only

rarely she didn't know a word; in Albania, she'd told me, most educated people spoke at least three languages. 'But I don't think I do, actually.'

She nodded. 'For sure. Making a joke like that, when the wind blew his ashes at us . . . That was very Jimmy. And now that your hair's getting longer – when you push it back with both hands, it's the exact same gesture.'

'That's probably why I prefer it short. I'll go to Sóller and get it cut.'

'I like it like that. It suits you,' she said, then blushed.

There was a short silence.

'Well, don't get too used to it,' I said breezily. 'One day soon, I'll come back as shorn as a sheep.'

Of course, now that she'd said she liked it, there was absolutely no chance of my changing it.

She stood up. 'We should probably get back.'

As we walked towards the car, she said, 'You know . . . the first time we met him, when he was telling us about his family, your father didn't call you Finn. He used a different name, I think.'

'That's right. He and my mother named me something different, originally.'

'I keep trying to remember . . . What was it?'

'I think I'd have to know you very well before I told you that.'

She pulled at my arm – she'd taken it again as we walked. 'But I *do* know you well, now. Don't I?'

'Not well enough.' We were both smiling now. 'Besides, it's a horrible name, and I know *you* well enough to know that you'd tease me by using it.'

'I promise I won't.'

'We'll see. In any case, I got off lightly compared to Jess.'

'Why – what's her real name?'

'Honeyblossom Strawberry Rain.'

Roze considered. 'That's actually a very nice name.'

'Yes, if my mother had given birth to a bottle of shampoo.'

'There you go again – sounding like your father.' She took her arm away and nudged my shoulder with hers. 'We should look serious now. For Mama's sake.'

'Of course.' The car was in sight, and, beyond it, the figure of Ruensa, standing by the wooden rails at the top of the cliff.

I tried to do as Roze asked and look serious. But it was hard to stop smiling, when I was so happy.

SEVENTEEN

As the days got warmer, we started taking longer breaks at lunch-time, and I started working through Tomàs's to-do list. I asked Ruensa where my father's bank statements might be kept.

'He wasn't exactly a man for filing – he threw most things straight in the bin. But there are some papers upstairs, in his paint room.'

'Paint room?'

She nodded. 'After we turned the studio into a bedroom, he worked in a room on the top floor. I'll show you.'

She led me up the stairs. The finca had three storeys; since I'd arrived, I'd only seen the ground floor and, briefly, the floor above, when I moved the scorpions from Roze's bedroom. It soon became apparent that it was only those first two floors that had been renovated. It was almost like stepping off an elegant stage set and discovering that backstage was a complete mess. Exactly on the turn of the third flight of stairs, where guests on the floor below wouldn't see it, the smart new paint ended and my father's awful frescos began, now mercifully faded with age. The floorboards up here were bare and full of holes, and the plaster on the walls was crumbling. Most of the bedrooms, too, were full of junk that hadn't been touched for fifteen years. Through one doorway, I glimpsed the beehives someone had persuaded my parents to get, telling them they could sell the honey; the bees had only lasted a day before decamping somewhere more hospitable, but the empty hives had remained. Another room contained a couple of rusty bicycles and an iron four-poster bed frame, the latter now colonised by a false-widow spider as a scaffold for its distinctively tangled web. A third held the remnants of a rotting tepee.

'We ran out of money to do up this floor,' Ruensa explained, as she led me down the corridor. 'We were going to wait until we had some income . . . In here.'

The room she showed me into took up one whole corner of the house. Next to a window was the leather armchair I recognised from the portrait of Ruensa and Roze hanging in my bedroom. The area around it was clear, apart from an easel, but the rest of the room was chaos – the floorboards randomly splattered with paint, like multicoloured bird droppings, the walls striped and smeared where my father had simply wiped his brushes on them to clean them as he worked. Against the far wall, boxes of loose sketches bookended what looked like a row of finished canvases.

But it was the daybed – an ancient chaise longue, its stuffing gaping through various slits and rips – that drew my eye. Piled up at one end was a thin duvet.

Ruensa followed my gaze. 'He used to sleep up here sometimes. In the afternoons, or when he'd been drinking. He said it was because he didn't want to disturb me when he'd been working, but I don't think it was ever really that.'

Subinspector Parera's words rang in my ears: *Would you happen to know if their relations were that of a normal husband and wife? For example, whether they shared a bedroom?*

I shook the thought away. So my father slept up here sometimes. It meant nothing.

'This is where he kept anything important,' Ruensa said, crossing to a bulging chest of drawers. 'But I don't think there was any system to it.'

'Thanks – I'll take a look.'

'I'll leave you to it.' She closed the door behind her as she went.

I looked around. More than anywhere else in the house, this room still felt crammed with my father's presence. I could imagine a supine figure on the chaise longue suddenly throwing off the duvet, sitting upright and roaring at me, *Fuck off out of here, you little runt. Can't you see I'm trying to sleep?*

Even now, it felt like I was trespassing.

I pulled open the first drawer. He'd clearly just pushed things in as they arrived – an electricity bill, a letter from the Ministry of Tourism acknowledging an application for a rental licence, a napkin from a bar with some illegible names and phone numbers on. And, I saw, a marriage certificate.

I pulled it out. The witnesses had been Ferid Karemi and Saban Flutur. Albanian names? They certainly didn't look Spanish.

Near the top of the drawer was a Santander bank statement, still in its envelope. It showed a balance of three hundred and twelve euros. There was nothing before that but outgoings.

I worked my way down through the layers. There were some letters to do with his application for citizenship; a newspaper cutting in what appeared to be Russian; and more bank statements, showing mostly outgoings until just over a year ago, when – as the police had noticed – a payment of almost forty thousand euros had come in and almost immediately started going out again.

Getting up, I went to the row of canvases and pulled one out. It was a seascape – a fishing boat bobbing in the sea at Port de Valldemossa. I took out another. The lighthouse at Portocolom. And another – the rocky cove at Deià. I counted them. Eight, in all.

He must have been meaning to sell them, I realised. That would have been his contribution to the household finances. Only the very last canvas was almost indecipherable, the paint smeared over it in great circular scrawls, as if to obliterate what lay underneath. Whatever it was, he'd evidently decided it was no good and abandoned it. Either he'd become disgusted by what he was painting, or angry, or drunk.

Or possibly all three, I reflected.

'They'd cleaned him out, you mean.'

'Actually, it looked more like the other way round. Ruensa told me they'd been trying to live frugally – only eating what they could grow or shoot, reducing their spending to the bare essentials so they could finish the improvements. Unfortunately, they hadn't budgeted for the brandy. It meant they had to put off sorting the access track. That was going to cost about five thousand euros, and, without fixing that, they couldn't really open to paying guests.'

Jess said thoughtfully, 'You know, the more I think about it, the weirder it feels that she didn't get some kind of receipt for the money she put in. If you knew the house wasn't yours, why *wouldn't* you do that?'

'She's quite . . .' I searched for the right word. 'Not impulsive, exactly, but trusting. And no one expects the sixty-four-year-old man they've just married to drop down dead. The OB always seemed indestructible, right?'

Jess sighed. 'OK. So what do you think we should do about this?'

'Tomàs says that, from a legal point of view, we have to pay her back. And, from the bank statements, it looks like she put in over fifty thousand euros.'

'So it would be an advance?' Jess's voice was suddenly wary. 'Which you want me and Leo to stump up?'

'Well, *I* don't have that kind of money—'

'How much *do* you have? You've been saving up for a deposit, right?'

'Well, trying to. I've got maybe seven grand in that account. Ten, if I count my unused overdraft.'

'All right, then – I'll talk to Leo about putting in forty, if you'll put in ten. It's called sharing the risk, bro. But unlike the merry widow, I *will* want a receipt. And I'm not transferring a penny until they've signed those waivers and fixed a date to leave.'

I started to protest, but she cut me short.

'Unlike you, I'm a worry-guts, OK? I don't know why you're giving them such an easy ride – if I'm being charitable, I might put it down to that saviour complex of yours – but I still smell something fishy about this.'

EIGHTEEN

As a short-term fix, I loaded the car with my father's canvases and the boxes of sketches and took them to Marc, his gallerist, in Palma. He agreed to put the best on display, and, if he sold any, transfer our share direct to my account.

'You know,' he said, pulling out a canvas and scrutinising it critically, 'your father was a talented artist, when he wanted to be. But he ended up despising the people who bought his paintings, and that's a sure way to destroy your talent.'

'He did a portrait of his new wife and her daughter that's really good. But that's not for sale.' Ruensa had told me that was the one keepsake she wanted, and of course I'd been happy to agree.

Marc nodded. 'That was painted before the problems started, presumably?'

I glanced at him. 'What problems?'

He looked discomfited. 'I assumed you knew ... A year ago, he told me he'd given up the booze completely. He seemed full of energy – a different person. But then I saw him at an opening, a few months ago, and he was so drunk, he could barely speak.

I asked him how things were and he muttered something about this marriage going the same way as the others. I thought that must be why he was drinking again – because he was unhappy.'

'Ah, Finn,' Tomàs greeted me. 'This is a surprise. Have you brought me the signed waivers?'

'Not yet . . . It's all been a bit hectic. I just wanted to talk something through with you. Do you have a minute?'

Tomàs brightened. 'Let's go next door for a glass of wine, and you can tell me all about it.'

When we were sitting in the sun with two glasses of Binissalem rosé in front of us, I relayed what the gallerist had just told me.

'The strange thing is, it's almost the exact opposite of the impression Ruensa herself has been giving me,' I concluded. 'I mean, she told me he'd been drinking again, but she made it sound more like an illness he was fighting than something he'd started doing all the time. Then there were those texts Jess was sent – now that I think about them again, they do seem to support what Marc was saying.'

Tomàs nodded. 'And you're worried there could be a sinister explanation?'

'Well . . . it's crossed my mind. It seems ridiculous even to think it, given what normal, likeable people they are, but what if Ruensa doesn't want to admit to anyone that the marriage had broken down, because she knows that, if she's honest about what a cantankerous, abusive bastard he really was, it'll appear to give her a possible motive for killing him?'

'The two aren't mutually exclusive,' Tomàs pointed out. 'They may have been genuinely in love, but having problems. Then he dies in tragic circumstances and the police are suspicious, so, out of simple self-preservation, she now emphasises how fundamentally happy they were.'

'OK . . . But, at the very least, it shows the police have been looking at this all wrong. They've been focusing on the idea that it was a sham marriage which somehow ended up as murder. If Marc is right, though, it was far more complicated than that – my father was genuinely in love with her, or at least with the idea of a fresh start with her, until, for some reason, the relationship soured.'

'Perhaps we will never know the full story.' Tomàs took a mouthful of wine. 'Even so, you might think it prudent to draw your own visit to a close soon and return to the UK. Or, if you feel you need to stay longer, to move into a hotel.'

I said awkwardly, 'Actually, I'm thinking of staying quite a bit longer. To help out on the farm.'

Tomàs regarded me quizzically. 'May I ask how long?'

'I haven't decided yet. Perhaps until the autumn.'

'The autumn?' Tomàs echoed, astonished. He shook his head. 'I may not have made this as clear as I should have done, Finn. Under Spanish law, probate must be wrapped up and all the taxes paid within six months. After that, you will be liable to a substantial penalty.'

I stared at him. 'How much are we talking about?'

He shrugged. 'A five per cent surcharge on the full value of the estate, payable every three months.'

To be fair, Tomàs had explained how the Spanish system worked at our first meeting, but I hadn't really been paying attention. At the time, the plan to sell up as quickly as possible had seemed so straightforward.

He sat back and looked at me, a little exasperated. 'Have they actually signed those waivers yet?'

'Not yet,' I admitted.

Tomàs sucked his teeth sharply.

'That's probably my fault,' I added. 'I wanted to talk to Jess first about agreeing some kind of compensation.'

'And have the two of you decided on an amount?'

'We think fifty thousand euros sounds about right.'

'Fifty thousand?' Tomàs looked as if he might fall off his chair. 'I must say, that is quite extraordinarily generous of you.'

I shrugged. 'It's what my father would have wanted. Whatever problems had arisen, he clearly loved Ruensa once. And it's not her fault she's inheriting absolutely nothing.'

Tomàs frowned. 'And your sister feels the same way?'

'Yes. That is, she understands why we have to do it,' I lied.

'Well, you must do as you both see fit. But I wouldn't write any cheques until those waivers are signed. And, even then, I'd be inclined to pay them in stages – so much on vacant possession, so much on sale, and so on.'

'Jess said something similar,' I agreed reluctantly. 'So I guess that's how we'd better play it.'

He nodded. 'Quite apart from anything else, knowing there's more to come will be something of an insurance policy for you, yes? If there *was* any possibility of foul play with your father, the prospect of a payout after you're safely home can only work to your advantage.'

NINETEEN

I drove back to the finca, thinking hard. So my little paradise had an expiry date. I was sad, of course – it would have been nice to draw things out until the end of the year, at least – but it raised a practical question, too.

Should I continue to leave my feelings for Roze unspoken, or declare them to her?

If I spoke up, there was the possibility of weeks, if not months, of happiness. But there was also the possibility of rejection, and all the awkwardness that might ensue. I was fairly sure she felt something for me, but what if she was still at the stage – as I myself had been not so very long ago – of thinking that a relationship would be inappropriate, given the circumstances? What if she said – God forbid – that it was better we just stay friends, and subsequently became wary of doing or saying anything that might undermine that – if she no longer bumped her shoulder against mine when we walked through the fields, say, or stopped resting her hand on my arm to make a point? What if she no longer thought it right to tease me, or to hurl oranges at me in mock-exasperation when I teased her in return? What if she backed away from having me work alongside her at all?

I lived for those moments, storing each touch in my memory like parched ground remembering rain.

Some words from a poem I was made to learn at school came back to me:

> *How many loved your moments of glad grace,*
> *And loved your beauty with love false or true,*
> *But one man loved the pilgrim soul in you,*
> *And loved the sorrows of your changing face*

Yeats, I remembered. That was one of the poems written to Maud Gonne, the woman Yeats had loved, unrequited, for almost his whole life.

I would say something, I resolved. How or what, I didn't yet know. It might be formal – *I think you should know that I'm developing feelings for you* – or flirtatious – *Well, this is a bit awkward. I seem to have got the hots for my co-worker* – or even just a simple but slightly mysterious, *Do you feel the same way I do?* But say something I must.

Not when the alternative was letting 'I dare not' wait upon 'I would'.

It was strange how much poetry was coming back to me these days.

The road through Cauzacs passes through the village square, where Alejandro's café is. He always puts a few tables and chairs out, but in low season they're rarely used – locals prefer to drink their coffee inside, standing at the bar.

So when, as I drove past, I noticed a young couple sitting at one of the tables, at first I assumed they were tourists. It was only when the woman gesticulated, in a way characteristic of Roze, that I realised it was her. She was wearing sunglasses, and her dark hair was tucked under a sunhat, which was why I hadn't recognised her immediately.

As for her companion, he was dark too, and sleekly dressed, his sunglasses tucked into the V of his polo shirt. Something about his face – his pronounced cheekbones, perhaps – made me think he wasn't Spanish.

I drove past, my mind churning. Then, on an impulse, I stopped and reversed back. There were *No Parking* signs all around the square, but nobody took any notice of them at this time of year.

I got out and walked towards the café. Roze was still talking animatedly. She laughed – I saw the flash of her teeth – then reached across and put her hand on the man's arm to make a point.

I felt as if someone had punched me in the guts, though I kept walking.

I was almost at the doorway now. Engrossed in their conversation, she still hadn't seen me. She laughed again, and the young man smiled, clearly pleased at the effect he'd had.

I stopped beside their table, as if I'd only just noticed them. 'Oh, Roze. Hi. I didn't see you there.'

She looked up. 'Finn! You're back quickly.'

'Yes.' I gestured into the café. 'I'm just getting a cortado, then I'm going back up to the house.' Then, as if the idea had only just struck me, 'I'll give you a lift, shall I?'

'Oh . . .' She shrugged. 'Thanks, but there's no need. I'll come later. I don't mind walking.'

I didn't move. 'I can wait a few minutes. I've got a couple of errands to run while I'm here, anyway.'

'It's no problem,' the young man said, in precise but accented English. 'I have a car. I'll run her back.'

'Thank you,' I said. I still didn't move. There was the briefest of pauses.

'This is Finn,' Roze said to the man. Then, to me, 'This is Ferid.'

Ferid waved in my direction.

'Hi,' I said pleasantly. I waited for them to ask me to join them.

Ferid said, 'Enjoy your cortado, Finn.'

I threw the little car around the track back to the house with barely controlled aggression, sending loose stones clattering down the hill. *This is Finn*. Now that I picked it apart, it spoke volumes that she'd introduced me to him, not the other way round. As if *I* was the stranger.

Or was it even more pointed than that? Had she actually said, *THIS is Finn* – as if she'd already been talking about me, and wanted Ferid to pick up on who I was?

There'd been something about him, too – something cocksure. Pleased with himself. He knew he was a good-looking bastard, that was certain.

I'd always assumed that Roze didn't have a boyfriend, though

I realised I'd never actually asked her. But she'd been in Mallorca for almost two years. She'd worked on the Strip. Even if she was keeping a low profile, she'd have friends, acquaintances, possibly lovers. She could be on Tinder, for all I knew.

Then I remembered something else. The names on the marriage certificate – the two witnesses. One of them had been called Ferid.

Roze's boyfriend, attending the service as her plus one? A family friend? Whatever the explanation, he clearly wasn't a recent acquaintance.

I strode into the house, crunching the car keys in my fist. Ruensa was in the kitchen, stirring something on the stove. She looked up, startled.

'Oh – Finn. How was your trip to Palma?'

'All good,' I said shortly. I was discussing the best way to give you and your daughter fifty thousand euros, I thought incredulously. I was being 'extraordinarily generous'. Had I been mad? Why was I giving them anything at all?

'I met Roze and Ferid at the café,' I added.

Ruensa nodded. 'Yes, they arranged to meet there. Did Ferid say everything would be all right?'

I stared at her. 'All right? In what way?'

Ruensa suddenly looked discomfited, as if she'd said too much. 'Nothing – I may have got confused—'

'Ruensa,' I said bluntly, 'who is Ferid?'

'He's a very good friend,' Ruensa began. Then, seeing my expression, she added quietly, 'He's also our lawyer. He volunteers with Acción de Refugiados. They've been helping us with our appeal.'

I frowned. 'You said you couldn't afford a lawyer.'

'We can't. They work for free – *pro bono*, they call it. Of course, it's not really his area, but he kindly agreed to give us some advice about our situation here, as well.'

I found an awkward smile twisting my lips. 'I thought you said you trusted me.'

Ruensa looked puzzled. 'Of course we trust you. But you mentioned that your lawyer thought we should have someone take a look—'

'They have to say that,' I interrupted. 'It's just something they always say.' But even as I spoke, I knew I was being unreasonable. As Ruensa had just pointed out, I had a lawyer myself. How could I resent them taking legal advice, particularly when my own lawyer had been the one to suggest it?

But I did resent it, all the same. It felt as if the close relationship we'd built was being undermined by an outsider.

And yet, I realised, the real outsider here was me.

'Ferid was at your wedding, wasn't he?' I added.

Ruensa nodded. 'He'd become a dear friend by then. When things were very bad – when we thought we might be put on a plane back to Albania at any moment – he was always there for us. I can't tell you how many hours and weeks he spent, fighting for us to stay. Without him . . .' She shook her head.

And I'd thought they'd be grateful to me, for my generosity in letting them stay in the house as long as possible. Not to mention lying to my own sister, in order to pay them back more than they'd put in.

Evidently, compared with what Ferid had done, I was doing almost nothing.

I knew I was behaving oddly – although, out of politeness, Ruensa had clearly decided to ignore it. I pulled myself together.

'What stage are your appeals at?' I went to the sink and poured myself a glass of water.

'Oh . . .' Ruensa said. 'It's only Roze who's appealing now – getting married to Jimmy meant I didn't need to. Ferid has submitted a new legal argument on her behalf, and we're waiting to see if it's accepted. If it is, he believes she has a very good chance.'

'Good for him,' I muttered.

There was the sound of a car. Through the open window, I saw a battered old Skoda come to a halt outside. Roze and Ferid got out and strolled easily towards the house. Realising he meant to come in, I bristled.

Ferid greeted Ruensa effusively, kissing her on both cheeks, then nodded to me. 'Hello again, Finn.'

Twirling his sunglasses in his hand, he looked around the kitchen admiringly. 'It looks even better than the last time I was here. What a fabulous job you have done, Ru.' He glanced at me. 'Along with your father, of course, Finn. And I apologise – I should have said sooner, at the café, how sorry I am for your loss. My condolences to both of you.'

'Thank you,' I said stiffly.

'I told Ferid about those documents of your lawyer's,' Roze said. 'He's offered to take a look.'

'How kind,' I said sourly.

They all three looked at me expectantly.

'I'll just go and get them, shall I?' I added.

'If that's all right,' Roze said, puzzled.

I went to the guest house. I was being childish, I knew, and, what was worse, I knew that everyone else was aware of it. But something in me rebelled at the way Ferid was muscling in and taking charge. No doubt he would now pick holes in everything Tomàs had done and turn it into some big legal drama, with himself as the one saving the day for Ruensa and Roze.

I paused to splash water on my face. When I returned, I handed the documents over with what I hoped was a casual gesture. 'Here.'

Ferid took the pages and scanned through them. 'Yes, that all seems very straightforward,' he said to Roze and Ruensa. 'It simply says that you acknowledge you are staying here as Finn's guests, rather than as tenants or inheritors. And I see the lawyer has attached the original *usufructo* . . . which also seems clear. Here is a copy of the waiver for Ru, and a copy for you also, Roze. He has omitted to ask either of you to date it, but that is easily put right. If you would like to sign and date them now, I can witness your signatures.'

Ruensa found a pen, and both women signed.

'There's one for you as well, and you should countersign their copies,' Ferid said to me. Roze handed me the pen.

'Yes, of course,' I said. I looked at the documents, found the space for my signature and put my name to it.

'Would you like me to post them back to your lawyer for you?' Ferid asked politely when he had added his own name. 'I can easily do that – the address is at the bottom.'

'I'll do it,' I said curtly.

'As you wish.' He turned to Roze and Ruensa. 'And now I must leave you.'

'Oh.' Ruensa looked upset. 'Can't you stay and eat with us?'

'I'd love to,' he assured her, 'but I have a case going to tribunal tomorrow, and I need to make sure all the paperwork is in order. Another time, perhaps.' He turned to me. 'It was nice meeting you, Finn.' His handshake was firm and dry.

'I'll walk you to the car,' Roze said.

I went to the sink and, under the pretext of refilling my glass, watched them. Ferid was talking urgently but quietly to Roze. She was nodding. When they got to the car, he embraced her – not the formal one-two of Spaniards kissing each cheek, but a hug. Then, still holding her shoulders, he stepped back, looked her in the eye and said something. She nodded again, and he got into the car and sped off.

Roze came back in. 'Finn, are you all right?'

I looked around, and realised Ruensa had made herself scarce.

'I'm fine,' I said. 'Why?'

'You seem a bit . . . off.'

Now is the moment, I thought. I have to say it now.

But how could I confess that I had feelings for her, when I had just been so childishly jealous? It would look as if my jealousy was what had prompted the confession. And Roze was hardly likely to give me a positive answer now, anyway – not after the way I'd just behaved.

'Really, I'm fine,' I said stiffly.

She nodded, and the moment was gone. 'OK. I'm going to have a shower. See you at lunch, yes?'

'Of course,' I said.

I went back to the guest house and lay on the bed. Across the room, from her place in my father's portrait, Roze regarded me solemnly, her dark eyes unreadable. I thought of her stepping into her shower, and the image was so painful, I almost groaned.

TWENTY

Time might be standing still, but the seasons didn't. That week, as we worked in the fields, the first heatwave of the year seared Mallorca like the breath of a dragon. We were at a reasonably high altitude at the finca, but, without any hint of a breeze, the glare of the sun was merciless even there. When we pulled oranges from the trees, they were almost too hot to touch, and the juice inside, when we moistened our parched throats, was as warm as blood.

It was too hot to think – too hot for rancour. The sun erased all thoughts of speaking out as completely as it would have shrivelled an unwatered seedling, even as it inflamed my simmering jealousy, my brain churning with fantasies of pummelling Ferid's girlish cheekbones until they bled. By lunchtime each day, it felt as if we'd done a full day's work, and we flopped into the swimming pool as soon as we got back to the house – neither of us bothering with towels or swimming costumes, simply stripping off our T-shirts and tumbling into the still-cool water in our underwear.

It was always uncertain who would splash the other one first, or which of us would be the first to try to push the other under.

The feel of her smooth wet skin as I put my arms around her to pull her down. Her wriggling and kicking to get free. The water closing over both our heads as we play-fought. Coming up, gasping and laughing, only to be splashed again for not letting go sooner.

I had been right to say nothing, I realised. Slowly, our relationship was rebuilding after my stupid fit of pique. I thought of the pine martens and almond-eaters I'd befriended as a child – how many months it took of offering them titbits before they were ready to trust me. You could never be too patient, or too slow.

After swimming came lunch, cooked by Ruensa and eaten on the veranda – cheap dishes, made with our own ingredients: tumbet, a kind of Mallorquín ratatouille, with peppers, onions, aubergines and potatoes, all grown on the farm and watered assiduously by Ruensa; or frito Mallorquín, using the same ingredients, but fried in olive oil this time, and flavoured with the liver, heart and kidneys of a rabbit. I felt I had never eaten food that tasted so good.

Waking up early, to begin work when it was cool – but never as early as Roze. While still in bed, I'd hear, among the other sounds of dawn, two loud bangs in quick succession. By the time I got to the kitchen for breakfast, there'd be a rabbit on the draining board, head flopped into the sink, blood dripping from its nose, to be eaten late that evening, when the air was once again cool. Then conversation, weariness, bed. And dreams – also delicious, and comforting in their vividness.

How long did that weather last? Honestly, I have no idea. Perhaps it was only a few days. Perhaps a week. Perhaps I only dreamt it. But suddenly, one day, the sky was full of thunder-clouds, the winds were rising, and the tops of the mountains had disappeared.

And then the police came.

TWENTY-ONE

'We have received the specialised toxicology findings,' Subinspector Parera said. 'The initial tests done in Valencia were inconclusive, so they were sent on to Madrid, where they have a more powerful machine.' He took a document from his papers. 'The reports confirm that your father's blood contained a substantial amount of oleandrin, the toxic compound in oleander. Onset of symptoms would have occurred between one and two hours after consumption, and may have included vomiting, intense abdominal pain, blue skin, cardiac arrhythmia, and death.'

'So it *was* the bonfire that killed him,' I said.

The subinspector and I were sitting on the veranda – Officer Castell and another young detective were in the house, speaking to Ruensa and Roze. As we talked, the wind sprinkled blossom from the lemon tree on the table between us, like confetti.

'His blood also showed high levels of alcohol and paracetamol,' the subinspector said. 'Paracetamol, like oleander, is hepatotoxic. That is to say, in high doses, it attacks the liver.' He glanced at me. 'In hindsight, it is unfortunate that the medical examiner who took the blood did not consider your father's symptoms merited a full post-mortem, and for that I can only apologise. But I think we can assume from what you told us that his liver might already have been impaired by heavy drinking . . . Do you know whether he was in the habit of taking paracetamol?'

I nodded. 'He used to take a couple of pills when he had a particularly bad hangover. Usually washed down with brandy, then pretty soon he'd be drinking seriously again.'

'This would have been rather more than a couple of pills,' the subinspector said. 'More like half a dozen. Is the bottle he was drinking from that day still available, by any chance?'

'You'll have to ask Ruensa. But I don't think it's likely. She had a big sort-out after his death, and I can't see her keeping something like that.'

There was a brief silence while the subinspector made a note.

'The thing that is still confusing me,' he said, looking up, 'is the timeline. As I said, with liver toxicity, it generally takes several hours before symptoms appear. But he was found next to the bonfire. It seems strange that he inhaled the smoke, then stayed in the same place for several hours until it killed him.'

'Unless he had a lot of oleander bush to get through and was feeding the fire continuously,' I suggested. 'Or he might have lit it and come back.'

The subinspector nodded. 'Yes, those are possibilities. It is also possible that someone laced his brandy with paracetamol and oleander sap, then dragged him to the fire after he collapsed.'

'Well . . .' I stopped, a little unnerved now that he'd put it so bluntly. 'Theoretically, I suppose.'

Subinspector Parera kept his eyes on my face. 'When you first came here, did you notice anyone with scratches or bruising on their arms?'

'Well,' I said reluctantly, 'Roze works on the farm. She gets scratched all the time.'

'I see.' He made another note.

'I was there when she scratched herself picking asparagus, for example. She shrugged it off – it was clearly something that happened a lot. And she doesn't wear gloves.' I looked at my own arms, now criss-crossed with scratches from the orange trees. 'Neither do I, for that matter.'

The subinspector wrote that down as well. 'Last time we spoke, you told me your father abused you. Would you be able to go into more details about that?'

'*What?*' I tried to remember what I could possibly have said to prompt that question. 'Oh – no. Not an abuser – he was *abusive*. I meant, verbally. He wasn't violent. But he could be unpleasant to people.'

The subinspector frowned. 'To women? Or just to you?'

'To pretty much everyone. But that was when I was growing up. By all accounts, he'd changed a lot since meeting Ruensa.'

But even as I said it, I could feel myself doubting it. Do people ever really change that much? And then there'd been what my father had told the gallerist, Marc, about this latest marriage going the same way as all the others . . . I should really tell Subinspector Parera that, so it could be weighed against all the other evidence.

But then he would seize on it, and Roze and Ruensa would fall under even greater suspicion.

The subinspector leant forward. 'Let me ask you this, and

please think very carefully before you answer. Did you have any personal, first-hand evidence of your father's . . . transformation? Had you seen it with your own eyes?'

'Well – no,' I admitted. 'But I was told about it by several people. The man who runs the café, for example.'

'Hmm.' Subinspector Parera's tone made it clear what he thought of café gossip. 'Have you ever seen his widow grieve?'

'What a bizarre question.'

The subinspector shrugged. 'Sometimes the police have no choice but to intrude on personal matters.'

'Anyway, the answer's yes. Many times. When we scattered my father's ashes, for example.'

'And your relationship with her is still cordial, as you described to me last time? You are still on good terms?'

'Very much so.'

'Well, that is fortunate,' the subinspector said quietly. He slid his pen inside his notebook. 'Thank you. If we have any more questions, we'll be in touch.'

He looked up at the house. 'What a beautiful property . . . There are so few of these old fincas that haven't been over-restored. May I take a look around, while I wait for my colleagues?'

'Actually,' I said, 'I'd rather you didn't.'

I was thinking of that painting room – so clearly my father's – and the signs that he'd slept there.

The subinspector gave me a thoughtful look and got up. 'Of course. I'll wait by the car.'

Relieved, I got up too. Just then, the two other detectives came out of the house, followed by Ruensa and Roze.

Officer Castell nodded at his boss. 'All done.'

'Thank you for your time,' Subinspector Parera said courteously to me, then turned to go.

The younger detective – the one I hadn't met before – said, 'Finca Síquia . . . Wasn't this the place where someone died?'

The subinspector swung back towards me.

'It must have been fifteen years ago,' the detective added. 'I remember it because she was the same age as me.'

'There was a girl who died here, yes,' I said shortly. 'I believe it was drug-related.'

He nodded. 'It was a kind of hippy commune back then, wasn't it? There was some sort of festival . . . I grew up in Sóller, just down the road, and everybody was talking about it.'

'Well . . .' I said. 'It wasn't exactly a commune. Or a festival. But my parents always had people coming and going.'

The detective clicked his fingers. 'She was here with her mother. That's right – there was a bunch of kids who'd got hold of some drugs—'

'I don't remember the details,' I lied.

The young detective nodded and turned towards the car.

But Subinspector Parera's eyes lingered on me a few moments longer, his expression once again thoughtful.

TWENTY-TWO

'He wanted to look around,' I said. 'I wouldn't let him.'

Roze glanced at me. 'Why not?'

'It looks like my father was sleeping in his painting room. And he told his gallerist he was only drinking because his marriage was falling apart. He sent Jess some drunken texts by mistake, too. He called your mother a bitch.'

We were loading my car with crates of oranges, to be taken to the cooperative in Esporles. Roze picked up another crate before she replied, carefully, 'And that makes you think what, exactly?'

'It's not what *I* think. It's what the police would think. They so clearly want to believe he was poisoned, they'll seize on any little scrap of evidence.' I paused. 'They asked about the scratches on your arms, too. I said you got them working on the farm.'

She put her crate on top of the one I'd just put in, then turned to me. 'Do you trust me, Finn?'

I looked back at her, surprised. 'Of course.'

'Then I'll tell you something you mustn't repeat to anyone else. Not to the police, or even to my mother.'

'OK,' I said, unsure where this was going.

'It was me who found him first. We'd seen him staggering about, so we kept out of his way – he could be horrible when he'd been drinking, and we could see he had a bottle stuffed in his pocket. Then he disappeared – we assumed he'd gone to sleep it off somewhere. Anyway, after a while, I went outside to look for him. Mama knows that part, but what she doesn't know is that, when I found him, he was still conscious. I tried to pull him away from the fire – like this.'

Roze demonstrated on me how she'd put her hands around his wrists.

'I knew I should try to get him on his side as well, in case he threw up,' she added. 'But he fought me – it was as if he didn't want to be moved. He clawed at my arms . . . It was so unlike him to be physically aggressive. Of course, I didn't know then it was probably because he was in a lot of pain. So yes, some of the scratches you saw were from him.'

'What happened after that?'

'I told Mama he was drunk. Later, she went out to put a coat over him – it was getting cold. She found him almost unconscious. He'd turned blue, too, and he could hardly breathe. That's when we called an ambulance.'

I tried to think this through. 'Why don't you want your mother to know he scratched you?'

'She likes to believe it was painless and quick – as if he'd just passed out. And she'd hate to think of him being violent to me. She has this . . . image of him. Of the man he could be. She doesn't like to admit he wasn't always perfect.'

I nodded. 'Well, I think you're right not to say anything. It'll only upset her, and the police will start pointing the finger at you, as well as her.' I paused. 'Thank you for trusting me with it.'

'And thank *you*, for not telling the police those other things,' she said quietly. 'I really am grateful, Finn.'

I felt a shiver of pleasure go through me. She was grateful to me. She trusted me. What was love, if not something very similar to this?

TWENTY-THREE

I don't think I was imagining it, but it felt as if there was a new depth to our relationship after that – the intimacy of a secret shared. When we worked in the fields, it was as if we sensed each other's thoughts – when one tree was finished, we both knew instinctively which we would pick next, or when we should stop for lunch.

Sometimes I worried that we were so attuned to each other, she could actually hear the clamour of my thoughts, running on just one subject – her. But of course she couldn't. As a wise person once said, there's a reason our skulls are soundproof.

Then the oranges were all picked, and the cooperative paid us for them – an astonishingly low amount. We'd harvested roughly two thousand, and our income was just over five hundred euros.

'The plan was never to make a living from the farm,' Roze said, when I pointed it out. 'The plan was to have tourists paying a little extra to stay on a working agroturismo – somewhere they could feel in tune with nature.' Her eyes took on a faraway look for a moment, then she shook her head, and it was gone.

After the oranges, we moved on to the apricots, for which there would at least be a higher price per kilo. But – disaster. Apricots are a notoriously fragile crop, and it turned out that the recent heatwave had turned the insides of ours to mush. We let them fall to the ground, gathering them with spades to sell for biofuel.

There was an interlude while we waited for the peaches to ripen – which would take another two or three weeks, Roze estimated. She said she needed to catch up on the MBA she'd been neglecting, and disappeared to her bedroom to work. I was always disappointed when she did that, waiting impatiently for her to emerge again in the evenings. In the meantime, I tried to concentrate on my own freelance work, but somehow all that seemed another world away now, and, as the days grew hotter again, I began to spend more time simply flopped beside the pool, sunbathing or swimming. Gradually, Roze began to bring her books out and join me. Her degree was taught in English, and occasionally she needed to ask me what a word meant. But she also wanted to learn Mallorquí, so sometimes we'd pull our sunloungers into the shade and I'd teach her.

'There are two words Mallorquíns use a lot: *uep* and *això*,' I told her. '*Uep* means "Hey", and we use it at the beginning of almost every sentence. And *això* just means anything you want it to. So if you say, "*Daixonem es d'això*," you're literally saying, "Thing me that thingy." You might mean, "Pass me that knife," or, "Give me the bread," or, "Walk me up the hill." It all depends on the context. We're a very chilled lot.'

'How do you flirt in Mallorquí?' Roze enquired sleepily.

'Well, you could say, *M'agrada estar amb tu*. That means, I like being with you.'

'*M'agrada estar amb tu,*' she repeated with a half-smile. Was she practising it, or saying it to me? Or both?

'And then the other person might say, *A jo també* – me too. And, if they were a woman talking to a man, they might add, *rei meu* – my king.'

'*A jo també, rei meu.*'

'And, if you really wanted to make it clear what a good time you were having, you could say, "This is honey" – *Això és mel.*'

She stretched luxuriously. '*Això és mel.*'

How I loved hearing those words on her lips, even if I had put them there myself, thinking about the day when she might say them unprompted.

There were tourists in Cauzacs now. The café tables were full, the roads clogged with drivers timid in their unfamiliar hire cars, terrified by the hairpin bends and the sheer drops down to the sea. It was unmistakably summer.

One afternoon, Roze was lying by the pool with a book – some heavy business-school tome on analytics. She was sunbathing at the same time – I'd rubbed cream into her back, and she mine, and I'd shivered at the lightness of her touch. But now I saw – or rather heard, from her gentle breathing – that she'd fallen asleep, her head resting on her forearm, her hand still propping the book open where it lay on the ground.

The sun was at its strongest by then, and it had been a good hour since I'd put that cream on her. I didn't want to wake her, but neither did I want her to burn. I went to cover her with a towel.

As I did so, I stopped, unable to complete the movement. To be able to watch her like that – sleeping and unguarded – felt such a privilege. For a few moments, I simply stood there and drank her in: the shape of her shoulder blades, like a butterfly's wings; the knotted braid of her spine; the gentle swell of her buttocks.

I was doing no harm, I told myself. She was asleep, after all.

And possibly burning. Tenderly, I laid the towel on her back, so lightly that she didn't even stir.

It was half an hour before she woke. She looked at the towel in surprise.

'Did you put this on me?'

I glanced up from my own book. 'You looked like you might be burning.'

'Thanks.' She rolled over and yawned. 'Fuck. I didn't mean to sleep. This is so lazy.'

'There's a Mallorquí saying that summer lunches last eight hours.'

She got up. 'I'm going back inside.' But then, with a laugh, she dived into the pool, deliberately soaking me, even though she could enter the water like a dart when she chose.

Another time, she brought me a fig – or rather, half a fig; she'd already eaten most of it, and the purple-grey skin still bore the imprint of her teeth.

'I think these are ripe enough to be picked now.' She held it to my mouth for me to try.

She was right – it was as sweet as jam, the skin soft, the flesh oozy, the seeds no more than a slight crunch in the texture.

'Your father always quoted some dirty poem when he ate a fig,' she added.

'Oh – God, yes. I remember that. D. H. Lawrence.' And I blushed a little, because, although I couldn't recall the exact wording, I could remember some of the language, something about a fig being like a woman's orifice, inward-flowering and womb-fibrilled. *That's why pussy's called a figa,* my father would say with gusto. *The sweetest fruit of all.*

In my embarrassment, I said, 'Figs were brought here by the Moors, originally. Some of the local varieties date back to the tenth century.'

'Really?' she said. 'So full of history, Finn.' But her eyes sparkled as she ate the last bit, and tossed the empty stalk into the bushes.

Fragments, moments, memories from that long, heat-licked summer . . . I should have said earlier, Roze and I were mostly alone together at the finca by then. Ruensa had decided that, now she was no longer doing up the house or sorting my father's things, there wasn't enough to keep her busy, and, with the tourist season underway, there was good money to be made cleaning villas. I tried to dissuade her – hadn't I promised to relieve her of that drudgery? – but she insisted that she enjoyed it.

'Besides, I simply can't lie around on a sunbed like you two,' she added. 'I'll ask my old agency for work. They'll pay me in cash, and we need the money.'

Much later, I asked Roze what her own memories of that time had been.

She thought for a moment. 'I remember the pine marten. And trying to get you to tell me your name.'

'Oh yes – the pine marten.'

One had been eating the peaches. They were good climbers, almost as good as squirrels, and had an infuriating habit of taking a single bite from each fruit. This particular one was audacious, too. Sometimes we actually had to chase it away from the trees, shouting and making shooing motions.

'That's it. I'm going to shoot it,' Roze declared after one such encounter.

'Please don't.'

'It's that pine marten or my peaches.' Technically, they were my peaches, not hers, but I understood why she felt ownership.

Rabbits were one thing – they weren't even native to the island; like the snakes and the tourists, they'd arrived on boats. But pine martens were special, somehow. And it wasn't as if the peaches were worth much – even for big ones, we'd only get thirty cents a kilo, and, unlike the oranges, they'd have to be handled carefully to avoid bruising.

'I'll tell you what,' she added, 'I won't shoot the pine marten if you tell me your real name.'

I shook my head. 'No deal.'

'That's crazy. Why not?'

'Well . . . I'll tell you the first letter. It begins with a D.'

I had a sudden recollection: my father mimicking my childhood stutter. For a while, he'd even called me Dodo, because that's what I'd say when I was asked what my name was, trying and failing to get my lips around the initial sound.

'Hmm.' She thought for a moment. Then: 'Dweezil!'

'No. I was spared that, at least.'

'Dylan!'

'. . . Would have been infinitely better than what I have. And my mother actually liked Bob Dylan – she used to strum "Lay, Lady, Lay" on the guitar.'

'I give up. Tell me.'

I shook my head. 'How do I know you won't cheat as soon as I've told you, and shoot it anyway? If not telling you keeps that pine marten alive, my lips are sealed.'

So that became another of our games – she'd shout out random words whenever one popped into her head. 'Dharma!' she'd yell as we were swimming past each other, or 'Dakota!' when we were lying by the pool. One evening, just as the three of us had started dinner, the sound of braying floated across the valley. 'Donkey!' she yelled triumphantly, and, with a forkful of food in my mouth, it was all I could do to shake my head helplessly.

'Damn!' she cried, making a frustrated gesture. 'I was sure I had it!'

Ruensa looked at us, clearly baffled as to why we were now both speechless with laughter.

Were there darker moments, as well? Yes, certainly. There was the time she wanted to go to a beach, for example. I explained there were nothing but rocky coves for miles, but she insisted; so, after our next trip into Soller for supplies, we made a small detour to the beach at Es Canyaret, just below Llucalcari. The path was steep, a scramble down through olives, carobs, pine trees and oaks, but we were eventually rewarded by the sight of a small inlet, a mixture of rocks and pebbly shingle about a hundred metres long, bordering a clear turquoise sea.

And people. Sitting on rocks, on towels, by the edge of the trees, swimming. Now that it was summer, crowding was inevitable.

Roze clutched my arm. 'What the fuck?'

'What is it?'

'You didn't say it was a nudist beach.'

'Oh – they almost all are, round here.' The early tourists being mostly German, and the Balearic Islands famously relaxed, there were few beaches that didn't have a nudist section. If they were small like Es Canyaret, most happily accommodated a mixture of clothed and unclothed, with the balance generally favouring the latter. Since my parents' house guests were often naked anyway, and I'd been coming to this particular beach since I was a child, I'd never thought anything of it.

A middle-aged man waded out of the sea close by, his rotund belly failing to mask his flapping member.

Roze stiffened. 'I want to go.'

I laughed. 'I didn't see you as uptight—'

'Anyway, *I'm* going,' she said sharply. 'You can stay if you want.' She turned.

'No problem – of course I'll come with you,' I said, a little mystified. I had an idea. 'Or we can walk to Deià – there's a trail through the woods. I doubt there'll be any naturists there. It's too smart, these days.'

As we headed towards the track, I added, 'It isn't Deià either, by the way.'

'What isn't?'

'My name.'

'Oh. Right,' she said flatly. In some strange way I didn't quite understand, the game had been suspended.

The path from Es Canyaret to Cala Deià is about three kilometres long, snaking mostly through pine woods, their cool shadows giving way to hot sunlit patches of limestone and sea. The heat made the air around us fragrant with the scent of pine needles, rosemary and thyme. In places, we joined old cobbled mule tracks, or passed houses built on rocky outcrops, their craggy terraces planted with vines.

'Those look familiar,' Roze said at one point, pointing at some distinctive rocks.

'That's probably because my father used to paint them. At one time, there were so many artists in Deià, this was known as *es camí dels pintors* – the path of the painters. After they all got priced out, he had the market pretty much to himself. That was before he really started to hit the bottle, of course.'

Where there was room, she walked alongside me, and slipped her arm through mine – not apologising for her strange reaction at the beach, much less explaining it, but, perhaps, indicating that it wasn't anything to do with me.

'These houses are nice,' she said, looking up at an old fisherman's cottage.

'Don't be fooled. They go for millions, to rich people who want to spend a few weeks every year pretending to live the simple life. That's the sort of person who'll buy Finca Síquia, unfortunately.'

She said nothing, and I realised how tactless I had been.

'Sorry,' I added.

'Finn,' she said suddenly, 'would you do something for me?'

'Of course. What is it?'

She stopped, and her eyes scanned my face. 'Just look at the business plan I drew up sometime, will you? I know it won't make any difference. But I'd like you to have seen it, all the same.'

TWENTY-FOUR

She showed me that evening, on her laptop – a simple spread-sheet with set-up costs, income, outgoings and net revenue, all precisely itemised and totalled. The rental figures were based on what other agroturismos were charging locally, she told me, the occupancy rates ditto.

'This is what we'd hope to make each year,' she said, pointing to the bottom of the revenue column.

I stared. 'Are you sure?' It seemed a very large amount – tens of thousands more than I'd expected.

'That's the great thing about agroturismos – unlike beach villas, we can expect a seven-month season.' She glanced at the spread-sheet. 'I haven't updated it since your father died. We'd have to take out the money from the painting lessons. But everything else still stands.'

'I could give guided walks,' I said, without thinking. 'I know the trails here like the back of my hand.'

She looked at me. 'You mean – you think it could work?'

I realised what I'd just said. 'No. I meant ... I was speaking hypothetically. The house still has to be sold. We still have to pay the transfer tax on the *usufructo*. There's no way round that.'

She gave me a long, searching look, then nodded. 'Well, thank you for looking at it, anyway. At least now you know what we'd planned together. Of course, I understand that it isn't going to happen.'

TWENTY-FIVE

'So, where are we, bro? I thought you'd vanished off the face of the earth.'

'It's time-consuming. You know what Spanish bureaucracy can be like.'

'But it's all basically OK? Nothing that could trip up the sale? What about the waivers – have you managed to get them to sign those yet?'

'Oh – yes, as it happens.'

'Really? Good work.' Jess sounded surprised.

'It wasn't difficult,' I assured her. 'You've got them all wrong, honestly. Neither of them is out to fleece us. Quite the reverse.'

'Good to hear, though I'll reserve judgement until they've actually left. And I'm still not handing over any money until then. So what's next on the to-do list?'

I let my eyes drift to the portrait on the wall. Ruensa, with her head turned to the window; Roze steadily meeting my gaze, urging me on. 'How would you feel about me buying you out?'

'What?'

'I like it here. I like them. They showed me their business plan. Places like this can make a very decent income.'

Jess took a few moments to respond to that. Then she said tartly, 'Well, putting aside the fact that they've clearly brain-washed you, what are you proposing to buy me out *with*? You told me you only had access to about ten grand. Which, if you recall, you've already pledged to give to the OB's widow, in exchange for a few roof slates.'

'You could come and stay whenever you wanted. I bet Leo and the kids would love to have their very own finca in Mallorca.'

'But you haven't answered my question. Where exactly would you get the funds to buy me out?'

'It would have to be in stages,' I admitted. 'So much per year, from the profits. And we'd need some money up front to pay the transfer tax, as well.'

'You don't say. How much are we talking?'

'About another thirty.'

At the other end of the phone, Jess gave an incredulous snort.

'If we call that part a loan, we'd pay you five per cent interest,' I added. 'Which isn't to be sneezed at, surely.'

'What about school fees? It won't cover those.'

'Let's face it, you can afford those already – it's perfectly obvious that Leo's loaded; it's what makes you love him. But you'd have the money I'd be paying you from the business, as well.'

'And your measly ten grand? Where does that go?'

'We'd need that to improve the access track and renovate the rest of the bedrooms.'

Jess was silent a moment. 'And this is the plan you've hatched up between you, is it? The three of you staying on at the finca, running a cosy B & B together with my money? How do you know they won't do to you what they did to our father?'

'We haven't hatched anything – I wanted to talk to you first. And they didn't do anything to our father.'

'Says you.'

'Not that I'd care much if they did,' I added.

'*Commit a sin more than once, and it will not seem to you a sin,*' she quoted loftily.

'Where's that from?'

'I don't know. The Talmud or something. The point is, if they did off him, and you fall out with them, you could be next.'

'Now you're being ridiculous.' A movement caught my eye – a flicker of light in the almost-darkness. I crossed to the window and pushed the shutter open, letting in the sounds of night – cicadas, wind in the pine trees, a distant owl. In the pool, the underwater light was on, illuminating the nearby branches. Roze was swimming underwater, her arms making wide, powerful swathes, her legs kicking, long as a frog's, her dark hair billowing behind her. Above the pool, a pair of bats fluttered and jinked in the ghostly half-light.

I turned back to the room. 'Anyway, will you think about it?'

Silence. Then she sighed. 'Look, I'll talk to Leo – see if it's even possible. But only on condition it doesn't hold anything up, OK? Keep doing whatever it is you need to do.'

'Thanks, Jess.'

'No promises, right? I'm finding out if it's possible. Nothing more.'

TWENTY-SIX

To be fair to Jess, she didn't make me wait long. She called back the next evening. I was with Roze, picking figs in the cool of the dusk, but I moved away when I saw my sister's name come up on my phone.

For all of that day, I too had dared to dream, just as Roze had once dreamt. It would be hard work, running an Airbnb as well as a working farm, but it was doable. I'd woken early, and felt an unaccustomed thrill of excitement at the prospect. As the cockerels and donkeys started their dawn chorus, I'd reached for my laptop and googled 'agroturismos around Cauzacs'. There were half a dozen, and all, according to their online booking engines, were fully booked until at least October. There was one on the other side of the valley that offered meditation, cookery lessons and therapeutic goat-herding. The latter sounded faintly ridiculous – but cookery! Ruensa's cooking was fabulous: she could teach our guests how to prepare local dishes, and cook lunch for them at the same time. Another farm was offering visitors the opportunity to get involved in the grape harvest. Our guests could pick our oranges and peaches, and we could squeeze fresh juice for them to enjoy with their meals. And, best of all, Roze and I would be together – her suitably grateful, me benevolent. Working on our shared enterprise like that, it was surely inevitable that we would become a couple . . .

'So I spoke to Leo,' Jess was saying. 'Sorry, but it's a no. He isn't up for it.'

It was a moment before I could reply. 'Why not?'

'Too risky. Your two compadres could move on or lose their immigration status, the rental licence might get turned down, some disgruntled guest might leave you a bad review on Tripadvisor and crash the bookings. Or there could be a pandemic, or an ash cloud, or even just a cold, wet summer. Compared with a lump sum he can put straight into our investment account, it's a no-brainer.'

'I'm your brother,' I said slowly.

'Well – obviously. What are you saying?'

I forced myself to speak calmly. 'I was hoping you'd do this for my sake. Because I asked you. Not because it was the most profitable option.'

A long pause. 'It doesn't really work like that, though, does it? When it comes to things like money, it's best to take the emotion out of it. Otherwise, you just end up in a really messy situation.'

'It's not messy. It's my dream.'

'Your *dream*?' Jess echoed incredulously. 'You said you'd rather cut off your hand with a rusty fish knife than live there.'

'Things have changed.'

'How, Finn? How have they changed?'

I was silent a moment. 'There are . . . possibilities now.'

'Exactly – possibilities. Not certainties. You're building castles in the sky and it isn't like you, bro. Which is why I can only conclude that the gold-diggers have somehow got you wrapped around their little fingers—'

'There's only one gold-digger in this situation,' I snapped. 'You.'

I was shaking with anger.

There was a long silence. Jess said quietly, 'One day, you'll thank me for this. Because, yes, this isn't just about the money. I don't know quite what's going on out there, but I think I can guess. And I know that sometimes my little brother has to be saved from himself.'

I still couldn't reply.

'There was a reason we had to come back to England,' she added. 'Or have you forgotten?'

Silence.

'Bye, bro,' she said.

On the line, I could just make out the chatter of static from some distant satellite. Then I hung up on her, and all I could hear was cicadas and frogs.

I went back to the fig trees. Roze's eyes searched my face, but she said nothing. We worked on in silence.

TWENTY-SEVEN

All that night, I was consumed by rage. Jess, I decided, as I lay awake fuming, had been not just materialistic, but condescending – calling me her little brother; insinuating that, in some vague, unspecified way, I was incapable of making financial decisions. As for implying that Roze and Ruensa had somehow put this idea into my head, rather than coming up with it myself – that was ridiculous, as well as insulting.

I regretted calling her a gold-digger, of course, but she'd been the one to use those words first.

But even through my anger, I couldn't help reflecting that what I was experiencing was exactly what Roze had gone through. She too had dreamt of a future at the finca. She too had had it dashed away from her. And, unlike me, she'd worked on those plans for almost a year – had sweated, day after aching day, to make them a reality.

No wonder she'd been crying when we scattered my father's ashes. She must have been crushed when she realised just what his death meant. It was extraordinary, really, that she hadn't been more hostile when I turned up out of the blue to claim my inheritance. Instead, both women had welcomed me with civility and hospitality – warmth, even.

I found myself comparing Jess with Roze, and realising that, as a person, my sister wasn't a patch on her.

Furious fantasies flitted through my head. I would simply tell Jess that I didn't consent to the sale of the house. We were co-owners, after all. If I refused to leave, she'd have to choose between dragging me through the courts – never an easy matter in Spain, as she herself had pointed out – or taking what was offered. Or Leo might die in a car crash, and her whole entitled lifestyle implode in an instant. Or . . . Or . . .

I think I went to sleep then, because I dreamt of the finca as it had been when I was a boy. The hole in the third stair down, the wood rotten yet also ringed with splinters, that I'd learnt to avoid whenever I came down in the night. The smell of cannabis and burning olive wood from the firepit, where the adults talked and played music. The chanting and the dancing and the bongos and the deep nasal groan of a didgeridoo. The guests, one male and two female, who decided to initiate a threesome on the veranda one night, their bodies streaked with paint and astral signs in honour of some pagan solstice or other, in full view of anyone who walked past.

And in the centre of it all – Lord of Misrule in his dashiki smock, his red fez akimbo on his head, his face ruddy with the firepit's flames; booming with laughter, bashing his thigh at a joke, scowling at anyone who was being insufficiently entertaining – my father.

'Can't you keep the noise down? I'm trying to sleep.'

In reality, I'd never have said those words to him – would never have dared – and, in any case, bedtimes were bourgeois and should be shrugged off like any other tokens of conventionality. But, in the dream, he turned to me.

'You can sleep when you're dead! Come and join the fun!'

I woke. The night was still and clammy – cooler air hadn't yet made its way down the side of the mountain. I lay and stared at the ceiling, wondering what the dream had meant – my mother had been a great believer in dreams always meaning things. Perhaps it meant nothing at all. But in some way that I couldn't explain, I found it had dissipated my anger at my sister. Instead, I felt for her only a cold and furious contempt.

TWENTY-EIGHT

I timed my gift carefully. Ruensa was out, cleaning. Roze and I had come back to the house for lunch – *pa amb oli* with a few slices of Mahón cheese, just soft enough to spread, the flavour nutty and sweet, followed by watermelon, deliciously cold from the fridge.

'By the way, I've got something for you.' I spoke casually, but my heart was pounding. I passed the cheque across the table. 'Here.'

She glanced at it, then did a double take. She looked up at me. 'But this is—'

'Twelve thousand euros. I wish it was more.'

She stared at the cheque, then back at me. 'Are you sure about this?'

I nodded. 'I wanted . . .' I took a deep breath. 'I told Jess about the business plan. I said I wanted to stay on here, with you and Ru, and pay her back from the profits we made. I'm afraid she didn't go for it. I'm sorry, Roze.' I gestured at the cheque. 'I know this is no compensation for all that, but at least it's something.'

'Where did this come from?' she asked quietly.

'It's the money I've been saving up for a deposit.'

She pushed the cheque back across the table. 'You can't give me that.'

'I want to. It's not as if I'm doing anything with it – it's just sitting in a bank account. Think of it as an advance on the sale of the house.'

'Well, if you're really sure.' She picked it up and looked at it again, as if by scrutinising every detail it would become more real.

'I expect there'll be something to sign – some kind of receipt,' I added. 'I'll talk to Tomàs.'

She looked at me. 'I do understand how generous you're being, Finn. Ferid told us . . . Legally, you aren't obliged to give us anything.'

'Not legally, no. But morally . . . And it means your mother can stop cleaning.'

'Oh – she actually likes cleaning; she says it takes her mind off things. She'll be thrilled about this, of course, but I don't think she'll stop. And . . .' Roze took a deep breath. 'Actually, we – I – need money right now. Quite a lot of money.'

'Why?' I said, puzzled.

'It's . . . it's best you don't know the details. It's to do with my asylum case.'

I frowned. 'I thought Ferid was doing that pro bono.'

'He is.' Roze looked torn. 'Please, Finn – don't ask me to say any more. You just have to trust me. It's something you mustn't know – that no one must know.'

'Is it a *bribe*?' I said slowly. 'If he's got you mixed up in that kind of stuff—'

'No – nothing like that. Please – forget I ever said anything.'

'It's my money,' I said hotly. 'I think I have a right to know.'

She pushed the cheque back at me for a second time. 'Take it back, then,' she said in a small voice.

There was a short silence.

'No.' I took a breath. 'Of course, it's nothing to do with me. The money's yours, now – yours and your mother's – and you can use it how you like. But please . . . Don't do anything illegal. It isn't worth it.'

She smiled, a little sadly. 'Being on the right side of the law isn't a luxury people in our position always have. But thank you, Finn. Thank you for being so generous.'

We went back to our separate rooms for siesta. For my part, I was still trying to get my head around what she'd just said. If I'm honest, I'd been indulging in a wild fantasy in which she'd be so grateful, she'd come to my room that same afternoon – not because I'd really thought that was going to happen, but because the fantasy itself was so delicious, I hadn't been able to stop replaying it over and over in my head. The soft knock on the door. My quiet, '*Entra.*' Her in white pyjamas – no, a strapless dress – no, a towel. Her smile – all she needed, when words were so redundant. Our urgent kisses . . .

I shook my head and exhaled. That wasn't happening. Instead, I seemed to be enabling some criminal enterprise.

Should I cancel the cheque? But it was too late for that. She'd already offered to give it back, and I'd said the money was theirs. I could hardly go back on my word now.

In any case, it wasn't really the possible criminality that

bothered me, I realised. It was the fact she wouldn't tell me why she needed it – that she was keeping a secret from me. However bad it was, whatever difficulty she was in, I wanted her to share it with me. Being told I mustn't know felt like a rebuff.

And, if she was capable of keeping one secret, were there others, too? When it came right down to it, how well did I really know her?

I stewed and seethed and bothered at it all afternoon, and when we went back to work at five, I was uncommunicative and curt with her. She tried hard to lighten the mood – 'Is it Dexter? What about Dodge? Dobby? Dimples?' – but I was having none of it, and eventually she retreated into a tactful silence.

TWENTY-NINE

In the morning, I didn't join them for Pilates as usual. I lay in bed instead, feeling bruised and exhausted.

There was a soft tap at my door. My heart jumped. Was it—?

But it was only Ruensa, still in her leggings and yoga top. 'I'm so sorry to disturb you, Finn. There's a frog in the pool, and I'm not sure what to do.'

I followed her outside. There was no sign of Roze. But, sure enough, there in the swimming pool was a bright green frog, nosing at the side with long, slow kicks.

'Will it be able to get out on its own?' Ruensa asked.

'No.' I crouched down. It was a water frog, originally introduced to Mallorca because they were endangered on the mainland; now, ironically, they were outcompeting the native frogs. 'If we leave it, eventually it'll get tired, and then it'll drown.' I added. I looked around for something to put it in. 'Could you get me a saucepan of fresh water?'

By the time she came back, I had the frog gently enclosed in my fist, its back legs feebly kicking against air. 'Before we let it go, we should wash the chlorine off,' I explained. 'They breathe partly through their skin, so it can be poisonous for them.'

'It's strange to think of a frog being able to drown.' Ruensa crouched beside me as I gently rinsed it off. Then, seeing its chance, it jumped out of the saucepan and into the shade of the lemon tree.

'Yes.' I watched it go. 'But it'll be all right now.'

'Finn . . .' Ruensa said, as we stood up, 'I just wanted to say thank you, for giving us that cheque.'

'Oh.' I shrugged. 'It's no more than what you were owed. Not even that, to be honest.'

'And, Finn . . . You mustn't mind if . . .' Ruensa seemed unusually sombre – awkward, even. 'Roze needs to make sure she doesn't get sent back to Albania. We know we can't stay here at Finca Síquia, of course. But for us, the priority now is simply staying in Spain. I'm safe, thanks to your father. But she – Roze – needs to make some difficult choices. I hope you understand.'

She reached out and rubbed my arm, and I was surprised to see that the expression in her eyes was unmistakably one of pity.

THIRTY

I went and worked in the fields on my own, after that. There was still no sign of Roze. The physical labour did me good, though, and gradually my sense of hurt dissipated and was overtaken by a renewed longing to see her again. I thought she must surely appear any minute – it was unlike her to miss a whole morning's work – but I worked on until lunchtime without a glimpse of her.

I went back to the finca hot and dusty, looking forward to getting in the pool. But when I got there, I saw there was a battered old Skoda parked at the front of the house.

I went around the corner. The table on the veranda had been laid with four places instead of the usual three. Ferid was sitting between Ruensa and Roze, relaxed and dapper in a Ralph Lauren shirt, his sunglasses pushed up on top of his head.

'Oh, Finn,' Ruensa said. 'You're here – good. I'll go and get the *arròz brut*.'

'I'd better shower first,' I said shortly. 'I didn't realise we had guests.'

'Ferid needed to go through some paperwork with Roze,'

JP DELANEY

Ruensa said. Was I imagining it, or was there a hint of nervousness in her quick smile? 'I'll go and take it off the stove, anyway – it's had long enough.' She bustled off.

'Aren't you going to swim, Finn?' Roze asked. She was wearing a dress – the same one she'd worn the first evening I came to the finca, I realised.

'Not today. In any case, it sounds like lunch is almost ready.' The pool was in full view of the veranda, and I didn't fancy swimming under their gaze. I nodded a curt hello at Ferid and went to shower.

When I came back, dressed in one of the shirts Ruensa had passed on from my father, the dish was on the table and they each had a glass of wine.

'Ferid was just telling us how he became a humanitarian,' Ruensa said, as she served the food.

'I didn't know that was an actual job title these days,' I muttered. Roze smiled, and I remembered her comment about sounding like my father.

'Back then, I was a corporate lawyer, in Athens,' Ferid said mildly. 'With a highly paid job, dealing with international shipping contracts. My girlfriend at the time persuaded me to go on vacation to one of the Greek islands – to Lesbos, as it happens.'

He was silent a moment. 'Like most people, back then, I was unaware that dozens, sometimes hundreds of refugees were reaching Lesbos every day on overcrowded, sinking boats, then staggering up through the sunloungers, trying to find someone to claim asylum from. Most of the holidaymakers simply ignored them. Can you imagine? They lay on their beach towels and read their magazines, trying to pretend these exhausted human beings didn't exist. I joined a group that patrolled the beaches every morning. And that was when I found . . .' His voice cracked, and he paused. 'I saw a small red object by a pile of rocks. At first, I thought it was just a discarded lifejacket. Then I got closer and I saw . . . there was a child inside it. A little boy, about three or four years old. He was dead. When I picked him up to carry him back to the others in my group, I realised why. His life jacket wasn't inflated – it couldn't inflate. It was a fake. The traffickers had saved a few pounds by giving out imitation life jackets. I phoned my office and resigned the same day. I spent the rest of that year pulling migrants out of the water.'

No one said anything.

'Now I work a few days a month, here in Mallorca, for a local law firm, to pay the bills. The rest of my time I donate to Acción de Refugiados. As for my girlfriend, she still lives in Athens and goes out with a corporate lawyer – one of my friends, in fact.'

There was another short silence.

'So you see,' Ferid said, 'every migrant I can help to claim asylum feels like one more who has been saved from the sea.'

Roze and Ruensa nodded solemnly. I felt slightly sick. My biggest achievement that day had been helping a frog out of a swimming pool. Ferid saved migrants from drowning. Of course it was no contest.

I glowered at him for the rest of the meal, drank too much wine too quickly, and, when I'd eaten, announced that I had to go and do some work in my room. I lay on my bed and tried to doze. For some time afterwards, though, I could hear the chink of glasses and the murmur of conversation from the veranda, until at last that too, mercifully, fell silent.

THIRTY-ONE

I had a brief, fitful siesta, then splashed water on my face and went into the kitchen, where Roze and Ruensa were sitting at the table, talking urgently in Albanian. A yellow folder lay between them.

Was it my imagination, or had Roze swept some papers into it just as I arrived at the door? I looked at her, but she didn't return my gaze.

Nevertheless, I was clearly coming in on some kind of disagreement. Ruensa seemed tense, while Roze wore an air of stubborn defiance.

'I didn't know Ferid was coming to lunch today,' I said conversationally, going to the tap for a glass of water. 'Does that mean there's been some news on your appeal, Roze?'

'Not really,' Ruensa began, just as her daughter said, 'Yes.'

'What's happened?' I asked.

'The tribunal have asked for more evidence,' Roze said flatly. 'Evidence we have no hope of providing.'

'She still has a very good chance,' Ruensa added.

Roze said, 'Ferid thinks we should prepare ourselves for the fact I might lose.'

'Which would mean what, exactly?' I asked.

She shrugged. 'I've already extended my red card once – that's the permit that allows you to stay in Spain while you apply for asylum. I can't extend it again. And my master's won't qualify me for a student visa beyond the end of August. This is my last attempt.'

I stared at her. 'You mean – if this goes against you, you could be made to leave?'

She nodded. 'I could be taken to an internment centre, like the one in Cádiz, then put on a flight back to Albania.'

Ruensa put her hand over Roze's. 'We won't let that happen.'

'So the alternative is just to disappear,' Roze went on. 'If I can manage to stay in Spain as an illegal for another two years, I can regularise my position through the *arraigo* scheme. But that rules out staying in Mallorca. It's too small. I'd have to go to Madrid or Barcelona.'

I was reeling. 'But . . . when would you leave?'

'Ferid thinks the sooner the better. That way, if we win, I can come back, but if we don't, I'll already be somewhere safe.' She hesitated. 'He's been telling me to go for some time, actually. I've just . . . I've been putting it off.'

All this time, I thought disbelievingly. All this time she'd been working alongside me in the fields, and she'd somehow been able to shut this out – to not even mention it. How could anyone not talk about something so big? Particularly with someone as close as I – surely – had become?

We were all silent for a while.

'There's still one other possibility,' she added. 'Not a nice one, but it would mean I could stay here, on the island. Or anywhere in Europe, for that matter.'

'Yes? What is it?' I demanded, when she didn't immediately go on.

Ruensa sighed and shook her head, as if to say that this other possibility was no such thing.

Roze said quietly, 'I could get married. To an EU citizen. Then I'd automatically get residency.' Her eyes went to the folder. 'It's not the kind of thing Ferid would normally get involved in. But he knows people who do . . . Of course, it's breaking the law. That's why he had to come in person – it's too dangerous to send information like this electronically.'

'Why? What's in the folder?' I heard myself say, although a part of me had already guessed.

Roze reached for it and took out some papers. The first page had a photograph clipped to it. It showed a dark-haired young man staring into the camera.

'This is Guillem,' she said. 'He's the man Ferid's found for me to marry.'

THIRTY-TWO

For a few moments, I found myself unable to react. Thoughts crashed into my brain. And images: Roze in a wedding dress, smiling under a cloud of confetti; Roze laughing for the wedding photos; a bouquet, tumbling through the air . . .

I shook my head to free it of this nonsense. Of course Roze's wedding would be nothing like that. It would be a quiet, miserable ceremony in a town hall. Any laughter or smiles would be fake, to fool the watchful eyes of the registrar.

But at the thought of her faking laughter for another man – any man – my stomach churned. In my head, I heard the words, *Vos podeu besar* – 'You may now kiss the bride' – and felt physically sick at what would follow.

'It would only be for a year,' Roze was saying. 'That's the minimum you need, to satisfy the authorities that it's genuine. After that, we could go our separate ways and never see each other again.' She picked up the photograph. 'Ferid says Guillem's a kind man. He needs the money to pay for an operation for his mother. So perhaps it will be bearable.'

She sounded as if she was trying to convince herself.

'Please, Roze,' Ruensa said quietly, 'don't do this. It's too risky. And besides, marrying for anything but the right reasons – for love – I think it will do something to you. *Change* you.'

I found my voice. 'Where would you stay?'

Roze shrugged, as if to say that was the least of her problems. 'There's cheap accommodation on Mallorca if you know where to look. We'll go to a campsite, if need be.'

'You can't share a tent with a stranger for a whole year!'

'Why not?' She gave a twisted shrug. 'We'll have to share everything else. If anything, it'll help prove to the authorities that we're for real. Young love will do anything to be together, right?'

'And what happens if one of you . . . if you meet someone else?'

She gave me a puzzled look. 'Well, we couldn't, obviously. It would be too risky. But like I said, it's only a year.'

'And this is Ferid's answer, is it?' My shock was quickly turning to anger. 'He's failed to get you residency on legal grounds, even though he's such a hotshot fucking lawyer that every single migrant he helps feels like he's personally pulled them out of the fucking sea. Although, in your case, it seems more like he's pushing your head under and watching you drown.'

She sighed. 'It's not Ferid's fault – he doesn't like this any more than Mama does. But I begged him to come up with some other options and this is what he's found for me. Don't blame him.'

'It's better to simply disappear,' Ruensa said. 'Surely—'

'Then I'd be leaving you,' Roze said softly. 'I can't do that. Not when you've already given up everything for me.'

Her mother didn't reply.

'It's a terrible plan,' I said hotly. 'You could go to prison.'

'Actually, the worst that would happen to me would be a fine and deportation,' she said. 'It's a much bigger risk for Ferid. He could be struck off.'

'As he bloody well should be!'

'I asked him as a friend,' Roze said. 'That's the only reason he's doing it. Despite the risks.'

'A real friend would stop you,' I retorted.

'I knew you wouldn't like it. That's why I didn't want to tell you what your money was going to be spent on. And, believe me, I don't want to be in this position.' She looked at me levelly. 'But tell me this, Finn. What other choice do I have?'

THIRTY-THREE

I didn't reply to that. Instead, I stormed back to my room, where I paced up and down like a caged animal.

What other choice do I have? Roze asked me again, from the portrait on the wall.

I stopped and spoke out loud to her: 'You could stop being such a fucking idiot, for a start.'

She nodded mutely, but I felt no better. What was so particularly infuriating, I realised, was that it was I myself who had enabled this madness. My gift to her, which I had thought so generous – so noble – was instead being used to facilitate some squalid arrangement with a stranger – a man who might be kind to his mother, but who was hardly likely to be the ideal partner in any other way, given that he'd already shown himself willing to break the law for money. And besides, I thought, my mind racing, wasn't it a bit creepy to still have that kind of relationship with your mother at his age? He might turn out to be one of those Spanish men who idolise their mothers, but despise any woman who isn't them—

My God, I suddenly thought. Would she have to sleep with

him, too? Would that be part of the price demanded, either in the upfront arrangement, or at some point along the way?

At the thought of Roze – my Roze – having to submit to Guillem's lascivious pawings, I felt physically sick.

And it might be even worse than that, I realised. Guillem might indeed turn out to be a kind, gentle partner – a humanitarian even, like Ferid, doing this at least partly out of principle. Such a man, over the course of a year, might come to seem like a knight in shining armour to Roze. What was there to stop her falling in love with him for real?

I imagined the two of them sitting on our veranda, hands entwined, glancing lovingly into each other's eyes as Roze explained, *You'll never believe how we two met – it's crazy, but now we couldn't be happier!*

I clenched my fist, and smacked my palm so hard it hurt.

What other choice do I have? Roze's portrait asked me again.

I whirled around and stared at her as an idea flooded my brain.

'You do have another choice,' I told her. 'Of course you do.' One that had been staring her in the face all along – was staring at her that very moment, in fact.

THIRTY-FOUR

I drove to Palma far too fast, taking the corners on the mountain roads at near-lethal speed. But somehow it was important not to stop and think, to hurtle towards this next stage like a teenager jumping off the eighty-foot cliff at Cala Deià.

There were plenty of jewellery shops in the city – clustered around the marina, mostly, their glittering displays positioned to catch the eyes of oligarchs' girlfriends as they strolled by on their way to lunch. I knew of some aimed more at locals, though, and walked through the door of the first one I came to.

'I need to buy an engagement ring,' I told the jeweller.

'Of course,' he said smoothly, pulling some trays out of a display cabinet and placing them on the glass counter. 'If you choose some you like the look of, I'll reserve them, so you and your fiancée can come and make the final decision—'

I shook my head. 'That won't be necessary. I'm going to choose it now.'

He raised his eyebrows. 'We find that usually, these days, couples like to select the ring together. It's the woman who has to wear it, after all.'

I pointed at one that had a dazzling white gemstone. 'How much is that?'

'That?' He picked it out and placed it on the glass. 'Nice, isn't it? That's a one-carat diamond. Extremely pure. A lot of people prefer sapphires now, but a diamond is the classic choice. The platinum band gives it a modern touch.' He waited for me to pick it up and examine it, so that it flashed tiny highlights of yellow and blue into my eyes, then added, 'It's four thousand euros.'

I must have flinched, because he said, 'The amethysts and garnets are more affordable. If you can give me an idea of your budget—'

'No,' I said. 'It's perfect.' I reached for my wallet. 'I'll take it now.'

'It's a laboratory diamond – guaranteed conflict-free,' he said conversationally, as he looked for a box. 'Some people still think they're not quite the real thing, but actually they're the only way to make absolutely sure—'

'Yes, yes, that's great.'

I waited impatiently while he boxed it. As I tapped my PIN into his card reader, he added, 'And if for any reason your fiancée isn't completely happy with it, you'd be very welcome to come back and look at some alternatives. She'll probably want it resized, in any case.'

'She's going to love it,' I said. 'Trust me, I know her.'

I drove back more slowly, thinking through how I was going to do this. There was so much to say – and yet, in some ways, so little that needed to be said. Not that I let that stop me from having a dozen different conversations with her in my head – a multiverse of different scenarios, each of them delicious or torture to me in different ways, sometimes both at the same time. Of course, I knew there was a chance she'd say no – that streak of stubbornness in her that could make her act against her own best interests sometimes. But I didn't waste too much time on that possibility. In my head, any hesitancy or doubts would be swept away by the force of my own feelings. But even if they weren't, there were – surely – compelling reasons for her to agree.

Even so, I felt my nerves rising as I neared Finca Síquia. So much was riding on this – not just my future happiness, but, I felt increasingly, hers as well.

And after all, every man is terrified when he comes to propose, I told myself.

I pulled up outside the house, then paused for a second or two. The finca seemed very still and quiet, and, despite its size, very small under the massive weight of the mountain that loomed over it, now washed a burnt-orange colour by the evening sun.

I will always remember this moment, I thought. This exact light, those shadows, that tiny quiff of cloud on the top of Puig de Galatzó.

I went around the corner. Roze was sitting at the veranda table, staring into the distance, lost in thought.

I paused for a second time, to watch her, before I spoke. 'Is Ruensa around?'

At the sound of my voice, she looked up, startled, then shook her head. 'She's gone to lie down.' She sighed. 'She's angry with me. I thought you must be, too. I saw your car wasn't here.'

'I'm not angry with you,' I said. 'I'm happy. And I'm glad your mother's not around. I want to talk to you alone.'

A puzzled frown flitted across her face. 'Why?'

'Because I've thought of a better idea than you marrying Guillem.' I pulled out the ring box and placed it in front of her, adjusting it so it was straight, like a fussy waiter positioning an amuse-bouche in front of an honoured diner. As I opened it, the light from the diamond seemed to explode into our faces. I got down on one knee. 'Roze . . . Will you marry me?'

Her expression of astonishment was almost comical. Was she *too* astonished? Was this something that had never even crossed her mind? 'But – Finn – what are you saying?'

'I want to marry you. That's got to be better, hasn't it, than someone you don't even know? Someone who might be kind to his mother, but horrible to you? Why take that risk, when you don't have to? And, from a practical point of view, I'm just as good as he is – I was born here in Mallorca, a pre-Brexit baby, so I have an EU passport too.'

'So it would just be – for me?' she said slowly. 'To help me out?'

'No,' I admitted. I got to my feet and sat down. The urge to touch her was irresistible, and, for the first time, I didn't resist it. I reached out and put my hand over hers. 'It would be for me, as well. I want to do this.'

'Because . . . you know . . .' she went on slowly, 'in some ways, it might actually be easier to marry a stranger than a friend. Someone who has no . . . expectations. Who I'm free to like or dislike, or get on with or not, because it's clear from the start that it's a purely financial arrangement.'

'That part's up to me, though, isn't it? I'm willing to take that risk – of you disliking me, I mean.' I was silent for a moment. 'Besides, I think I can make you happy.'

'Happy!' She shook her head, almost in disbelief, as if happiness was now beside the point. 'And what about *you*, Finn? Will I make you happy?'

'You already do,' I said softly. 'You see, you wouldn't be marrying a friend. That's not what I am. Not only that, anyway.'

'What are you, then?' Her voice shook a little.

'Something more.' I paused. 'I'm in love with you.'

She gave a little gasp. Of delight, or surprise? Horror, even? Or simply because, after so long, I'd finally put into words what we'd both been thinking?

She put one hand unsteadily to her face. 'I've been trying to think of you as family.'

I noted that *trying*. 'Well, don't,' I said shortly.

There was a brief silence.

'In any case,' I added, 'you can't marry Guillem now. That cheque I gave you will bounce.' I nodded proudly at the ring. 'That's a one-carat diamond I just bought you. But there'll be enough left in my account to redo the access track, and probably to renovate the top floor, too.'

She glanced at me sharply. 'What about Jess? And selling up?'

I shrugged. 'It's a package deal. Me and the house. It was high time I stood up to her, anyway.'

Roze thought for a moment. Then she nodded, and for a second or two my heart soared, before she said, 'There's something I need to tell you, Finn. Something I – we – didn't tell you the whole truth about before. And then, if you want, you can ask me again, and I'll give you my answer. But you need to hear me out first.'

'OK,' I said. 'I think I can probably guess what it is, anyway.'

She glanced at me again, puzzled.

'About your mother and my father . . . ?' I suggested.

'Oh.' She shook her head. 'No. It's about me.'

I was about to prompt her with another question when she jumped up.

'Can we walk somewhere while we talk? This is . . . difficult for me.'

'Of course.'

We walked towards the fruit terraces. I offered her my arm, but she didn't take it.

'When we told you, that first night, that we'd come to Mallorca by chance because we were running away from someone in Albania, that wasn't quite true,' she began. 'But we knew you'd be curious, and there was no way I could tell you the truth, not when you were still a stranger.'

'Why not?' I asked, when she didn't go on.

'Because it's too painful to talk about. But I'm going to try.' She sighed. 'When I was in my last year at college, I had my first serious relationship. His name was Dion. He was beautiful. And wealthy – he had an incredible car and so on – though I never really found out where his money came from. He didn't seem to have a job . . . He was generous, though. Always taking me out, always buying me nice things. I loved him so much. I even brought him home to meet Mama. We started making plans together – what we'd do after I finished college . . . Then he found this incredible master's for us both to enrol on, here in Mallorca – an MBA. He showed me the website. It was in a beautiful old building, with really good lecturers . . . He'd never shown any sign of being interested in business before, but I was so happy at the idea we'd be together. I even sent them a deposit.'

She fell silent again. Her voice, when she went on, was flat, all emotion drained away.

'When we landed, there was a car with three men in it, waiting. They said they were taking me to the college, to register. Dion told me to go with them – he even said something about how he could vouch for them because they'd all been messaging each other on Facebook. He blew me a kiss and said he'd see me later . . . That was the last time I ever saw him.

'They call it the Romeo trick. It's how most of the girls working here get trapped into it – the ones from Eastern Europe, anyway. That evening, they sat me down and told me Dion had already gone back to Albania with twenty thousand euros in his pocket. When I'd earned back the debt, they said, I'd be free to leave too. Until then, I had to do everything they said.'

She stared sightlessly into the distance. 'Brothels are legal in Spain – did you know that? They're called *puticlubs* and even teenagers go to them – it's completely normalised here; part of their culture, like bullfighting. At first, I was made to work in an apartment with two other new girls, where they could make sure I wouldn't run away. Everything was charged to my account – food, rent, clothes, even condoms. However much I earned, the debt hardly went down.'

'Roze . . .' I said helplessly. 'I'm so sorry.'

She nodded in silent acknowledgement and went on, 'In the apartment, there was always the threat of violence to keep us in line. But in the clubs, they have to step back – sex work isn't illegal, but pimping is, so they rely on the management to tell them if a girl isn't pulling her weight. I worked in a club near the marina. One day, I asked a teenage customer if I could borrow his phone, and used it to text my mother the address. She flew to Mallorca the very next day and got me out.

'When we told you we couldn't go home, that was the truth – one of the threats was always that they'd go after your family in Albania if you tried to escape, and Dion had given them the address of our apartment. That's why we had to get a friend to sell it for us. Neither of us would ever have been safe there again.' She was silent a moment. 'That poor kid whose phone I borrowed. He couldn't get out of there fast enough when he realised. But really, what do they imagine? All the women in that place had been forced into it one way or another – either trafficked, or bullied into it by pimps. The men who went there weren't customers, whatever they pretended to themselves. They were rapists.'

'Jesus,' I said. '*Jesus*. Roze, I can't even begin . . . It must have been horrific.'

'Yes,' she said simply. 'It was.'

We'd stopped walking by then – we'd come to the end of one of the terraces, the low wall a natural stopping point.

'Sometimes I think I'm starting to get over it,' she added. 'Then something will remind me . . . Like that guy on the beach.' She nodded in the direction of Es Canyaret, far below. 'For a moment,

I thought I recognised him . . . I hadn't, of course. It was just the type. Fat, hairy, old, with his dick out. So I freaked. Sorry.'

'You've got nothing to apologise for.' At the thought of a man like that pressing his paunchy body against hers, my blood boiled. 'But if you ever *do* recognise someone, tell me, and I'll happily kill them for you.'

She shrugged. 'To be honest, after a while you stop looking at their faces.'

There was another long silence.

'I don't normally talk about this,' she said in a stronger voice. 'Not even to Mama – it upsets her too much. But you need to know why . . . to understand . . . I don't think I'll ever fully trust a man again. I'll certainly never have the kind of relationship I had with Dion. So you see, you would basically be marrying a nun. A really fucked up, angry nun.' She turned sideways, so she could study my face properly. 'I'm telling you because I don't want there to be any false . . . expectations. I like you, but not in that way. It's nothing personal. But I care about you enough to want you not to get hurt.'

'If anyone can mend you,' I said quietly, 'I think it would be me.'

She smiled then – a sad little smile. 'Perhaps you're right. But I can't make any promises about that. So, really, the simplest thing would just be for you to take the ring back to the shop, I'll cash your cheque, and then I'll go ahead and marry Guillem.'

'That's not going to happen,' I said firmly. 'For one thing, I don't think the jeweller would be too happy if I turned up on his doorstep demanding a refund. And for another . . .' I knelt down and plucked a blade of grass from where it was growing against the wall. Twisting it into a makeshift ring, I looked up at her for the second time that day.

'Marry me,' I said simply. 'Marry me for a year and a day, and I promise it'll be the happiest year of our lives.'

THIRTY-FIVE

'I don't think you appreciate just how difficult it will be,' Ferid said. 'It certainly won't be some schoolboy adventure. It is deadly serious, with unpleasant consequences for all of us if we get found out. Most especially for Roze.'

He gave me a sour look, and I tried to wipe the grin off my face.

'Sorry,' I said. 'I was thinking about something else.' But I couldn't help reflecting gleefully that the lawyer's nose had clearly been put out of joint by the discovery that it was me, rather than his protégé Guillem, Roze would be marrying. I'd been feeling cheerful enough already, but Ferid's bad temper was the icing on the cake.

'For several years now, any non-EU foreigner marrying an EU citizen in Spain has been required to attend an interview, six weeks before the wedding, together with their fiancé,' he continued. 'The officials will take you into separate rooms and present each of you with a questionnaire. One section will be basic information about yourself and your partner – birthplace, date of birth and so on. They will ask about your financial affairs – who is the breadwinner, which bills do each of you pay, that sort of thing. But there will also be some everyday questions designed to trip you up. What is your partner's favourite meal? What is the recipe? Who are your best friends as a couple? And some of those questions will be intimate and even intrusive. Which side of the bed does your partner sleep on? Do they have any scars or tattoos? Do they wear pyjamas?' He paused. 'To make it harder, they change the questions every few weeks. We can prepare you, to some extent, from old ones we have seen, but they will only be a start. You should think of this as a very important examination, one for which you must study intensively.'

I thought of being a student again, with Roze as my only subject, and had to fight to stop the smile from coming back. My eyes kept going to the ring – I noticed how she kept her left hand on top, so the diamond sparkled in the brilliant Mallorquín sunshine, and how her own eyes kept going back to it as well, as if to check that this was really happening.

I'd offered her the chance to change it, of course, after she'd said yes. But she said she loved it – as it happened, even the size was right. She wore the grass one I gave her for a day or so too, even though it was never going to survive our regime of hard labour very long. But it had given me almost more pleasure to look at than the other one. The diamond was necessary, at least in part, for the rigmarole of proving we were genuine – Ferid had been going to find a fake one for Guillem to give her, he'd told me tetchily – but the grass ring was for us, plucked from the earth of the farm we both loved, and for our eyes alone, rather than any town-hall official.

After she'd said yes and I'd put it on her finger, we'd walked quietly back to the house. Just before we got there, she laced her fingers in mine.

'When we tell Mama . . . I have a feeling that she'll worry. I'm not going to tell her the exact details of our arrangement, but I am going to say that you've promised to be good to me. She's more romantic than I am, so this will be hard for her. We can't suddenly pretend to be passionate lovers who can't keep our hands off each other, but we should show her that we can be affectionate and kind with each other.'

'Of course,' I said, raising our joined fingers to my lips and giving them a kiss. 'Kindness and affection. That should be the bedrock of every marriage, anyway.'

As it turned out, Ruensa had already come across the ring, which I'd left on the table when we went to the orange grove. We found her staring at it fearfully. As we approached, she looked up at Roze. She said nothing – that look, and her silence, asked the question for her.

'I'm going to marry Finn,' Roze said defiantly.

Ruensa spoke to her in Albanian – four or five sentences that sounded like questions. Roze nodded and answered in the affirm- ative each time.

A little reluctantly, Ruensa turned to me. 'Thank you, Finn. I think you know that I don't like this idea. But I'm very glad that it's you and not some stranger.'

It was the following day when we sat down with Ferid to dis- cuss how it would work. Ruensa joined us, listening without comment to his description of the process – having married as a foreigner herself, of course, she would already have been familiar with most of it.

It was her who asked quietly, 'And remind me – what happens if the officials become suspicious?'

'Then they will refer the information to the police, who will decide whether or not to open an investigation,' Ferid said. 'The police, in turn, can prevent the marriage from going ahead while they gather more evidence, and, if necessary, take what they have found to an examining magistrate, to authorise criminal charges.'

He turned to Roze and me. 'It is quite possible that the officials will refer you in any case. The fact you have known each other for only a few months will be a clear red flag. And you can hardly lie about that, given that the police have been in contact with Finn ever since he came. Then, once the police are involved, there are many other investigative tools at their disposal. They could turn up here at any time, for example, to check whether you really are living as a couple. Or they may ask to see your phones, so they can examine your messages.'

Roze and I looked at each other, puzzled. 'We haven't sent each other any messages,' I said. 'Working together as we do . . . if we want to communicate, we just talk.'

Ferid nodded. 'Well, you might want to start now, to build a picture that supports this fiction. You should take photographs, too, that demonstrate how close you are. And they may want to know when you told your friends and family this happy news.'

I was silent. Telling Jess and Tomàs was an ordeal I hadn't yet faced.

Ferid kept his gaze on me. 'I imagine this may be difficult for your sister, Finn. Presumably she still thinks you are only here to organise the sale of the house.'

'It's going to be awkward,' I admitted. A thought struck me. 'Is there any way I could come up with some legal obstacle to selling? Something that might plausibly hold her off for a year?'

'Hmm.' Ferid considered. 'Have you sent those waivers to your lawyer yet?'

'Not yet,' I confessed. The envelope was still in my room, unposted.

'Let me take another look at them, then, and at the original agreement as well. Perhaps there is some ambiguity we can exploit ... But, really, it shouldn't be me advising you on this. You already have a lawyer.'

'That would also be difficult,' I said. 'Tomàs is a family friend.'

'Ah.' Ferid nodded. 'Then I can certainly take a look and give you, as it were, some unofficial advice.' He gestured at the village below us. 'What about your neighbours? The police may question them. Would they support your story of falling in love among the oranges?'

Roze looked at me. 'I haven't met most of them. I've been trying to keep a low profile.'

'Leave that to me,' I said. There was a time-honoured way to let the whole of Cauzacs know about a new relationship, and we could do it straight away.

THIRTY-SIX

Later that morning, Roze and I drove down to the village, and held hands as we walked into the square. At the pharmacy, she peeled off, blowing me a kiss as she did so, and I continued into the café.

'Finn!' Alejandro greeted me. 'What can I get you?'

'Just a quick cortado. I'm waiting for Roze while she gets a few things from the pharmacist.'

'Yes, I saw.' He gave me an enquiring look, and I nodded.

'We're together. It's been a while now, actually. Pretty much love at first sight.'

'Love!' Alejandro echoed. 'I thought you were just here to sell the house.'

'So did I.' I shrugged, allowing my grin to spread from ear to ear. 'Turns out life had other plans.'

'Wow . . . You'll have to introduce her to Aina.'

'We'd like that.' I left a pause. 'We'd love the two of you to come to the wedding, actually.'

'Wedding?' Alejandro looked shocked, then amused. 'Well, congratulations, Finn. That's pretty fast work.'

I nodded. 'Sometimes you just know, don't you? And, with

Roze, it was exactly like that. The moment I set eyes on her, I thought, That's the woman I'm going to marry.'

Alejandro looked serious for a moment. 'You were always like that. I remember how, at school, you were always completely in love with one girl or another.'

'We all were, at that age,' I said lightly.

'And following in your father's footsteps, too. *De tal palo tal astilla* – a splinter off the old stick.'

'Well . . .' I said. 'It's not quite the same, I hope. Given that he was a drunken oaf who couldn't keep it in his trousers.'

'Oh, sure. But you know what's funny? Just over a year ago, when he came in here and said he was getting married again, he used almost the exact same words you did just now – "You just know".' Alejandro nodded. 'Anyway, I'm really happy for you. It's great news.'

As he turned away to serve a customer, I became aware that someone else had just come in. It was Miquel, my less-than-cheerful neighbour.

I gave him a nod. '*Uep.*'

'*Uep,*' he grunted back.

'I was just telling Alejandro – I'm engaged now.'

'Congratulations,' he said dourly. 'Who's the lucky woman?'

'Actually, you'll have seen her – it's Roze, the one who helped my father clear our terraces. You've probably seen her out there with me, as well.'

'Oh.' He made a face. 'Sure, I've seen her with you. But never with him. Well, maybe a couple of times. It was her who cleared the terraces – her and her mother.'

'I think you're mistaken,' I said lightly. 'My father helped her. And with the harvests, too, just like I do.'

'Your father?' Miquel looked scornful. 'He barely raised a hand to those fruit trees in thirty years. But I'll say this for those women – they're hard workers. Day after day, they were at it. I assumed they were hired labourers when I first saw them. They say you can get black-market fruit pickers for around thirty euros a day, if you know who to ask.'

I gave him a thin smile. 'They're not black-market workers.'

He shrugged. 'If you say so.' He tapped a coin on the bar to attract Alejandro's attention.

Roze walked in, a paper bag from the pharmacy in her hand. Coming up to me, she kissed me on the cheek. 'I'm done.'

'So am I,' I said shortly. 'Let's go.'

Roze nodded politely to Miquel, who ignored her, before I took her arm and guided her out.

'We have a saying,' Roze observed as we turned up the road towards Finca Síquia. '*Ti glóssa sou katápies?* It means something like, Say what's on your mind.'

'Sorry.' I sighed. 'Just something Miquel said, back in the bar.'

'About me?'

'Not exactly . . . He was just being unpleasant.'

'He gives me the creeps. When I'm out in the fields, sometimes I see him staring at me.'

'I don't think he's a fan of migrants.'

'It's more than that. He wanted those fields for himself – did you know that?'

I glanced at her. 'What makes you say that?'

'Your father told us – he'd been on at him about it for years. Miquel's argument was that, since your father didn't use them, he might as well let Miquel add them to his own terraces, so the land could be worked as one block. Your father said Miquel wouldn't be happy when he saw us clearing them.'

As a proposition, it actually made sense, now that I came to consider it. Miquel's was the only property that bordered ours on that side. And, once our fields were amalgamated with his, it would become much easier for him to hang on to them – possibly even to buy them – when the finca was sold.

'Your father was very close to saying yes, before we came along,' she added. 'He knew Miquel wouldn't pay him much for them, but he didn't have many other sources of income left.'

No wonder Miquel claimed not to like migrants, I thought. As so often with old-school Mallorquíns, it was partly about self-interest.

I decided to tell Roze what was bothering me. 'He said it was you and your mother, mostly, who cleared the land. Not my father.'

She glanced across at me. 'Yes, that's right.'

'Oh – I thought . . .' I was trying to remember. How had I formed the impression that my father had helped her?

'I said your father *backed* me doing it – getting the tractor, that is,' she corrected me. 'And then, later, when I needed a bit of extra help with the fruit picking, he started doing that too. Not the initial clearing, though.'

'Apart from the oleander,' I pointed out.

'What do you mean?'

'Well – he was burning the oleander when he died. There was a big mass of it in among the fruit trees, your mother said, that he'd been clearing out. I think that's why I just assumed—'

'Oh . . .' Roze said. 'Yes, he did do that part. Maybe because he knew it was dangerous to handle, and he didn't want me doing it.'

'Right.'

We drove in silence for a little while.

'Why is this feeling like a police interview all of a sudden?' she demanded. There was a steely edge to her voice that I was becoming familiar with – the tone she used when she thought I was crossing a line.

'It's not meant to, really. I was only wondering—'

'Sometimes, Finn, you have to choose who to believe.' The steely note was getting more pronounced.

'Of course,' I said.

As the house came into view, another thought occurred to me. If Miquel had been frustrated by not getting the answer he wanted from my father, could he conceivably have hastened the sale of the land along by killing him? My father could be a rude bastard, after all – even ruder than Miquel. He'd have made a terrible neighbour, and that was even before you factored in all the late-night parties and didgeridoo music from the hippy years. What if Miquel had harboured resentment against him for decades, but forced himself to hide it because he hoped to get something from him one day? Could the prospect of this new, more settled phase in my father's life have caused that to boil over?

I wondered if Subinspector Parera had ever considered that possibility. But even as I asked myself the question, I knew it wouldn't be to our advantage to raise it. However suspicious the police were about my father's death, officially it was still a tragic, self-inflicted accident. Any investigation now would inevitably rebound on Ruensa and Roze. Better to let sleeping dogs lie.

'That's probably all it was, then,' I said as I parked outside the finca and turned off the engine. 'Pure spite on Miquel's part. I won't give it any more thought.'

THIRTY-SEVEN

Finn to Roze, 09:18:

Thank you for last night xx

Roze to Finn, 09:22:

No, thank YOU. It was beautiful X

Finn to Roze, 09:23:

Even though you snore . . .

Roze to Finn, 09:26:

Ha ha. That isn't true of course

Finn to Roze: 09:27:

Don't worry, I could watch you snore for hours (and probably did, given that sleep was impossible)

Roze to Finn, 09:32:

Well, I slept VERY well. I think we both know why xx

Finn to Roze, 09:33:

Glad to be of service xx

Roze to Finn, 09:36:

Aixos es mel, my beautiful lover xx

Finn to Roze, 09:37:

Aixos es mel xxxx

THIRTY-EIGHT

'What make of phone do I have?'

'An iPhone. And me?'

'A blue Samsung Galaxy, with cracks in one corner.'

'Very observant, Finn. Which corner? How did I break it?'

I stretched luxuriously. 'Bottom right. And you dropped it on the kitchen floor, which –' I glanced down – 'like the floors in most Mallorquín kitchens, is made of hard tiles.'

'OK . . . What's my favourite meal?'

'Rabbit. Preferably trapped with your own hands and slowly tortured to death.'

'Be serious.'

'Tumbet.'

'Correct. How many pairs of shoes do I own?'

'Only four.'

Roze glanced up from the questionnaire Ferid had given us, frowning. 'How come you know that?'

Because I want to know everything about you. 'Like you said, I'm observant. Do I use an electric toothbrush or manual?'

'Hmm.' She thought, her head on one side. 'I'm going to say manual. Originally you only packed for a few days, after all.'

'Wrong – I always travel with my electric toothbrush. What's the most romantic thing we've ever done together?'

She screwed up her face. 'I've no idea.'

I said softly, 'I took you on the old railway that runs from Sóller to Palma, when the orange blossom was out. First it goes through a whole valley of fruit trees, then through the mountains – a long, long tunnel, as cold as the deepest cave – and, when you eventually come out, suddenly you're on the other side of the island, with the sea far away and the plain below you.'

'It sounds lovely.'

'It is.' I was silent a moment. 'We should do it for real sometime.'

'Good idea. It might help if I can talk about some of the land-marks along the route.' She made a note on her questionnaire. 'How do you usually celebrate Christmas?'

A part of me knew it wasn't real, of course – that our court-ship was just another of our games, albeit a deadly serious one. Yet even the pretence was so dizzyingly enjoyable that it created a reality of its own, a kind of mutual daydream. When my phone pinged with a romantic text from her, my heart leapt as if it were the real thing; when she squeezed my arm, or gave me a quick kiss on the cheek, it was easy to forget that it was just for her mother's benefit. And, besides, I'd already convinced myself that the pretence and the reality would grad-ually converge; that the more I proved to her she could trust me in executing this charade, the more she would trust me in every other way, too.

When I laid a trail of crumbs to entice a pine marten or an almond-eater to come to my hands, the crumbs didn't lead anywhere near me to begin with – didn't even look like a trail. It was only when the animal had overcome its initial fear and become accustomed to my distant, unthreatening presence that I let the crumbs fall a little closer. But even then, I made no sudden movements, no gestures or demands. It was all about building its confidence, so that – slowly, slowly – it chose of its own volition to edge a little more in my direction. That was the crucial thing: it had to make that decision on its own. So I waited patiently, trusting that, if I laid enough tiny crumbs of kindness, one day Roze would want to say those words to me for real.

THIRTY-NINE

I sometimes think that learning a new person is like learning a language – to begin with, you stutter and fumble for the most basic of phrases. But, gradually, the work becomes less about vocabulary and more about the subtleties of inflection and meaning. So it was with us – as we became more attuned to each other, we could often guess each other's answers correctly, without having to be told.

'What are you planning to get me for my birthday?' she asked me.

'I haven't decided yet. After all, I've got until November the twelfth. But I was thinking of a puppy. One that could come out to the fields with us while we work.'

She stared at me, astonished. 'That's actually a really great present!'

'I know.' I was smiling now, at the thought that she liked it. 'Have I ruined the surprise?'

She shook her head. 'Anyway, I don't like surprises.'

We sat in silence for a few moments.

'Finn . . .' she began.

'Yes?'

'You realise I'm going to have to know your real name now, don't you? It would be crazy to have memorised your date of birth and so on, then tell them you could be called Donald Duck for all I know.'

'Donald Duck?' I sighed theatrically. 'Oh, if only.'

'Finn!'

'I suppose you're right,' I admitted.

'Well . . . ?'

It was genuinely hard to do this – secrecy about my name had become more than just a habit; it was a way of compartmentalising everything I despised about my parents' way of life.

I took a breath. Once again, I felt like I was about to leap off a high rock.

'My real name – my birth name, I should say, since I don't think there's anything remotely genuine about it – is Dolphin Oberon Siddhartha Hensen.'

'Your name is Dolphin?'

'Yes. "Finn" was Jess's way of shortening it, when she couldn't say the whole word. So, gradually, my parents started calling me that too.'

'OK . . . But what's so bad about that?'

'Apart from the fact that calling your child after an endangered cetacean is narcissistic, selfish and almost guaranteed to get them bullied at school? Nothing.'

'Perhaps they thought it wouldn't matter in a Spanish-speaking school.'

'Well, they were wrong.' I felt almost light-headed at having confessed so much. 'Anyway, now you have to tell me something about you, in return. Something secret.'

'Me? I don't have any secrets left.'

'Somehow I doubt that's true.'

She only smiled and shrugged.

That afternoon, I was lazing in the pool when I saw Ferid's battered Skoda coming up the track. I watched as he got out. I assumed he'd go into the house, to see Roze, but when he saw me, he turned and headed in my direction.

'I need to speak to you, Finn,' he called.

'Couldn't you have phoned?'

Reaching the pool, he stopped and looked down at me. I saw he had a thin folder in his hand. 'I told you – there must be no communications between us on this subject, not ever. Proceed on the assumption that the authorities will one day scrutinise every text, every photograph, every call log and every email. Because the likelihood is that, yes, they will. Have you heard yet when your marriage interview is?'

I nodded. 'A week tomorrow, at the town hall. The letter came this morning.'

'Well, that's something, to have a firm date.' He pulled a chair out from the veranda table and sat down. 'You asked me to take a look at the *usufructo*, to see if there was anything we could use to delay the sale of the house.'

'Oh – yes.' I climbed out of the pool and wrapped a towel around myself. 'What do you think? Is it possible?'

'You must understand, this isn't my area. But I showed the

document to a colleague . . . By coincidence, he worked in international house sales before he joined us, so he has some idea of the different legal systems here and in the UK.'

'And? What did he say?'

Ferid hesitated. 'It seems there is a discrepancy, of sorts. The document itself, as I'm sure you're aware, is mainly in Spanish, but it also contains an English translation, for clarity. The Spanish version says that you and your sister own the freehold as *inquilinos conjuntos*, which the translator has rendered literally as "joint tenants".'

I shrugged. 'And?'

'In English law, unlike Spanish, that phrase has a very specific meaning, quite distinct from the more usual "tenants in common". It means, for example, that your sister cannot force you to sell your share if you don't want to.' He grimaced. 'Well, she probably could, if a Spanish judge ordered it. But it would be a complex and difficult case, with lawyers from both countries racking up fees. She would be much better advised to come to some kind of agreement with you.'

I was silent as I processed this. True, at one point I had fantasised about somehow cutting Jess out. But I had never seriously imagined it might be possible. And she was the only close relative I had.

Then I thought about the prize that awaited me if I did. Living at the finca, and married to Roze. Business partners in our own little paradise, and lovers in all but deed. Once again, I felt almost dizzy at the prospect.

'Please understand, I am not advocating this course of action,'

Ferid added, 'any more than I am advocating that you get married. In fact, my advice is almost the exact opposite – I think both actions are fraught with risk.'

'But it's possible,' I said softly. 'If we do this, there's a chance we might get away with it.'

'Yes,' he said, equally quietly. 'There is a chance.'

We were both silent, contemplating that.

Then he added, 'Of course, I understand why Roze might be drawn to this. For her, there are few alternatives, and all of them present difficulties. But you . . . I am not sure why you feel compelled to go along with it.'

I looked at him, unabashed. If his intention was to embarrass me into admitting the strength of my feelings for Roze, he was failing.

'Perhaps I'm just a humanitarian,' I suggested.

'Perhaps,' he agreed. 'Or . . .'

I waited. Whatever he had been about to say, evidently he had changed his mind.

'You know,' he said eventually, 'during that terrible time when I was pulling people from the boats . . . often they were overcrowded. The traffickers would force forty people to get into a fishing vessel with room for no more than a dozen. After a few hours, the boat would be awash and on the verge of sinking. In the worst cases, there would be dead bodies down in the bilges, and the ones who had survived had done so by standing on them. Of course, they would always say those poor people had drowned long before they did that, but I sometimes wondered . . . It's a simple truth that some migrants survive and some don't. Once,

I found a baby floating in the sea, clutching at an empty water bottle, because it somehow instinctively knew that, if it could only cling on, it would live. And it did – when we checked it over, we found it was perfectly well, despite its time in the water. A triumph of the human spirit over adversity, you might say. The thing is, you can't tell just by looking who has that instinct – to survive at any cost – and who does not. I don't think a person even knows themselves, until they are in that position.

'Roze has an astonishing instinct to survive. Something in her, something perfectly hidden, burns fiercely ... As her lawyer, it makes her a very good client, always willing to take a suggestion or a strategy and run with it. But I would not like to be the person she needs to stand on to avoid drowning, if you take my meaning.'

There was, I realised, a touch of bitterness in his voice. I regarded him calmly. I did indeed understand him perfectly. He was in love with her himself – hopelessly infatuated, with no hope of her ever returning his affection. That touch on the arm she gave him outside the café, which at the time had made me so jealous – that wasn't because she had feelings for him, but rather because he had feelings for *her*, and she needed his help. She had used him and moved on, and he was feeling sore about it.

I felt sorry for him, of course, but, now that I had bested him, I no longer felt threatened by him. I even found myself quite liking him. We had competed for her, but he had lost.

He sighed and pulled something from his folder. 'This is a draft of an email you could send your sister, if you decide to go down that path. I would ask you to be so kind as to destroy this piece of paper once it has served its purpose – as I said, there must be no record of any dealings between you and me.'

I took the document and read it. It was written in legalese, but the meaning was clear. I was informing my sister that I had decided not to sell, and that, under the terms of our parents' agreement, she had no right to force me to.

Wordlessly, I placed the draft on the table. Ferid was watching me closely.

'To love someone you are with almost every minute of the day, and not be loved in return . . . that would be a kind of living hell, I think,' he said softly.

'I don't know what you're talking about,' I said shortly. 'If you have inappropriate feelings for your client, that's not my problem.' I tapped the document. 'Thank you for this. I'll let you know what I decide to do.'

FORTY

I almost didn't do it. I'd got so used to being bossed around by Jess that the thought of standing up to her seemed an enormity, almost a betrayal. Alone in my room, I wrestled with the decision for the rest of that afternoon. But then, just before Roze and I were due to go back to work in the fields, my phone pinged.

It was a WhatsApp message. A photo – a selfie. She was in her underwear, smiling at the camera.

The caption read, *Couldn't resist sending you this x*

I drank the image in for a few moments, then tapped back, *I love you x*

Her reply, after an agonising minute, was equally simple.

Love you too, dolphin boy xxx

FORTY-ONE

Jess to Finn, 17:03:

WTF is that email you just sent me? And why aren't you answering your phone?

Jess to Finn, 17:07:

Ffs pick up. Is this some kind of scam?

Jess to Finn, 17:12:

For Christ's sake, tell me what's going on out there. This is complete bullshit and you know it. Have you got Stockholm syndrome or something? Whatever it is, we need to sort it out, so YOU NEED TO ANSWER YOUR PHONE

Jess to Finn, 18:32:

Can't go on leaving you voicemails. You need to call me NOW

Jess to Finn, 19:02:

Now what the fuck? My texts aren't getting a 'delivered' note and my phone cuts out when I call you. HAVE YOU FUCKING BLOCKED ME?? Your own sister?

Jess to Finn, 19:03:

Fuck you, Finn. Just fuck you. You've fucking gone too far this time

FORTY-TWO

The next morning, Roze and I were having breakfast on the veranda when a car made its way carefully up the track – a smart Audi, very different from Ferid's beaten-up Skoda.

'Who's that?' Roze asked as it pulled up.

'I don't know.'

The driver's door opened and Tomàs got out. He paused for a moment, looking up at the house, then strode purposefully towards where we were sitting.

'It's my lawyer,' I said. 'You'd better go. I have a feeling Jess may have called him.'

'Of course. I'll be inside if you need me.' As she left, she put her hand on my shoulder and squeezed briefly.

'Good morning, Tomàs,' I called. 'I was just about to make coffee. Would you like one?'

'No,' he said shortly. 'Finn, what is this nonsense Jess has been telling me about? Is it true?'

'I've decided not to sell, if that's what you mean,' I said defiantly. 'I'm going to stay here for the time being, with my future wife and my mother-in-law.'

'Your *wife*?' He stared at me. 'But who . . . ? My God. Is this your father's widow and her daughter we're talking about?'

'Yes. There's no law against that, is there? We intend to run this place together, as an agroturismo – a business.'

'A business?' he repeated incredulously. He waved a piece of paper under my nose – I recognised the email I'd sent Jess the afternoon before. 'And this? Where in God's name did this come from?'

'I'm correct, though, aren't I?' I was watching him carefully. 'The *usufructo* has been badly worded. I don't have to sell if I don't want to.'

With a visible effort, he controlled his anger. 'You could try to argue it that way, but the intention is clear. Any judge would see that in seconds.'

'And how long does it take to get a case like this before a judge in Spain?'

Tomàs shook his head in frustration. 'Finn . . . Surely you can see this isn't fair on your sister?'

'But that's not your concern, is it?' I asked. 'Strictly speaking, you're *my* lawyer, not hers. You have to do as I instruct you.'

'I'm a friend of the family!'

'Who somehow drew up an agreement for our mother that turns out not to have been watertight. Or am I wrong about that?'

He frowned. 'Have you been speaking to another lawyer about this?'

'I took some informal advice,' I admitted.

'Then I resign,' Tomàs said bitterly. 'I'll send you a letter to that effect.' He looked at me sadly. 'This marriage you're talking about ... It's a marriage of convenience, I take it? An illegal enterprise?'

'No,' I said firmly. 'I love her.'

'You can barely know anything about her!'

'Actually,' I said, 'I know everything. Test me, if you like – her date of birth, her hobbies, her favourite job on the farm, anything.'

'I'm not talking about the *facts*,' he said incredulously. 'I'm talking about the person – her *character*. Did they at least sign those waivers?'

'Yes, they did,' I shot back. 'Without a murmur. Which proves that you and Jess were wrong to be so cynical about them.'

'Where are those documents now? I certainly haven't received them.'

I hesitated. 'They're no longer relevant to the situation.'

'Oh, Finn. *Finn.*' He shook his head. 'What have they done to you?'

'I'm in love. I refuse to apologise for that.' I saw the opportunity for a low blow, and took it. 'Just as you were in love with my mother once. But, instead of pursuing her, you sent her away to England.'

Tomàs's face darkened. 'There were other reasons for that. Or have you forgotten?'

It was my turn to remain silent.

'At least your father had self-knowledge,' he added. 'He knew he was a womanising, egotistical drunk. But you – when you came here, you made such a show of wanting to do the right thing. And now look where it has led you – into betraying your own sister.'

'I *am* doing the right thing,' I retorted. 'Sometimes matters of the heart trump matters of law. Or family solidarity, come to that.'

Tomàs sighed. 'Well, if you insist on this, there is nothing more I can do for you. I suggest you hire a specialist criminal lawyer next time. Because you will certainly need one, when the police come knocking. And, when that happens, you may discover that, in the courts, matters of law always trump the heart.'

Turning on his heel, he left. As he passed the hallway, he glanced inside and nodded a curt acknowledgement to someone.

Roze came back out. 'Finn? Are you all right?'

'I'm fine. You heard that?'

She nodded. 'Most of it.'

I went to hug her. 'Don't worry. Tomàs was always a bit of a drama queen. Quite honestly, I'm relieved to be rid of him.'

She put her arms around me. 'Thank you,' she said softly. 'Thank you for everything you're doing. I know it can't be easy.'

For several long moments, we held each other, and I remember thinking that, even if our adventure ended there and then, it would still have been worth it.

FORTY-THREE

'For the record, I am showing Señor Hensen a series of texts sent by his father to his sister, apparently in error,' Subinspector Parera said. 'Señor Hensen, were you aware of these texts at the time of our previous conversations?'

It was with a sense of inevitability that we'd watched the police arrive at the finca the day after Tomàs's visit – two cars in the yellow-and-red insignia of the Policía Nacional, from the first of which Subinspector Parera had emerged, closely followed by a stern-faced Officer Castell. Roze and I had been taken to separate rooms, and it was immediately clear that this interview was going to be very different in tone from my previous dealings with the police.

I glanced at the printout Parera was showing me and nodded. 'She'd mentioned them to me, yes.'

'Why didn't you tell us?'

I shrugged. 'I didn't think it was relevant.'

Parera raised an eyebrow. 'Withholding evidence from a possible murder investigation is a serious crime.'

'First of all,' I retorted, 'you made it clear when we spoke that there *was* no actual investigation – that you were simply looking at the circumstances around my father's death. And second, those texts aren't evidence of anything, apart from the fact that he was an abusive drunk – which, if you recall, I did tell you. It would be ridiculous to make the leap from a few drunken texts to murder.'

The subinspector regarded me thoughtfully. 'And yet here you are. Engaged to be married to the daughter of the woman your father married. At the same time as she appeals against a decision to refuse her asylum, too. That's a remarkable coincidence, is it not?'

'We're in love. And, yes, marriage happens to be the only way to ensure that we can continue our relationship. That doesn't make it fraudulent.'

'Were you aware that, according to her latest evidence to the tribunal, your fiancée previously worked in Mallorca as a prostitute?'

With an effort, I controlled my anger. 'I was aware that she was trafficked into debt bondage and forced by threats of violence to become a sex worker, yes – a crime which the police have apparently done nothing to investigate.'

'Many men would find that background difficult to overlook. Many Spanish men, anyway.'

'That's ridiculous,' I scoffed. 'You can't legalise prostitution on the one hand, and demonise prostitutes on the other. And you certainly can't blame trafficked women for what happened to them.'

Parera reached for his folder and took out another document. 'As it happens, the town hall had already alerted the police to a potentially suspicious marriage. So now it will be us, rather than them, who carries out the pre-wedding formalities ... Can you tell me the date of your fiancée's birthday?'

'November the twelfth,' I retorted.

He made a note. 'How many siblings does she have?'

'None.'

'In what month did she come to Spain?'

'August, two years ago,' I said, without missing a beat.

The subinspector nodded again. I saw him turn the page, as if dismissing the rest of that section as too easy. 'In what room do you both sleep?'

I hesitated minutely, then said, 'In the *caseta* – the old olive press. It's been turned into a guest suite.'

The subinspector's head lifted up, as if scenting blood. 'On which side of the bed?'

'Me? On the left.'

'What colour is her underwear today?'

I met his gaze. 'I don't believe that question's on your list.'

'No, it isn't.' He smiled. 'But a man notices these things, wouldn't you say? Especially a young man in love.'

'A Spanish man, perhaps. One who objectifies women. I really don't care what colour her knickers are, for God's sake.'

He looked at me thoughtfully. 'Have you ever bought her any lingerie? As a romantic gift, perhaps?'

'No.'

'Would you describe yourself as a romantic person, Señor Hensen?'

I shrugged. 'Not particularly.'

'And yet, here you are, marrying so quickly, with all the haste of young passion. Again – it's a remarkable coincidence, wouldn't you say?'

'Remarkable, yes. But criminal? No.'

The subinspector got to his feet. 'I should like to take a look at this *caseta* where you both sleep, please.'

I blinked. 'Don't you need a warrant to do that?'

Subinspector Parera raised his eyebrows. 'Why would I need a warrant to look at your bedroom? I don't want to search it. You are simply showing me informally, in order to allay any cynical suspicions I might have. Or, perhaps, to confirm them further, by refusing.'

With a sinking feeling, I got to my feet. 'I don't know what you hope to learn from it, but very well.'

He made a courteous gesture. 'After you.'

I walked slowly down the hallway, thinking furiously. Discovering that the olive press, despite its king-size bed, bore no traces of Roze's presence was hardly evidence of an illegal conspiracy, but it would certainly reinforce the subinspector's scepticism.

I said casually, 'By the way, I have the receipt for the engagement ring. It cost four thousand euros.'

Behind me, Parera's footsteps didn't falter. 'How very generous of you. And practical, too, to keep the receipt. One never knows when one will need such things. To show to cynical policemen, for example.'

We reached the back door, and the heat of the day hit us like an oven. That wasn't why I was breaking into a sweat, though. I was desperately trying to think of something – anything – in my room that I could point to as evidence that Roze and I slept together. But there was nothing. Even the clothing piled up on the chair was unmistakably male – my father's chinos and linen shirts, my own T-shirts and boxers.

I reached for the door handle. 'In here.'

As I opened it, I glanced inside and almost stopped dead. The floor and bed were strewn with Roze's clothing. It couldn't have been her who'd done that – she was being interviewed by Officer Castell. It could only have been Ruensa. Had she been listening at the door? Even so, it was quick work to have gathered an armful of her daughter's laundry and thrown it in before we got here.

Recovering quickly, I added, 'I'm not marrying her for her tidiness, as you can see.' I opened the door fully to let Subinspector Parera look.

He only said, 'Hmm.'

'Seen enough?' I asked.

His eyes turned to search my face. 'What kind of contraception do you use?'

I blinked. 'I'm sorry?'

'It's a simple enough question, isn't it? I assume you *are* using contraception.'

I thought quickly. If I said condoms, he might ask to see the packet. The same for the pill. Had Roze bought contraception when she visited the pharmacy that time? I hadn't thought to ask.

'Actually,' I said, 'we ran out of condoms just last night. Young passion, as you say. I'll get some more when I go to the village this afternoon.'

We both knew I was lying.

'That text your father sent, or rather tried to send, to his wife . . .' the subinspector said. 'What did you take it to mean?'

I frowned. 'Mean? Nothing. He was just being drunk and aggressive.'

The subinspector opened his folder, glanced inside and read aloud, '*If you will not be a WIFE to me* . . . Why do you think he used those words?'

'I've no idea.'

'Could he have meant that their relationship was not a physical one, do you suppose? And that he was unhappy with that?'

I shrugged. 'As I said to you before, I don't consider it any of my business. You'd have to ask Ruensa.'

Parera gave the room another pointed look, then slid something else from his folder. 'One final question. Do you know this man?'

He was showing me a headshot of Ferid.

'I don't believe so.' I scrutinised the photograph carefully, as if trying to refresh my memory.

'You surprise me. This is your fiancée's lawyer, the one who has drawn up her appeal. They must have had many meetings.'

'Oh . . .' I said vaguely. 'Now that you mention it, I believe I've seen them at the café together.' I gestured at the access track. 'As you can see, we're not exactly easy to get to.'

'Indeed.' He took the photograph back.

'Why do you ask?' I added.

'Ferid Karemi is currently on bail, awaiting trial in Greece for crimes of human trafficking,' the subinspector said. 'If you do happen to come across him, I urge you to have nothing to do with him, or any schemes he might propose. He is most certainly not a man to be trusted.'

FORTY-FOUR

After the police had left, I sat in the *caseta*, dumbfounded, trying to process what Parera had just said.

Ferid was not who he claimed to be. He was an imposter – no, more than that, a criminal, engaged in the very activity he purported to condemn.

And if *he* was a fake, then what were Ruensa and Roze?

Suddenly, like a photograph that surprises you by revealing itself to be a mirror image, I realised that there could be another version of everything that had happened at Finca Síquia. In that version, the three of them had been in league all along. Roze and Ruensa were desperate women who would stop at nothing to get themselves new lives in the EU, and Ferid was their enabler – well, I realised, that much was true whichever way you looked at it. But, in this new version, they were all tricksters, liars, swindlers.

Crooks.

Roze had already admitted they'd been lying to me that first night, when they claimed to have been fleeing some all-powerful criminal mastermind in Albania. It had been a crazy story, now that I came to think about it, full of holes – yet they'd told it so convincingly, and at the time I'd swallowed every word.

Guillem – did he even exist? And, even if he did, had Roze hoped all along that I'd step in and offer to marry her myself, rather than see her given up to a stranger? I'd been so childishly jealous of Ferid, after all – had that been noted, and built into the plan, so that my jealousy became the very thing that would propel us all onwards to the next, most crucial stage?

Had I been played? Or, rather, *was* I being played, right at that very moment?

I recalled wondering how much Ruensa had known about the *usufructo* before Tomàs made his initial phone call to her. I'd decided that no one could be quick enough to sound unsurprised if they were hearing about it for the first time. Yet Ruensa had just proved she was exactly that – not only quick-witted, but resourceful as well. Look at the cool-headed way she'd outsmarted the police, by throwing Roze's laundry into my room.

I tried to think back. Had there ever been even the smallest proof of anything Roze and Ruensa had said? But there was nothing, I realised – just words; words that built into stories; ever-shifting stories at that, like a net that shimmered and changed form even as it draped itself around you.

Did I trust her?

I knew that I loved her. How could I not trust someone I loved so intensely? And yet somehow I found the two could coexist quite easily in my mind – the love and the doubt, like the six-foot-high yin-yang symbol, painted by my father, that was still there somewhere, buried under layers of white paint at the bottom of the stairs.

With a heavy heart, I pulled open the door of the *caseta* and went to confront Roze with what the subinspector had just told me.

'But I know all this,' Roze said impatiently. 'Ferid told me the first time we met. He said the authorities would use it to try to undermine him, and now here's the proof he was right.'

I stared at her. 'But – a *people trafficker*? How could you have got involved with someone like that?'

She shook her head. 'He isn't a trafficker, not in the way you mean. One of the organisations he was working with on Lesbos had a boat, and they went out on search-and-rescue missions to try to find the migrants' dinghies before they sank. Of course, the authorities hated that – they were trying to make the crossings harder, not easier, even if that meant people drowning. So they charged all twenty-four members of the organisation with facilitation of illegal entry. Ferid was granted bail, but his right to travel in Greece was revoked. That's why he came to Mallorca. He has to inform the authorities if he leaves the island.'

'Oh . . .' I felt a little stunned that there could be so simple an explanation. 'So when will his trial be?'

Roze shrugged. 'It's already been almost two years, and no date's been set. He suspects it'll never happen – that the charges were more to scare off other organisations, to stop them saving lives, than to get a conviction. It succeeded, too – for a while, there were no rescues at all, and he's been told that, even now, the NGOs have to be very careful about what they do. But it means he could be ordered to hand himself in at any time. That's why he has to be so careful about helping us.'

'I see.' Relief washed over me. For a brief time, I'd felt sick at the thought that I might be some kind of love-befuddled patsy. Now, I felt guilty that I'd ever doubted Ferid, and by extension Roze and Ruensa as well. And a little envious, too, if I was honest. Compared with him, I'd done so little to help my fellow human beings.

But at least I was marrying Roze, I reflected. For one human being, I was making a difference.

'How did you do on the marriage questions?' she added.

'Oh – pretty good, I think. He asked about contraception, though, which threw me. I said condoms, but that we'd run out.'

She nodded. 'Condoms is what I said, too. That's what I bought in the pharmacy – two packets of a brand called Control.'

'Thank God we said the same. Even so, I'd better go into the village and buy more.'

The truth was, I realised, that, even before the subinspector's comments about Ferid, the police's visit had rattled me. Before, it had been possible to think of all this as a kind of game – a delicious romantic fantasy, half real and half pretend. Being questioned by a seasoned professional who suspected me of a criminal conspiracy had not been a pleasant experience.

For the first time, I wondered if Tomàs might be right, and I was making a terrible mistake.

'Finn . . .' Roze was saying. 'I think we're going to have to share a room from now on. The next time they come, we might not even be awake.'

I gave her a quick look. 'And you'd be OK with that?'

She shrugged. 'I have to be, don't I? After all, we can't go on sleeping apart once we have guests here, not if we're trying to make it look like we're a normal married couple.' She managed a smile. 'At least I'll have someone to protect me from scorpions. I'll sleep on my yoga mat.'

'Don't be ridiculous. Quite apart from anything else, if you slept on the mat, you'd be right at scorpion level. Take the bed – I'll use the mat. I insist.'

'Well . . . maybe we take it in turns, or something.'

'And you're sure you're all right with it?'

'With turns? Or scorpions?'

I shook my head. 'Sharing with a man. It won't be . . . triggering for you?'

'Oh . . .' She took a deep breath. 'I guess we'll find out. Put it like this . . . I'm glad it's you.'

She moved in that night, filling my wardrobe and two of the drawers with her things. It gave me a jolt of pleasure to see her toothbrush standing next to mine in the bathroom, like two little sentries on guard, and her shampoos and conditioners in the shower. She tried again to insist she should sleep on the mat, and I got a little fierce with her until she caved in and took the bed. The mat was hard and uncomfortable, and I found it difficult to drop off, but my reward was to listen to her breathing as it became more regular, and to smile to myself when she eventually slept, which she did as deeply as a child.

I woke in the darkness, panting and clammy with sweat,

something ringing in my ears like the echo of a shout. Dimly, I became aware that Roze was crouching over me, shaking my shoulder.

'Finn! Finn, wake up.'

'My God . . .' I struggled upright, trying to breathe.

'What happened? Were you having a nightmare?'

'I guess so. Sort of.' I could remember, now – something to do with being in the pool, underwater, and my father aiming some kind of harpoon at me. Or had it been Subinspector Parera standing there on the decking? Already the details were becoming unclear. 'They're night terrors. Like a panic attack, but when you're asleep. I haven't had one for years.'

'Is it because of me, do you think?' she asked quietly. 'Because of what I'm asking you to do?'

'No,' I said shortly. 'It's just a coincidence.'

She touched my shoulder again, but gently. 'Come to bed. You'll sleep better.'

'Are you sure?'

She nodded. 'Yes. It'll be . . . I have nightmares too, sometimes. I know what it's like.'

So I crept into bed beside her, making sure to leave her plenty of room. For the second time that night, I listened to her breathing, but this time it was me who felt my body relaxing first, as I fell into a deep and dreamless sleep.

FORTY-FIVE

After that, we existed in a kind of limbo. The police were under no obligation to hurry, Ferid told us, but at some point they'd have to convince a magistrate a crime was being committed. Following that, there'd be timescales to gather more evidence, and either charge us or close the investigation.

In the meantime, because no formal allegations had been made, we were able to book a provisional day and time for our wedding. We took the first available slot, four weeks later, and kept our fingers crossed.

It was a limbo, but it was also a time of acute, intense pleasure – and acute pain, as well. *To love someone you are with almost every minute of the day, and not be loved in return . . . that would be a kind of living hell,* Ferid had said. It wasn't hell – far from it – but neither was it easy. Night after night, I lay with Roze in our bed, and, night after night, I was true to our pact and never once touched her. Did she know just how painful that was, how every cell of my skin yearned to fuse with hers, how every nerve and sinew strained and hummed with longing? By unspoken agreement, neither of us mentioned it – there was no point; it would simply

245

have made things more difficult. I just had to be patient, I told myself, and hope that it wouldn't be too long before she came to trust me fully.

Sometimes, when I woke in the night, I'd find her arm flung casually around my waist, or that she'd rolled so close, I could feel the warmth of her on my back. Then I would lie awake and try to silence the hoarseness of my breathing, for fear she'd hear me in her sleep and move away.

Sometimes I thought about the men who had done this to her – used her body so casually, for a hundred euros a time, and destroyed her heart as they did it – and felt a wave of fury wash over me. And something else, too, because those men had been able to get what they wanted, and for such a paltry cost, when I would have given literally all I had.

But there was a right way and a wrong way to do this.

So what's the right way, bro? Jess demanded mockingly in my head.

Unfortunately, I haven't figured that out yet.

Then I would shift, suddenly too hot, and wish that blocking my sister from my thoughts was as easy as blocking her from my phone.

Tomàs was there too, in my feverish imaginings. *You can barely know anything about her!* And Alejandro: *He used almost the exact same words you did just now!* De tal palo tal astilla, *right?*

You're all wrong, I told them. *I simply have to learn to trust her, the way she's trusting me.*

The conversations you have in your head, at three o'clock in the morning.

And then sometimes I'd wake up and realise she was awake too – awake, and trembling. At what we were going to do? At what she had already done? At her betrayal by the boyfriend she'd thought had loved her? She always refused to say, but she permitted me to put my arms around her and hold her close until the trembling had subsided, and those were perhaps the happiest times of all.

FORTY-SIX

We'd started work on the top floor by then – clearing out the junk and painting the rooms. It took three coats before my father's erotic frescos were obliterated from the landing – I was going to add a fourth, certain their outline was still visible if you looked hard enough, but Roze convinced me it was just my imagination.

The plan was for us and Ruensa to have our bedrooms up there, to give ourselves some privacy from our guests, as well as a little longer to compose ourselves if the police turned up unannounced. It also meant the rooms could be more spartan than the ones below, which speeded things up. My father's painting room we left untouched, for the time being – the blobs of hardened oil paint would have to be painstakingly scraped off the floor and walls, and, besides, it felt too soon to exorcise his presence from the finca altogether.

As we dragged the tepee out from the second bedroom, the threadbare canvas almost shredding in our hands, Roze looked at it curiously. 'What was this for?'

'Oh . . .' I shrugged. 'Every summer, my parents used to have what they called a Gathering. For about a week, there'd be forty or fifty people lying around, smoking weed and making music. Even a house this big couldn't accommodate them all. So they got hold of this tent from somewhere.'

I had a sudden image of the last Gathering I'd been around for: the skinny half-naked bodies daubed with paint; the smells of vegetable curry, patchouli and hash; and the sounds of someone playing badly on an old guitar, the throb of a tom-tom as it picked out the beat. Sophia, threading braids into Jess's hair, hour after hour, smiling at me as I walked by. Her mother, Nina, dancing with the Old Bastard. Our own mother nowhere to be seen, having retreated to her room, and then my father emerging from this very tent, early one morning, when no one was up but me . . .

'To be honest, I think it was mainly so he could shag people away from the house,' I added. 'And, of course, it always got left up until autumn, then put away wet. Even back then, it was starting to rot.'

'We should do it!' Roze exclaimed.

'Shag in a tent?'

'No, you crazy . . . We should get some tents like these. So we can fit in more guests. We couldn't charge the same price as the bedrooms, obviously. But they'd be popular in summer, and they'd give the place a cool vibe, like a festival. There's a word for it in English – I read it on one of the websites . . .'

'Glamping?' I suggested.

'That's it!'

I looked at the torn, stained fabric in my hands. 'We'd have to get new ones. This is well beyond repair.'

'Of course. Do you have enough in your account?'

'I'll do some research, find out how much they are.' But I already knew I would say yes. I found it almost impossible to refuse Roze things.

She was extravagant – I was aware of that, by then. Not for herself – as I had observed, she had few shoes and even fewer good dresses – but for the business. She was always finding something on a website that had to be ordered to make the house look nice, and, to be honest, indulging her was a pleasure, nesting for our first home.

Work also began on the access track – the last major project before we could start taking bookings. But, within a few days, the workmen hit a problem. Beneath a loose covering of scree, their digger encountered unyielding rock – the mountain's granite core, pushing through the softer limestone here like a hernia. The original plan, to lay a bed of crushed hardcore, would, the foreman told us, have to be abandoned; instead, they'd have to jackhammer into the granite to break it up. The original estimate, he warned, now looked way off; the final cost was likely to be double or even treble that amount.

I stared at him. 'But I thought the cost was fixed.'

He shrugged. 'The figure I gave your father was an estimate. I always said it would depend on what we found once we started.'

I fumed, but there was nothing to be done; we had to have that track built, or our guests would never make it to the finca. I agreed to spend more money on a survey, and resigned myself to finding even more to build it.

That evening, Roze, Ruensa and I sat despondently around the veranda table and tried to make a plan.

'You should take back the engagement ring,' Roze said. 'It's served its purpose now, and it was a ridiculous amount for you to spend on me in the first place.'

I shook my head. 'I wouldn't dream of it.'

She started to protest, and I cut across her.

'I'm not doing it. That ring is the only thing I've ever given you. I'll dig that track with my bare hands if I have to, but I'm not taking it back.'

There was a silence.

'The painting, then,' Ruensa said quietly. 'The one of Roze and me. We could sell that.'

I looked at her. 'Are you sure? You said it was the only keepsake you wanted.'

She shrugged. 'Jimmy would have understood.'

'No—' Roze began. But, at her mother's look, she stopped.

'That's settled, then,' Ruensa said, with an air of finality. 'And now I must go and see to supper.' She got to her feet a bit too quickly, and as she hurried off I saw her hand go to her eyes.

'I'll take it to Marc tomorrow,' I said to Roze, when she was gone. 'But however much he likes it, I don't think it'll cover the whole cost of the track.'

She nodded. 'You'll think of something, Finn. I know you will.'

The next day, I took the painting from the wall of the *caseta* and drove to Palma to show Marc. Taking off the old sheet I'd wrapped it in, he carried it over to the window and whistled.

'You're right. It's in a different league to that other stuff you left with me.' He nodded to where one of my father's landscapes was displayed. 'They do sell occasionally, as you know, but they're not exactly flying out of the door. If you could bring me some nudes, of course . . . Nudes always sell well.'

I shrugged. 'Possibly, but there weren't any nudes.'

'Are you sure? He'd done the preliminary studies, after all, and it wasn't like him to abandon a painting.'

'Well, he must . . .' I began, then stopped. 'What preliminary studies?'

'Some sketches.' He went over to the box of my father's drawings that I'd given him and reached inside. 'I went through and sorted them all by subject,' he explained. 'Sometimes people will pay a bit extra for the drawings that go with a painting – they like to see how it developed.'

He laid out four sketches on a plan chest. I recognised my father's hand immediately, even on charcoal studies as quick and fluid as these. They were indeed nudes. But not of Ruensa, as I'd assumed they must be. The drawings Marc was showing me were of Roze.

FORTY-SEVEN

'Yes, I posed for him,' Roze said in an exasperated tone. 'He asked me if I would and I said yes. Why shouldn't I? He was a professional painter, after all. He told me he'd painted dozens of women like that.'

'Most of whom he slept with!'

'Well, again – why not, if they agreed? But he never, ever suggested anything like that to me. In fact, he was always incredibly respectful. And my mother was there too, most of the time . . . What's this about? Is this why you've been so bad-tempered ever since you got back from Palma?'

I stared at her. 'You let me think you were traumatised!'

'Yes,' she said, frowning. 'Or are you accusing me of lying about that, too?' She gestured at the drawings, spread out on the table between us. 'What you see there is completely different. And, if you must know, it helped. It felt as if I was taking decisions for myself again about what I do and when. I felt *safe*, Finn, and in control. Like it was *my* body again, and not just something that had been hired out by one set of bastards to another.'

I raised my hands helplessly. How could she not see what was so blindingly obvious to me – that, whatever he'd claimed to her, my father's motives had undoubtedly been grubby? 'He slept with anyone and everyone. He was completely amoral like that. You know how the police were talking about Sophia – the girl who died during the Gathering? She'd posed for him, too. He slept with her mother first, then her. And all that was going on right under my mother's nose.'

'So what exactly are you accusing me of, Finn?' Roze said, angry now. 'Are you saying I slept with my mother's sixty-four-year-old husband right under her nose? Because, if so, that's disgusting.'

'That's exactly my point – he *was* disgusting.'

She shook her head firmly. 'Not to me. And not to Mama. Anyway, at least you're being clear now – you *are* accusing me of that.'

'No!' I protested. Her mind was too quick for me – she had a rebuttal for every point I tried to make, confusing and bewildering me until I couldn't think straight. I tried to cling to the one thing I knew for certain – that my father had been an entitled, selfish lecher. 'All I'm saying is, if he hadn't made a pass at you by the time he died, he was certainly about to.'

'I refuse to believe that,' she said loftily. 'He never showed me anything but respect and kindness. And, after what happened to me, I think I'd know if that wasn't genuine.'

I smacked my fist into my palm, and she flinched.

'Sorry,' I said. 'That was . . . You had a lucky escape, is all I'm saying.'

But even as I said it, I realised that Subinspector Parera would say it was far too lucky to be a coincidence.

He would say that, if Ruensa discovered that her husband had designs on her daughter – the same daughter for whom she had already abandoned her life in Albania, to rescue from sexual coercion – she would surely have been prepared to kill, to stop it from happening again.

I added, 'You do realise – if it *was* more than a lucky escape – if my father said or did something inappropriate – you *could* tell me. It would make no difference to how I feel about you. Or about him, for that matter.'

'I know, Finn. But there was nothing. So please can we just drop it now?'

'All right.' But something made me add, 'What happened to the painting?'

She frowned. 'What painting?'

I gestured at the sketches. 'The one these were the preliminary studies for.'

She shrugged angrily. 'How should *I* know? He never said anything, so I assumed he'd put it on hold while he concentrated on those landscapes. Or perhaps he thought people might misinterpret it, the way you just have.' She gave me a furious look. 'Anyway, I'm disappointed in you, that you'd even think something like that.'

All that evening, she continued to be angry, and, since it was impossible for us both to be in a bad mood at the same time, I found myself tiptoeing around her. Ruensa gave her some puzzled looks, but said nothing. Clearly, she was a little afraid of her daughter's moods too.

Over supper, Roze was monosyllabic, and afterwards she

announced she was going straight to bed. When I followed, an hour or so later, her back was turned towards me and she was asleep – or, at any rate, giving a very good impersonation of someone who was.

FORTY-EIGHT

Next morning, I apologised.

'I'm sorry if it seemed as if I was accusing you of something. I suppose I jumped to a conclusion when I saw those sketches . . . That was wrong of me.'

She sighed. 'I'm sorry, too. I was being defensive. A part of me knows how it could look to an outsider, which is why I never mentioned it before. But your father was always completely professional about it.'

And so harmonious relations were restored – a good omen, I felt; I'd read somewhere that psychologists believe effective conflict resolution is one of the best indicators there is for a successful marriage. I put the sketches away, and tried not to think about the tenderness, bordering on reverence, that my father had conveyed with a few swift movements of his charcoal when he gazed at Roze's naked form.

I'd assumed that our actual wedding would be some mean little formality – a suspicious civil servant speaking a few perfunctory sentences over us, the bare minimum required to legalise our union. But Ferid was adamant it should be more than that.

'Think about it,' he urged. 'You're creating a narrative here – two lovebirds who have fallen for each other so hard, they want to get married at once. For the story to seem real, the wedding should be romantic.'

Needless to say, I took little persuading, and I was pleased when Roze, too, seemed to enjoy planning our ceremony together.

'We should have music as we enter. The first song we ever slow-danced to.'

'Which was . . . ?'

She thought for a moment. '"A Sky Full of Stars".'

I said softly, 'I prefer "Fix You".'

'"Fix You" it is, then,' she said with a smile. 'I like that one too. What about vows?'

'We should each write our own. But show each other beforehand, obviously, so we can work on them together.'

'Our parents had a handfasting ritual as part of their ceremony,' she said. 'We could do something like that – something symbolic.'

'They did? Really?' I looked at her, perplexed. Even allowing for the fact that my father seemed to have changed beyond all recognition once he met Ruensa, the idea that he'd have wanted a handfasting – a ritual in which the couple bind their wrists together with ribbons of many different colours to symbolise life-long togetherness, a piece of bogus hogwash taken from Wicca, or Druidism, or some other bullshit sub-branch of general hippy bullshit – seemed unlikely. He tolerated a certain amount of all that in his guests, but mainly so he could enjoy himself being scornful about it. And he particularly loathed sentimentality of any kind. I don't think he even wore a wedding ring when he was married to my mother.

Unless, of course, it was all part of creating a narrative around his wedding. And, if a narrative had been judged necessary – by who? Ruensa? Ferid? – what else did it say about the parallels between that wedding and my own?

My marriage to Roze was a leap of faith, after all, and, like any faith, it required me to willingly step into the unknown; to believe that my love would eventually be returned in a kind of blissful afterlife, the existence of which was as unknowable as any heaven. In part, it was precious to me precisely because it *was* irrational – a commitment as devotional, and as ecstatic, as a martyr's.

But there was also a part of me that still thirsted to know the truth. Because I loved her, I wanted to see her fully; more fully even than my father, when he first gazed on her naked form, and put the tip of his sharpened charcoal to the paper.

FORTY-NINE

But, of course, wanting to know the truth and being able to know it were two completely different things. I had crumbs and fragments, no more – like having a small handful of jigsaw pieces, and trying to guess from them what the bigger picture might be.

And then, sometimes, a new piece would turn up that seemed to fit nowhere at all. What did it mean, for example, that, when I went to the hardware store in Esporles to buy more paint, I heard an American voice calling, 'Finn? Finn, darling, is that you?'

I turned. It took me a moment to recognise her – she'd had so much plastic surgery done, her face looked like a balloon that had been overinflated, all puffy lips and bulging eyes. It was the floaty sarong and jewellery-encrusted fingers that did it as much as anything, and her name came back to me.

'Sandra!' I said. 'How are you?'

My father's second wife swept me up in an embrace. 'It's sooo good to see you. You're here because of what happened to your poor father, I suppose.'

'Well . . . in a way,' I said vaguely.

'And those terrible women. Have you managed to get rid of

them yet?' She lowered her voice. 'I insisted on going to the funeral. They hated that, of course. They wanted to get his body into that oven as quickly as possible, in case the police changed their minds and demanded an autopsy.'

'Um . . .' I said. 'Funerals are usually pretty swift here, aren't they – forty-eight hours at most. I guess it's a hangover from pre-refrigeration days.'

She swept that aside with an impatient gesture. 'It was everything he would have hated. No music, no eulogy, just the bare minimum. And that cold-eyed woman staring at the casket as if she'd have liked to have killed him all over again. I was the only one who shed a tear, I can tell you that.'

I must have looked puzzled – not because of what Sandra was telling me, or because her eyes looked incapable of shedding anything very much, but because I seemed to recall that her own break-up from my father had been bitter and acrimonious.

'Oh, I know I probably hated him for longer than I loved him,' she added. 'But life with your father was never boring. His funeral should have been fun, for Chrissake! I've spoken to so many people who said they wished they'd known. But she wasn't having any of it. I asked her when the wake would be and she said she'd let me know. But she never did.'

'That's a shame,' I said. 'But I'm not sure they're big on wakes in Albania.'

'Albania! Well, that's another thing. I might not look it –' here, she pointed to her peroxide-blond hair – 'but my parents are Greek, so I speak it pretty well. I heard them talking to each other – that woman and her daughter. I don't suppose they realised anyone could understand them. But I'm quite sure they were speaking Greek. The daughter asked her mother who the awful woman was, and the mother said, "I think it's his last wife."'

There was, of course, a simple explanation.

'Not Greek,' Roze said. 'Epirot. Mama's family are from the Greek-speaking part of Albania, in the south, so that's where I grew up. It was officially designated a Greek minority area under the communists – it might have been the other side of the Iron Curtain once, but on a clear day you could see Corfu from our house, and all the schools are dual-language. It's no different from the way people round here speak Mallorquí as well as Catalan and regular Spanish – it doesn't mean they're not Spanish, just that they have other identities, too. If barbarians like Sandra don't get that, that's not our problem. And, yes, I probably did call her an awful woman.'

'Of course,' I said. And yet I was puzzled. All those hours we'd spent memorising each other's pasts – how was it that this aspect of hers had never come up? I knew that the Balkan countries were a complex mix of ethnic and linguistic groupings, fragments of half a dozen ancient empires splintered further by communism and its fall, but why had she never mentioned having Greek heritage – when I tried to teach her some Mallorquí words, for example?

It was partly because I was still puzzling over this myself that I didn't say anything about it when Subinspector Parera phoned. Besides, he was the enemy now, and I wanted to weigh up anything I told him very carefully before I said it.

As it turned out, it was a very short call.

'The prosecutor has decided there is not enough evidence to charge you or your fiancée with an offence,' he said curtly. 'As a result, our file will remain open, pending further developments.'

'What does that mean for us, exactly?'

'It means we will not be using our powers to postpone or halt your marriage.' He paused. 'Of course, if the marriage does go ahead, and it *is* primarily for the purpose of securing residency for one of the parties, you will both still be committing a crime, and we may well charge you at some point in the future.'

I felt almost dizzy with relief. 'Thank you.'

He grunted. 'Forgive me if I don't wish you and your bride good luck. Indeed, I strongly urge you both to consider your actions very carefully. There's still time to change your minds.'

'Good day to you, too, Subinspector,' I said politely, and hung up. Then I walked over to where Roze was putting up curtains, in what would one day be our bedroom.

'That was the police,' I told her. 'We can get married.'

The expression on her face was everything I'd hoped for – amazement, and joy, and delight, all mixed together in one wide-eyed, open-mouthed gasp. Then we were laughing and whooping, and I was whirling her round and round with her arms around my neck. We were getting married. Everything was going to plan, after all.

FIFTY

The day before the wedding, I went to visit Tomàs. He saw me in his office, his face stern – no more slipping next door for a glass or two of wine.

'If you've come because you want me to reconsider firing you as my client, that won't be possible,' he said curtly. 'There'd be a clear conflict of interest now.'

I shook my head. 'I've come because I'm getting married tomorrow, and I want to invite you. My mother can't be there, of course, but it would be nice to have someone to represent her, as it were.'

He regarded me for a moment. 'Unfortunately, that won't be possible either. Whatever my personal feelings on the matter, I have to consider that there's a high likelihood a crime is being committed. Professionally, I can't be seen to be getting involved.'

'Of course. I understand.' I reached into my pocket. 'There's something else. I'd like you to have a copy of my will.' As I handed the envelope over, I added, 'I want it to stay sealed until the event of my death.'

He looked at it thoughtfully, weighing it in his hands. 'Has this been registered with the public notary?'

'Yes,' I lied.

'Very well.' He put it to one side. 'I'll put it in our safe, with a note of your instructions.'

As I stood up, he added, 'And, Finn, for what it's worth . . .'

'Yes?'

'You'll say this is none of my business, but this . . . infatuation of yours – obsession, one might call it – it isn't healthy, you must see that. As a boy, you sometimes had . . . crushes on girls, didn't you? Well, we all do, at that age. But marriage can't be based on some juvenile calf-love. It's so much more – a partnership, a union between equals. And a legal contract between two parties as well . . . Whatever's going on with you and Roze, please don't complicate it further by bringing marriage into the picture.'

'You're right,' I said. 'It's none of your business.'

And then it was our wedding day. We took the old fruit-pickers' train through the mountain to Palma, just as I'd described it to Roze. She was wearing a new dress and carrying a small posy of flowers from the farm, and I was wearing my father's only suit – I was amazed to discover he owned even one, until I realised it had probably been purchased for his own wedding to Ruensa, the previous year.

It was a short ceremony, but a beautiful one. As I slid the ring up Roze's finger, I spoke the vows I had written for her.

'As this ring encircles your finger, so will my love encircle you forever. From this day forward, my heart will be your country, and my arms will be your home. I give you my adoration, my respect and my commitment, from now until the end of time, which, like this ring, has no beginning and no end.'

By the time I'd finished, tears were running down my face, and, when we reached the end of the ceremony, with the traditional Spanish cry of '*Que se besen! Que se besen!*' – 'Kiss! Kiss!' – and my lips touched hers for the very first time, it was all I could do to remember our fiction that we were a cohabiting couple who had kissed each other a thousand times already, and not devour her hungrily with my mouth.

Once the paperwork was completed – I saw Ferid, who was a witness, quickly look over Roze's shoulder to check the marriage certificate for any mistakes before stepping back – Roze and I returned to the finca for a late lunch. We left the others behind – Ruensa had offered to stay elsewhere for a few days, to give us a short honeymoon, and Alejandro and Aina went back to the café at Cauzacs.

When we reached the house, though, there was an unfamiliar car parked outside. It looked like a hire car – and, sure enough, when we got closer I saw there was a Sixt rental agreement on the passenger seat.

'Did you invite anyone else?' I asked Roze, who shook her head, puzzled.

Just then, Jess came around the corner. She took one look at Roze – at the dress and the posy – and at my suit, and said, 'Oh, Jesus. Am I too late? Have you already done it?'

'I'm afraid you've missed our wedding, yes,' I said lightly. 'But you can be one of the very first to congratulate us.'

Jess ran her hands over her face. 'Damn. *Damn.* Tomàs told me there wasn't much time, but I thought – if I came out and warned you myself—'

'I know exactly what I'm doing,' I said. 'It's my choice—'

'Not *you*,' she interrupted. 'It wasn't *you* I came to warn, Finn.' She looked at Roze. 'I think you may have just made a terrible mistake.'

FIFTY-ONE

'This is ridiculous,' I said.

'Hear me out,' Jess said to Roze. 'Has he told you yet how he and Lauren broke up?'

Roze looked at me, confused. Jess added, 'His last girlfriend. I take it that's a no, then. She had to get a restraining order against him.'

'Jess is bitter,' I said to Roze, 'because I've told her I'm not selling the finca. Of course she's going to try to undermine our relationship. If she can somehow drive a wedge between you and me, you won't pass the one-year matrimony test to get residency, and I'll have no reason not to sell up.'

'There was a court hearing,' Jess said. 'I went along, to support him. I'm used to him, of course, but some of it shocked even me. In the week after they broke up, he sent her over six hundred texts.'

I closed my eyes briefly. 'Lauren didn't know what she was doing. And she was doing it for all the wrong reasons.'

'One of the texts simply said, *You look nice today.* Lauren told the court that was when she realised Finn was stalking her.'

'*Following* her,' I said firmly. 'Not *stalking*. I saw her safely home from a late shift at the hospital a couple of times, that's all. Stop trying to twist things like she did.'

'Then he stood outside her flat and rang the bell continuously for forty-five minutes.'

'If she'd answered sooner,' I pointed out, 'it would never have had to be that long. And we needed to talk.'

'It's not even like it was the first time something like that had happened,' Jess said. 'Finn has a pattern, you see. They're usually lost causes – waifs and strays, our mother used to call them. Druggies, anorexics, strippers, rebounds ... He likes a project. Someone he can rescue and put right. But woe betide them if they come to their senses and decide they don't want to be rescued anymore.'

I was starting to get angry now. 'Says the woman who's had years of therapy. Most of it trying to work out why she's such a nymphomaniac slut.'

'Thanks, bro,' Jess said calmly. She turned back to Roze. 'And yes, I have had therapy. Mostly because of what happened *here*.' She gestured up at the house. 'For years, I felt obligated to have sex with pretty much anyone who asked. It took me a long time to realise that, actually, I'd been through a kind of abuse myself. You have to remember that, until eight years ago, the age of consent here in Spain was thirteen. And the people who came to this house all believed in what they called "free love". By which they actually meant, freely available to *them*.' She glanced in my direction. 'Has he told you why we had to leave?'

'He said your mother had finally had enough,' Roze said quietly.

272

'Well, that's true, in a way. But it wasn't my father she'd had enough of. He slept with a girl just a couple of years older than me, but that had happened before. The real problem was, it was a girl Finn had a crush on.' She paused. 'She was found dead of an overdose – someone had spiked her drink with MDMA. It was a drink Finn had given her.'

'Roze . . .' I said. 'You know how I've always believed in you. Even when I thought you might be lying, I always went along with it, for your sake. What was that thing you said to me once? "You have to choose who to believe." And I chose you. Now I need you to do the same for me. Don't listen to any more of these pitiful insinuations. She's just jealous we've got the house and she hasn't. It's a sibling thing – she'll say anything, however hurtful, to get her own back.'

Roze said nothing. She stayed rooted to the spot. For once, she seemed to have no idea what to do.

'You know me,' I added. 'You know what kind of person I am. How could I even be capable of something like that?'

'She was my friend, Finn,' Jess said. 'Sophia was my friend, and when she wouldn't sleep with you, and you found out who she was sleeping with instead, you killed her. That's why my mother had to get us out of here – people were starting to ask questions.'

'This is so not true,' I said to Roze.

'It's a form of attachment disorder,' Jess said. 'Stalking, I mean. What I had, too – the hypersexualisation. We grew up without any real parents, only a narcissistic drunken bully and a doormat, and it screwed us both up.'

'Speak for yourself,' I said.

'Finn always wants to be some helpless victim's saviour, but once they don't want to be victims anymore, they become *his* victim. Not that he sees it that way, of course – he thinks he's saving them from themselves. That's when he turns into a bully – like our father, but with a halo. Because he always knows what you really need better than you do. Does that sound familiar?'

Roze frowned. I could almost see her mind working.

'Go inside,' I said to her. 'I don't want you listening to any more of this poison.'

'No!' Roze said. 'Finn, I need to say something. And you need to hear me say it.' She turned to Jess. 'Thank you for coming. I know you genuinely mean well, and, as one survivor of abuse to another, I'm grateful. But I do know the man I've married. He's good and kind – I would never have fallen in love with him otherwise. And I *do* love him, whatever Tomàs might have told you. So I'm standing by him. I hope that one day you and I can be friends, but today I'm choosing him.'

She put her arm through mine. I felt a great swell of triumph wash through me – triumph and love. We were sticking together. We had won.

Jess stared at her for a moment, then, without another word, turned and walked back towards her car.

FIFTY-TWO

We went inside. Ruensa had left food for us in the fridge – cold meats and tumbet. *The wedding breakfast*, it was called, I dimly remembered. I wondered how many owners of Finca Síquia had done this – had brought their brides back to the house after the ceremony. I felt I was part of a long unbroken chain, somehow. Of course, most of those weddings would have been followed by a deflowering. Another ancient word. Silently, I rolled it around my tongue. *Deflowering.* Such a delicate term for such a physical, almost animalistic act.

Roze, I noticed, was unusually quiet. 'Are you all right?' I asked. For my part, the confrontation with Jess – so long overdue – had left me with a huge adrenalin rush and a pounding heart. Or was I simply delirious with happiness? After all, my wife had just told my sister, my only family, that she loved me.

'How much of that was true?' Roze asked. 'About your father, I mean, and the girl.'

I poured a large glass of wine to calm myself. 'It's true I liked Sophia a lot,' I admitted. 'Her mother, Nina, was a typical Balearic hippy – she'd dragged Sophia here for the Gathering, when she should have been studying for exams. And it happened like I told you – first, Nina slept with my father, then he got Sophia to pose for him. I told myself it would be different this time, because of Nina. But the truth was, things like that never stopped him – it probably even gave him a thrill, to have the daughter as well as the mother. So yes, that part's true. But the idea that I killed her – that's just Jess being cruel. And the stuff about restraining orders and so on – I've been unlucky in some of my relationships, that's all. There may be a grain of truth in what she said about wanting to help people. It's like I told your mother when she asked me why I was single – sometimes I want more from the relationship than the other person does. That's why this is so nice, quite honestly – knowing that you want to be married to me just as much as I want to be married to you.'

She gave me a strange look. 'I'm very grateful to you for helping me, Finn. But, as I said before, I don't want to be responsible for you getting hurt.'

'I'm not going to get hurt.' I reached out and ran my finger along her arm. 'I'm glad Jess told you, actually. It makes things simpler, to have everything out in the open. And it's probably the right time, anyway.'

She frowned. 'The right time for what?'

'To consummate our marriage.' *Consummate.* Another lovely word.

She sighed. 'I told you, Finn – I've been very clear. That's not going to be a part of this.'

'I think you're healing,' I said softly. 'I think you're ready. But you won't know for sure until you try.'

She shook her head. 'I like you very much,' she said firmly. 'But not in that way. I don't think I'll ever like someone—'

'Yes,' I interrupted. 'I know. But you have to trust me on this. Just like you're going to have to trust me on so many things.'

When you laid a trail of crumbs for a pine marten or an almond-eater, and they trusted you enough to come and nibble at them, there was still a moment when you had to commit – to grab them. When they felt your fist close around them for the first time, they'd always struggle to begin with – of course they would. You just had to hold on and not let go, and wait for the struggling to die down as they realised it was useless. That was when you could show them a crumb again, and slowly relax your grip, even as you stroked them gently with your other hand. It was only after that – when they realised being stroked wasn't so bad after all – that they really began to depend on you, and you could start taming them properly.

'This may not have occurred to you yet,' I added, closing my fingers gently around Roze's wrist, 'but, for the next twelve months, all it would take is one phone call from me to Subinspector Parera, telling him that you and I have separated, and he'll have you sent back to Albania. That's if you're lucky. If I tell him the marriage was bogus from the start, he'll probably open a formal investigation into my father's death as well.'

She stared at me, her eyes wide.

'And you, Finn?' she said at last. 'When did that occur to *you*? Just now? Last night? Or have you been thinking about it all along?'

She was trying to pull away now, but I had her tight. 'Let's just say that, when I put that engagement ring on your finger, it was never just for show. I always knew we'd end up having this conversation. I'd hoped it wouldn't be necessary to be quite this blunt about it, of course – it would have been so much easier if you'd been a bit more flexible about things. So, in a way, you've only yourself to blame.'

'*Blame?*' she said. 'Blame for what, exactly?'

'And, by the way,' I added, 'I still don't know exactly what happened with my father, but the more I learn about it, the more suspicious his death feels to me. So I've taken the precaution of giving my lawyer an envelope, to be opened in the event of my own death. Inside, there's a letter to Subinspector Parera. It tells him everything he needs to know – about my father and your mother, why he was drinking, how you and I faked our marriage . . . There's even Ferid's draft of the email I sent Jess, to show his role in all this.'

I could see her trying to process it – looking for the way out. She'd always been able to find one before, after all. It must have been hard to realise that, this time, there wasn't one.

'What do you want, Finn?' she said slowly. 'Why are you saying all this?'

'It's very simple,' I said. 'I want you to love me. Properly, I mean.'

She shook her head. 'But I don't. Not like that.'

'But I think you can.' I let go of her, but she didn't move away. 'I think you can make yourself. Fake it till you make it – that's what they say, isn't it? And besides . . . I've realised, from our little games these past few weeks, that when you pretend, it's almost as wonderful to me as if you really meant it. That I can manage to ignore the fact it isn't one hundred per cent genuine some of the time.'

'*All* of the time,' she said firmly. 'It's never genuine, Finn. What you're talking about – it would be rape.'

'No.' I shook my head. 'It would be a *deal*. Like I said – stick with me for a year and a day, and you'll qualify for residency. That's what a marriage is, after all – a contract between two parties. *Vows.*'

As this ring encircles your finger, so will my love encircle you forever . . .

'And how often would you need to rape me, Finn?' she asked softly. 'Just the once? Every month? Every week? Every day? Because sex through coercion is always rape, however much you pretend otherwise.'

'Don't use that word again.' I spoke sharply, but she had to understand how this was going to work from now on. 'I forbid it. Anyway, this is different. I genuinely love you.'

'*Love?* And this is the way you show it?' she said incredulously.

'You just have to accept that sometimes I know best.' I managed a smile. 'Like when you tried to insist that you slept on the yoga mat that time. Or wanting to give back the ring. Or marrying Guillem . . . You need to trust my judgement.'

'Trust you!' she said. 'When everything you've just said shows the exact opposite – that I was an idiot for trusting you as much as I did?'

I shrugged. 'You thought you were so clever. You and your mother – luring me in. Well, I forgive you all that – I forgive everything. But the game's over now. King takes queen.'

'*Luring* you? Is that what you think it was?' She shook her head. 'Other way round. You *groomed* me, Finn. I thought you were my friend – my fucking *stepbrother* – and all the time you were actually grooming me. Even though you know what I've been through . . . How could you bring yourself to add to all that?'

'Because it will *heal* you,' I said. 'And loving someone isn't grooming them. Being loved – being treated respectfully by someone who has your best interests at heart – it will make you strong again. I'm sure of it.'

'My God,' she said. 'Your sister was right. You've convinced yourself I'm a project – one I no longer have any say over.'

'I know it's for the best,' I said simply. 'I mean, I hold all the cards now, so of course you have to do what I say – that's a given. But I truly believe that, once we're over this initial hurdle, it will be to your benefit, too.'

'At least those men in the brothel knew they were just using me for sex. They didn't feel the need to dress it up with *bullshit*.'

'That's enough,' I said sharply. 'You're spoiling the mood.'

'The mood? What mood is that, exactly?'

'This is the happiest day of my life.'

She sighed. 'You're living in a parallel reality, Finn. Surely you can see that? We can't live like that – not for a whole year.'

'You've made your bed. Now it's time to lie in it.' I gave her an encouraging smile. 'I expect you'll want to shower. I'll give you five minutes before I come in, shall I?'

For a long time, she stared at me. Then, abruptly, it was as if all the fight went out of her, and her shoulders sagged. I recognised that moment – it was the moment when the struggling stopped, and the creature was no longer truly wild.

'All right,' she said. 'It can't be any worse than what I've already done, I suppose. Give me five minutes.'

FIFTY-THREE

I gave her five minutes while I ate tumbet straight from the bowl – the strain of so many plans coming to fruition on one day had left me ravenous. Then I went to join her.

The *caseta* was quiet, but the shower was running. I undressed and got into bed, listening to the hiss of the water with a half-smile on my face. Then, because I could, I decided to go and share her shower. I went into the bathroom—

The cubicle was empty – she wasn't there. In the steam on the mirror, she'd written with a finger, *Fuck you, Finn.*

Pulling on my clothes again, I ran outside. I hadn't heard the car leave, but maybe she'd managed to get to it without me noticing.

But it was still where I'd left it, parked near the house. I almost laughed with relief as I realised the keys were still in my pocket. I hadn't had time to hang them up with the others in the kitchen.

I relaxed. So she was hiding in the house somewhere, or possibly in the fields. Sooner or later, she'd have to reveal herself. But – impatient to get things started – I began to scour the place anyway.

'Roze? Roze?' I called as I searched. 'You must realise this is pointless. Hiding from me now doesn't change anything. The fact is, for the next year at least, you need me more than I need you.'

Silence.

Then an awful thought hit me. I ran to the hallway, where my father's shotgun was kept, tucked behind the door, along with the backpack I'd seen Roze carrying that time she ran away from the birdwatchers.

Both were gone.

I'll go up there . . .

I looked up at the mountain, towering over the farmhouse and still illuminated by the late afternoon sun.

She was up there somewhere, and now she had twenty minutes on me.

FIFTY-FOUR

The Serra de Tramuntana isn't just a few mountains – it's a whole mountain range. Puig de Galatzó, the peak that looms over the finca, might be over a thousand metres high, but it isn't even the highest point – that lies to the east. And, although it's only eight or nine kilometres wide, the range stretches all the way from Andratx on the west coast to Pollença on the east, a distance of some sixty kilometres. At one time, villages like ours were accessible from the rest of the island only by boat, or by the network of old mule trails that wind around the peaks in tight, precipitous spirals. Some of the trails are little more than rocky ledges, but many more are astonishing constructions of quarried stone, built over a thousand years ago by the Moors and as intricate as any Roman road, with large cobbles underfoot and stone walls on either side. They were built just wide enough for two mules to pass each other, and stepped every six feet or so to make them easier for the animals to manage.

Really? So full of history, Finn.

Because of the way they intersect every few miles, the paths form a labyrinth, a warren of possibilities. You could use them to go almost anywhere; but, because so few are signposted, it would be equally easy to get lost.

I knew the ones around Cauzacs like the back of my hand.

The first question, of course, was where Roze thought she was going. I remembered something she'd said, when I asked her about the backpack: *Even a four-wheel drive can't get much higher than this . . . I could go in any direction. Or simply stay up there until they gave up.*

And something her mother had mentioned, my very first evening here: *The trails go all the way to Esporles . . .*

Esporles. It made sense that she'd be heading in that direction – it was one of the largest and best-marked routes. If I took the car, I could simply drive there, then walk back along the trail, cutting her off from the other direction.

I imagined her surprise when she saw me strolling towards her. *Hello, babe. Out for a hike?*

I strode purposefully towards the car, then stopped. Was this too easy? Knowing her as I now did, might there actually be more to it than there seemed?

What if those words had themselves been misdirections, carefully dropped into the conversation against just such a day as this? What if, all the time I'd been preparing my glue of sticky lime, she'd been weaving her net of mist – tiny threads of fiction so fine, I never even saw them?

She wasn't going to Esporles.

She would keep going up, I decided. Towards the summit – that's where she would feel safest.

If so, she was quite wrong, but she couldn't know that.

I got into the car, but, when I reached the road, instead of going down to the village and the main road, I turned uphill. Carrer sa Síquia zigzagged up past two other properties before petering out. It wasn't quite a dead end, though – at the very top, a rough forest track led onwards through pine trees towards the Coll de Cauzacs, a paved mule path on a natural saddle between Puig de Galatzó and its neighbouring peak.

Even though the car was four-wheel drive, it was slow going round the narrow bends. And once I'd passed the highest property – a finca even more remote than ours, screened by tall security fences and guarded by dogs – and got onto the track, it was slower still. I was bottoming out on rocks every ten metres, until the holes became too deep and I was in danger of getting stuck completely.

I left the car there and continued on foot.

The forest up here was only partially managed – abandoned stone farmhouses, crumbling back into the mountain from which they were built, showed where previous generations had given up the unequal struggle. When I found her, I decided, I'd take her to one of the ruins and we'd spend the night there. It would be easier than trying to get her back to Finca Síquia, and even more isolated for what I was planning to do.

I wasn't too worried about the fact she had a gun – a .410 was almost useless for shooting anything larger than a rabbit. Besides, she couldn't risk killing me with a shotgun, let alone one so identifiable. If she threatened me with it, I decided, I would laugh at her, and pluck it from her hand.

I was hurrying, but even so it was a couple of hours before I reached the mule path on the col. One direction wound down to Esporles, the other led on towards the Puig de Galatzó. I went that way.

After about forty minutes, I came to a place where a narrow path forked off to the right. Beside it, climbers had made a cairn of piled-up rocks, to indicate the way to the summit. I paused again. Onwards, or upwards? Once again, I tried to put myself in her shoes. But there was also the question of which route gave me the best chance of stopping her. If she'd taken the mule path, and I continued to follow her, it might be morning before I caught her up. If, on the other hand, she'd headed towards the summit and I followed her, eventually she'd be trapped, with no further height to gain.

I went upwards. The path I was now on was nothing like the mule track; where that had been built to skirt around the mountain, this one was steeper and less defined. There were tight squeezes between boulders, and ledges with precipitous drops; more than once, I almost slipped on a loose rock, and the smaller stones I dislodged skittered away, falling hundreds of feet below.

Then I stopped dead, because, just ahead of me, another stone was tumbling past. But I hadn't dislodged that one. It could only have come from the foot of someone directly above me, where the path looped back on itself as it coiled towards the summit.

Of course, it might have been a goat. But the mountain goats were amazingly sure-footed; and, besides, there was almost no grazing to tempt a goat up here.

I moved purposefully but silently forward. There was an overhang, and another tight squeeze, then I was around the corner—

Suddenly, a rock the size of a football crashed on to the path beside me. I looked up and saw her face – she was kneeling on a ledge above me, by another cairn. Even as I watched, she took a rock and dropped it over the edge, sending me leaping out of the way. I caught a glimpse of it as it bounced down the mountainside. It was big enough to have staved my head in.

'Who's the victim now, Finn?' she called down. 'Who needs saving? Fuck you!'

Another massive rock hurtled down the mountainside. Then she was away again, climbing up the mountainside on all fours, as agile as a monkey. That damned Pilates.

I thought frantically. She must have calculated that, while a shotgun wound would be hard to explain away, death from a falling rock could be accidental. There'd still be the letter I'd left with Tomàs, of course, but she must have – or thought she had – some plan to deal with that.

Keeping to the inside of the path, where the mountain afforded me some protection, I crept back under the last overhang I'd passed and settled down to wait. It might be late summer, but at this elevation, with no shelter, the temperature on the summit would soon be barely higher than freezing. She'd have to come down then.

Another sound – a rattling noise, fast-approaching. I looked up—

With a yell, she swept downhill past me on a mountain bike.

She must have hidden it up there – the rocky landscape was full of hiding places.

For a moment, I cursed myself for not having realised she might do something like this. But then I reconsidered. Having a bike would hardly benefit her. Yes, she'd make it back to Finca Síquia before me, but, without a car, what then? Once on the roads, I'd soon be able to catch her. What she was doing made no sense . . .

And then I realised. She wasn't going back to Finca Síquia. She wasn't going back down the mountain at all – or, at least, not the way she'd come up.

She was going around it.

From here, after she rejoined the mule paths, she could just as easily go down the mountain's southern flank, to the little town of Puigpunyent, as back the way she'd come. Once at Puigpunyent, she could either ditch the bike and catch a bus into Palma, a journey of no more than twenty minutes, or, more likely, simply continue to coast downhill, and get there in around half an hour.

It was clever – brilliant, even – but I still didn't see why—

Then a lightbulb went on in my head.

So the alternative is just to disappear . . . Ferid thinks the sooner the better. He's been telling me to go for some time, actually. I've just . . . I've been putting it off.

Once again, I almost stopped dead as it dawned on me just how clever she was being. It would take me hours to get back to the car – if the growing darkness didn't slow me up still further – then another thirty minutes' driving on the rough forest track down to Cauzacs. Even then, I'd still have to go around the mountain by road to reach Palma – around a fifty-minute journey. By the time I got there, she'd be on a ferry or a plane, halfway to Valencia or Madrid.

My only chance was to stop her now, before she reached the relative safety and better surface of the mule tracks.

There was, I knew, a small torrent that cut down the side of Puig de Galatzó, not far from where I was – a stream course, dry at this time of year, that carried meltwater in the spring. It intersected the zigzagging path in several places. If I simply ran straight down it, there was a faint – very faint – possibility that I might be able to get ahead of her and cut her off.

Running to the small ravine the stream had left, I jumped in with barely a pause, accelerating still more as I tried to use gravity to go even faster. I knew within moments that I was out of control. But it was like the feeling when I bought her the ring, or when I told her I loved her – it was that or nothing; embrace the earth's pull or lose her, my darling Roze, possibly forever.

There were boulders underfoot I could barely see, any one of which might have tripped me up, but none did, and I laughed with exhilaration as I went faster still, my arms pumping, my legs churning beneath me as they tried to keep up. I thought I glimpsed two wheels, a figure hunched over the handlebars, as something flashed across my path, and I pressed on at full tilt. Was I falling, or flying? Running, or gliding? Then my toe caught on stone, the mountain choosing sides like the meddling bitch it was, and there was no longer any doubt – for a brief, terrifying second, I *was* flying, but it might it might it might still be all right, until my head met rock and everything exploded.

FIFTY-FIVE

How long I was unconscious for, I have no idea, but when I came round, it was dark and the air was freezing. I moved, and the pain in my head – both sharp and throbbing – along with an ache like the very worst hangover I'd ever had, told me I almost certainly had concussion.

Gingerly, I reached up, trying to assess the damage. My fingers felt blood and damaged tissue; possibly damaged bone, as well.

Of Roze, there was no sign. I doubt she'd even realised I was coming down the torrent after her.

I used a boulder to pull myself upright. It wasn't only my head I'd hit – my ribs were hurt too, and I could barely put any weight on my left leg.

I started to hobble in the direction of the path.

How I got as far as the mule track, I've no idea. How I retraced my steps to the car, I understand even less, unless there was a kind of homing instinct that somehow guided me back. The pain in my head was so excruciating, I thought I might vomit or pass out at any moment.

I drove with my head at an angle, so that the blood dripped

down my jaw rather than into the only eye I could keep open. By the time I got back to the finca, the clock on the dashboard told me it was gone midnight. Gasping with pain, I hobbled to the barn where the agricultural machinery was kept. At the back was a loose pile of earth. I rummaged around in it until my hands met wood and glass. My father had always kept his supplies of brandy in here – not the best hiding place, but the one providing quickest access. And it seemed I was in luck. There was a crate of Veterano, with only two bottles missing.

I opened one and tipped the contents down my throat.

FIFTY-SIX

I think I collapsed into unconsciousness again, after that. I woke up – or perhaps I came to; it was hard to say – in the full heat of the day. I was lying on the *caseta*'s bathroom floor – but how I'd got there, I had no idea. I dimly remembered hitting my head, but had I really walked through the woods afterwards, in the dark, then driven back?

I staggered to my feet, fighting the urge to retch as a bout of dizziness gripped me, and looked in the mirror. There was a blood-encrusted gash down one side of my forehead, the tissue around it already dark with bruising, the area around my left eye so swollen, the eye itself was almost invisible. I looked down at the floor. Where I'd been lying, the tiles were wet with blood.

The mirror – something about it triggered a memory. I tried to focus on it. *Fuck you, Finn.* It was still there, if you looked hard enough, the mark of her finger almost invisible now against the glass, like secret writing on paper. So she was gone. We'd had a row and she'd run away. Or had she? Had we made up and she'd come home? I felt a sudden sense of hope that that was what might have happened.

I went back through to the bedroom. My father was standing at his easel, over by the window, where he always worked because the light was better, a colourful bandana tied around his hair. His African smock was spattered with paint.

'What do you think of this?' he asked. 'I think it's bloody good.'

'What are you doing here?' I said, but he ignored me.

I went to look at the painting. It was of Roze. Roze, naked, lying on the bed. My father grunted at my reaction, then turned to squint down the length of his arm, using his paintbrush as a measure to check her proportions. I followed his gaze towards the bed, but she wasn't there. I felt a surge of jealousy that he could see her naked body and I couldn't.

'Of course, I told them you were a pervy little runt,' he said conversationally. 'We had a good laugh about that. No wonder she ran away from you.'

'I'm going to drink your brandy,' I told him. 'All of it. See how you like that.'

He licked his fingers, then pinched his brush bristles into a point. 'Haven't you heard? I've given up. I'm a reformed character. The point is, they saw you coming a mile off.'

Of course, that wasn't true. Roze loved me, or as near as dammit. But then I remembered that backpack, waiting by the back door for emergencies, and the bike hidden on the mountain. Was it the trafficking gang Roze been afraid of, or me? I couldn't remember. Did the trafficking gang even exist? It was so hard to work out what was a lie and what wasn't. Had all that stuff about sex work simply been a convenient fiction, to forestall the – perfectly reasonable – expectation that, having given her my hand in marriage, I might want to sleep with her, too?

I thought furiously of all those nights when I'd lain in that bed, my senses ablaze with the closeness of her, my loins straining. Had she been smiling to herself, unseen by me, before drifting off into a contented sleep, happy that the poor besotted fool beside her was so easy to manage?

No – it was real, I told myself. That horseplay in the pool. Those games when she threw oranges at me. Her arm slipping through mine as we strolled out to the fields. That much had been genuine, surely. She loved me. Well, liked me. Or some strange hinterland between the two . . .

'She was seeing how far she could draw you in, you idiot,' my father said. His voice was muffled – he had his paintbrush clenched between his teeth now, like a pirate's cutlass, as he smeared paint on the canvas directly with his fingers. 'Vulvas are pink, my thoughts are blue, I'll just finish this painting, and then I'll fuck you,' he sang to the unseen figure on the bed.

'Fuck off and die,' I snarled.

He snorted. 'Been there, done that. Your turn next. Well, not the fucking bit, obviously. But the dying, maybe.' Raising his voice, he called towards the bed, 'Smashing tits, by the way. Just how I like them.'

'And don't talk to her like that.'

He looked surprised. 'Oh, she doesn't mind. We met in a brothel, after all – I was one of her punters. We got chatting and she told me she and her mother might have to leave the country.

So I offered them a place to stay, in exchange for doing some work around the place.'

'No!' I said. 'You're lying. That never happened.'

He laughed. 'Maybe. But what's undeniable is that she played you, chum. Saw right through you from the start and outsmarted you, like the sucker you are. You always did go gaga over pretty girls, Dolphin. Ga-ga-ga-ga.' He imitated my childhood stutter. 'Fuck and forget, that's my motto.'

'You and Ru were in love,' I said desperately. 'You were happy together. You were going to give painting classes at the agroturismo—'

'Was I?' He snorted. 'I'd rather cut off my arm with a rusty fish knife.'

I squeezed my eyes shut. 'Go away. That isn't how it was.'

'How was it, then, duck-brain?' he demanded. 'If you think I'm lying, what was the truth?'

I couldn't answer that.

He laughed again. 'Quack. Quack quack quack. *Think*, duck-brain. Think!'

But I couldn't think. Instead, the hammering in my brain and the dizziness swept me up again, and I fell over.

FIFTY-SEVEN

The next time I came to, I was lying face-down in the barn, my hand clasped around a half-empty bottle of brandy. Had I actually hallucinated that conversation with my father, or had it only been a drunken dream?

As I staggered to my feet, I saw there was a second empty bottle on the floor. Nearby was a pool of vomit. It reeked sourly of spirits. I retched again.

I staggered towards the house. As I rounded the corner, I saw Roze. She was sitting at the veranda table, scrolling through her phone.

I stopped. 'Is this for real?'

She looked up. 'What do you mean? But yes – if you're asking, have I come back, I have.' She held up her phone. 'Forgot this.'

'God,' I said, 'I thought I'd lost you. I thought—'

'I know,' she said. 'You look terrible, by the way. I tried to wake you, but you were completely out of it. I left you to sleep it off.'

'Thank you.' My head was hammering, but I pulled out a chair and sat down. 'Roze, I'm so sorry.'

'Yes,' she said simply. 'You should be.'

'Everything I said – it was so wrong of me. And it wasn't even true, most of it. I was just trying . . . I was so desperate . . .'

She gazed at me with her dark eyes. 'You lied to me, Finn. You let me trust you. When, all the time, you were only plotting how to rape me.'

'No,' I protested weakly. 'It wasn't like that, honestly. Not at first . . . I just wanted to help you. But then I fell in love with you, and I think it sent me a little bit crazy.'

'Love!' she said incredulously. 'How can it be love, if it makes you want to treat someone like that?'

'I only wanted you to love me back,' I said miserably. 'And, when you didn't, I just wanted – well, as much as possible, I suppose. As much as I could get. Please, forgive me.'

'Well, if I'm even to consider coming back, there's going to have to be a new deal,' she said crisply. 'For starters, we won't be sleeping in the same room. We'll work separate shifts in the fields. You're not to go anywhere near the swimming pool. And then, at the end of the year, you can leave.'

'Leave the finca?' I stared at her. 'But it's mine!'

'You thought I was yours, once. Anyway, your sister's bound to force us out eventually. I just want to make sure I can stay here as long as possible, and you're not part of those plans anymore. Agreed?'

I hesitated, but only for a moment. 'And you swear it was all true? Everything you told me?'

Was it my imagination, or was there a tiny hesitation before she nodded? 'Everything. The important stuff, anyway. So, what's it to be, Finn? A year here, on my terms, or shall I pack my things and go?'

'No,' I said desperately. 'Stay. I want you to stay. Please stay.'

'Good,' she said. 'I'm glad that's clear. And now I'm going to swim. I'm filthy.' She went to the decking and started peeling off her clothes. 'Take a good look, Finn,' she called, 'because you're not going to touch this body ever again. And, by the way ...' A pause. 'Your father was right. I *have* got smashing tits.'

She dived in in her underwear, sending water flying in all directions. I was confused. How did she know what my father had said about her tits? Unless he'd also said it to her, when she posed for him? But that meant ... but no ...

Roze hadn't surfaced again. She must be swimming under-water. But as the moments turned into almost a minute, I became concerned. Was she all right?

I ran to the pool.

She was lying on the bottom. She must have hit her head when she dived in. I jumped in after her, pulling her lifeless body to the surface.

'Roze? Roze!' There was no response. Frantically, with one hand still under her back to stop her from sinking and the other sup-porting her head, I fastened my lips against hers, forcing air deep into her lungs. Then I pulled her to the steps and started compressions on her chest. You were meant to use the rhythm of that Bee Gees song, 'Staying Alive', I recalled. 'One, two, three, four, staying alive,' I grunted. 'Six, seven, eight, nine—'

She spluttered water, and her eyes opened. 'My God! Finn, you saved my life,' she said.

I looked down at her tenderly. 'I did, yes.'

'Then I love you,' she said, wrapping her arms around my neck – they were still cool from the water. I laughed, and she playfully pulled me down, under the water with her, as she had done so many times before . . .

I found myself standing in the pool, fully dressed. Roze was nowhere to be seen. 'Roze?' I called. 'Roze? Where are you?'

Nearby, an empty brandy bottle floated past. I stared at it. Where had it come from? Then I looked at the decking and saw her clothes weren't there.

'No,' I said. 'Please, no. Roze, come back.' And I cried to dream again.

FIFTY-EIGHT

'Think, duck-brain,' my father said impatiently. '*Think*.'

We were sitting on the ground outside the finca, our backs propped against the stone wall, soaking up the morning sunshine and sharing a bottle of brandy.

'I can't think,' I said wearily. 'I just want to sleep.'

He grunted. 'You always were a feeble little shite. Anyway, the point is, I've told you what happened.'

'You have?'

He reached across and plucked the bottle from my mouth. 'My turn. Yes, I told you – I said to my lovely wife and her even lovelier daughter that my son was a pervy little runt.'

'So? You used to say stuff like that all the time.'

'Oh, for God's sake.' He sighed. 'Do I have to spell it out? I told them about that girl – Sophie something. The one you killed.'

'I didn't kill her,' I said automatically. 'It was an accident. She died of an overdose—'

'Which you'd given her, so you could perve over her,' he interrupted. 'Anyway, they were fascinated. I told them about the animals you used to rescue, too, and the way you used to run off crying when I was nasty to you, and the girls in the village school you used to stare at . . . I didn't know about the restraining order, of course, because you and I had lost touch by then. But I'd heard enough from Jess over the years to know you hadn't changed.'

'It was your fault,' I said bitterly. 'You fucked me up.'

'Oh, for God's sake. Be a man and stop whining. The point is, they knew all your weaknesses. Mine too, come to that.'

I looked at him as he passed the bottle back to me. 'They played you, too?'

He shrugged. 'I assume so.'

'So who killed you?'

'Ah,' he said. 'We're not at the point, yet, where I can tell you that.'

'But you do know?'

'Yes,' he said. 'I know.'

I thought for a moment. 'But, just because you told them that about me, it doesn't prove they were out to trick me. They might not have believed you. There was no proof I killed Sophia, after all. No police investigation. It was put down to a bunch of druggie foreigners and a party that got out of hand, wasn't it? The Gathering was broken up, people either slunk away or got thrown off the island . . . And Jess and I went back to England.'

'Yes.' My father was silent, then said, 'I really hated you after that.'

'What do you mean?'

'If it hadn't been for needing to get you away from here, your mother would never have left me.'

I looked at him incredulously. 'You slept with Sophia *and* her mother, for Chrissake. You were a drunken, foul-mouthed, chaotic bully.'

He shrugged. 'Doesn't mean I wanted to divorce your mother. She kept the show on the road. I loved her.'

'You got married again quickly enough!'

'I'm not good at being alone.' He took a long pull of the brandy. 'Besides, I don't think I ever really loved Sandra. I just got excited about her for a while, because I thought things would be different with her. But they weren't. Same old same old.'

'And Ruensa? Was that to avoid being alone, as well?'

'No, Ru was different.' He tipped the bottle up and drained the last drops from it. 'Fuck, I've missed this stuff.'

'Different how?'

'That's what you have to work out.' Getting up, he hurled the empty bottle as far as he could over Miquel's terraces.

I sighed. 'Why? It won't bring Roze back.'

'Won't it? Maybe you've got a bigger hold over her than you think. I'm going inside.'

'I'll see you later, then.' I closed my eyes. The darkness lurched, and the wall against my back seemed to roll from side to side. 'Too much brandy,' I murmured.

FIFTY-NINE

That's what you have to work out, my father had said. But I didn't have the energy – not for a long time. Exactly how long, I couldn't say. I remember looking in the mirror at one point – my hair still matted as the wound in my head oozed a seam of fresh blood; the bruise less swollen now, but turning a vivid yellow-green colour.

Some of my hallucinations I remember only dimly. Like the time Roze made me beg for forgiveness on my knees. Or the time I walked in on her pleasuring my father. Or the time we had rapturous make-up sex on the veranda . . . These were the fragments I couldn't get out of my head, along with the tiny bits of bone I could still feel moving under the surface of my wound.

Maybe you've got a bigger hold over her than you think. Sometimes, I felt mildly curious about that. Did he mean there was something that might help me get her back? But then, my father wasn't even real. At best, he was a figment of my imagination; at worst, an indication that my head was in an even worse state than I was letting myself admit. Anything he said to me was hardly to be relied on.

Eventually, I dragged myself to Son Llatzer hospital, where

a doctor informed me that I was lucky not to have developed a serious infection. He cleaned me up, put two stitches in my wound and gave me antibiotics.

'You should rest,' he told me. 'We have no other treatment for traumatic brain injury, only rest. You shouldn't even be driving. Is there no one you can ask to come and get you?'

I shook my head, then regretted it – the stitching had made it throb. 'No one.'

'Then for God's sake, take it easy.' He looked at me. 'It'll probably be a couple of months before you're right again. Are you forgetting things?'

'Sometimes I can't even remember the passcode for my phone,' I confessed.

He nodded, unsurprised. 'You may not have any memory of this conversation, either, so I suggest you make a note of everything I'm telling you. And don't make any big decisions until you're better. Head trauma is unpredictable at the best of times.'

I agreed with him that I would make no major decisions for at least two months, and went back to the car, feeling better now that I'd actually done something about getting myself patched up.

That's what you have to work out.

It was early evening, and the hospital was only ten minutes or so from the centre of Palma. Instead of driving back to the finca, I made a snap decision and went in the other direction – towards the marina.

SIXTY

I worked in a club near the marina . . .

According to the maps app on my phone, there were at least half a dozen nightclubs close to the marina. Some might not have links to prostitution, of course. But, in a country where selling sex was legal and nightclubs were the main outlets, I knew that many places deliberately blurred the line, tempting ordinary clubbers in with cheap drinks and DJs at the front, with strippers performing in a discreet area towards the back, and the actual sex happening upstairs or in nearby apartments. Many were completely open about it – any club with 'Girls', 'Angels' or 'Dollar' in its name, for example, was likely to operate at the seedier end of the market.

I decided to start with the more sophisticated ones and work my way down from there, not least because it was still early and those were the ones that were open.

I swiped through the photos of Roze on my phone. There were dozens – after Ferid told us to embrace the idea that we were a young couple desperately in love, she'd sent me a selfie almost every day.

I chose the very first one – her in her underwear.

Couldn't resist sending you this x
I love you x
Love you too, dolphin boy xxx

Tears pricked at my eyes as I reread the messages. Oh, God – why had I gone and ruined everything? If I'd only waited a little longer, perhaps it would never have been necessary. Perhaps she would have come to me of her own accord.

We'd been so happy.

YOU WEREN'T HAPPY, my father roared at me. *HOW COULD ANY MAN BE HAPPY, CUTTING OFF HIS OWN BALLS LIKE THAT?*

At the first club, I paid a twenty-euro entrance fee and went inside. Three or four bored-looking women were hanging around by the bar. I beckoned one over. She came eagerly, clearly thinking she'd made a quick sale.

'Do you recognise her?' I asked, showing her my phone.

She looked at the photo. 'I'm not sure. Why? Is that your girlfriend?'

'It's someone who might have worked here. It would have been about eighteen months ago.'

She smiled at me. 'Are you going to buy me a drink?'

'No, but I'll give you twenty euros if you'll tell me whether you've seen her.'

The woman took the money, then shook her head. 'No, never.'

At the second club, I repeated my question, and waved another twenty-euro note. This time, the woman said, 'I don't recognise her, but you could ask Mila. She's been here the longest of any of us.'

Mila took two of my twenty-euro bills before saying no, she was sure she'd remember someone that pretty.

'Were you trafficked here?' I asked her. 'Are you under any kind of coercion to work? A fake debt, for example?'

Mila's eyes went dead and she glanced over to where a bouncer was watching us from beside the bar. He immediately set off in our direction.

'It's all right,' I said quickly. 'I'm going.'

As the night progressed, and the bars became seedier, the music got louder and the veneer of sophistication thinner. Some of the clubs were tiny – little more than a stage and an outer ring of banquettes, where a mostly male clientele lolled around with their legs spread apart, the dancers gyrating between them.

'Are you the police?' one girl asked when I showed her the photo, and I couldn't tell whether that was fear or hope I could hear in her voice.

I shook my head, and she shook hers. 'I've never seen her,' she said despondently, handing my phone back.

I'd just left that club when I noticed two burly bouncers hurrying after me. I kept going – although it was after midnight, it was still early by Spanish standards, and there were plenty of people around.

As they caught up with me, one of the bouncers grabbed my arm and spun me around, just as the other slammed his fist into my stomach. I doubled up and my head came down, straight into a quick, jabbing uppercut to my jaw delivered by the first one, flipping me over. I was left lying on my back, tasting blood, as they continued on their way. It had taken about five seconds, and they'd hardly broken stride.

I lay there, winded. It seemed easier than trying to get up. A passer-by made a detour in my direction.

'*Només va gat*,' he called to his friends cheerfully, going on his way. Just drunk.

I got up and staggered on. At the next club the entrance fee was thirty euros – prices had been going up as the night progressed. Once my eyes got used to the red light that saturated everything, I could see this was one of the larger places I'd visited. The dancers seemed younger and better-looking than in the previous clubs, too, as did the clientele.

They're called puticlubs *and even teenagers go to them . . .*

As soon as I'd sat down, two women came over. After I'd agreed to buy drinks, and one had gone to the bar to get them, I showed the other woman the photograph of Roze.

She shook her head. 'Sorry. I've never seen her.'

'She's from Albania,' I added, hoping to jog her memory.

'Really? I'm from Albania.' She looked at the photo again. 'She doesn't look Albanian.'

'Why not?'

She shrugged. 'The hair, I guess. Do you miss her?' She nodded at the other woman, returning with our drinks. 'We're good friends. Have you ever had sex with two girls at once? It's great. We'll do you a special deal.'

'No,' I said. 'I'm just here to look for my friend. You're sure you've never seen her?'

'I'm sure. We have somewhere we could go. An apartment, next door.'

'No, really.' Suddenly sick of the whole business, I stood up. 'Look, if you're friends, share this, will you? I'm sorry I can't help you more.' I put the rest of my money on the table. They nodded their thanks, and the notes disappeared.

When I reached the door and looked back, I could see that they'd already sat down either side of someone else.

SIXTY-ONE

I sat at the veranda table and tried to make a list of everything in Roze's story that I thought was true. And then another, of everything that might be a lie.

When it was done, I stared at the pages, the letters crawling across the dazzling white paper like ants. The two lists were identical. There was no real proof of anything. Everything was supposition. Trust, or its mirror image, doubt.

In one of his rare bouts of parental engagement, my father once taught me about perspective – how you could draw lines from all the objects in a picture, and how they should all eventually meet up in one spot, called the vanishing point. It was a kind of trick, he said; before anyone knew the trick, people's minds just didn't think like that, and they saw nothing wrong with pictures that didn't work that way. But, once you'd seen perspective, you couldn't unsee it. Every picture, every vista, demanded a vanishing point. And if you were really good at it, really exact, you could paint on walls or ceilings so precisely, people would mistake what they were seeing for the real thing. He even took me to see a pediment over a door in Palma that looked as if it was carved in stone, until you gave it a second glance and realised it was just paint on a wall.

It was like that with Roze, I realised. Seen from one point, everything was true. She had been trafficked. Her mother had rescued her. By chance, they'd met my father and fallen in love – my father with Ru, Ru with the house, Roze with the farm. Then I'd come along and tried to protect her – from Jess's cold-heartedness, from Subinspector Parera's borderline racism, from scorpions in her room, from marriage to a stranger.

But shift your stance only the tiniest amount, and all that was *trompe l'oeil*. They'd seen my need to protect the vulnerable and taken advantage of it, just as they'd exploited my father before me. Perhaps they planned my entrapment in minute detail; perhaps it had developed piecemeal, as they tried to make the most of a fast-moving situation. Perhaps they'd simply hoped to charm me into making them a slightly more advantageous offer than the one they deserved, then got in deeper than they'd expected, once the extent of my infatuation with Roze became clear.

The one thing that was undeniable was that she'd left me.

Who's the victim now, Finn? Who needs saving? Fuck you!

And I wept then, because I would rather be a deluded fool with her beside me than a wise and lonely cynic.

The bottle by my hand was empty now, and I went to get another.

The new bottle tasted foul – even fouler than normal. And I was distracted by the realisation that there was toast burning in the kitchen.

I wasn't surprised to discover I'd put on some toast and then forgotten about it – since my injury, I'd been forgetting the simplest things.

It was only when I went into the kitchen and looked around that I realised I'd forgotten something else, too – there *was* no toaster at Finca Síquia. But the smell of burning bread was stronger than ever.

I smacked my lips together. Why was I doing that? But it felt so good, I laughed out loud. For the first time since Roze left, I was happy – almost ridiculously so. I had survived! I had a future! The finca was effectively mine, the gold-diggers had been ousted, and I was on top of the world!

But my joy was quickly clouded by fury at the thought of just how close I'd come to being robbed of all that. I imagined my hands closing around Roze's throat – how I'd lift her right off her feet, and slowly squeeze, and watch the bitch's eyes roll back in her head before I let her fall to the ground . . .

I'd raised both my hands to make the shape, but now I saw they weren't fastened around an imaginary neck at all. My fingers were curling into claws and stiffening, my wrists turning upwards as if I was offering them to be bound. I stared at them. Why weren't my hands doing what I wanted? And why did I have a sudden sense that all this had happened before – that I knew exactly what was about to take place, but had somehow forgotten it?

Pins and needles danced up my legs. My thighs cramped. Then a sensation like an electric shock hit both sides of my body at once – like jarring the funny bone in my elbows, but a hundred times worse. I fell to the floor, bouncing on the terracotta tiles the way a landed fish trampolines on a riverbank, my throat paralysed, my arms flapping uncontrollably . . .

And then, as abruptly as it had come, whatever it was left me, and I threw up.

SIXTY-TWO

'You had a seizure,' the doctor said. 'It's not uncommon after a bad head injury.'

'Could it happen again?'

'Quite possibly.' He glanced at me. 'You're lucky in that you had some warning. The mood swings, the cramps, the disruption to your sense of smell, even the déjà vu – those can all be what we call prodromal symptoms. If any of those occur again, you should get somewhere safe and lie down in the recovery position as quickly as possible. And, needless to say, it's imperative that you don't drive now. How did you get here today?'

'By bus,' I lied.

'OK. Well, I'll prescribe an anti-epileptic drug, but the most effective thing is still to get plenty of rest. Have you been drinking at all?'

I shrugged. 'A bit.'

'You need to stop altogether. Apart from anything else, the AED I'm giving you interacts badly with alcohol. If you do drink, you may experience extreme confusion.'

'I'm already confused,' I said. 'About a girl.'

He smiled. 'Medical confusion is a little bit different. It's more like being –' he paused, then used the Catalan word – '*estupefacte.*'

Stupefied. I quite liked the sound of that.

SIXTY-THREE

That night, she came and slipped into bed beside me. I'd been asleep, but when I felt her pressing against my back – the hard points of her nipples, the sweet softness of her breasts – I stirred and turned over. Our love-making was swift and urgent, then she padded away on bare feet, leaving me sated and drowsy. In those moments, I had felt no hatred of her, only love, and it was that as much as anything that prompted me to say loftily to my father, next morning, 'I have decided to believe her. Her feelings for me were real and she spoke the truth.'

He cocked an eye at me over his newspaper – no one had delivered a newspaper to Finca Síquia in decades, but somehow he'd got hold of one. 'More fool you. You're forgetting the basic rule of testimony – if someone's lied about one thing, it makes it more likely they're lying about everything. Find one demonstrable fib, and your job's done.'

'More likely, perhaps,' I said. 'But not certain.'

'That's where you've got an advantage over me,' he continued as if I hadn't spoken. 'I became obsessed with finding out if the story about their past was true. You've got much more to work with – whether they lied about *me*.'

'You were obsessed?' I said, surprised. 'I didn't realise.'

He grunted, as if annoyed he'd let that slip. '*De tal palo tal astilla.* My demons lay in a different direction, mostly. But I'm just as capable as you are of making an idiot of myself, it seems.'

'So, if you know what happened to you, and whether they lied to me about it, why not just tell me?'

'Uh-uh. It's not that easy. You have to work it out.' He shook out the pages of his newspaper, then added, 'This is a clue, by the way.'

'What is?' I said, puzzled.

'Oh, for God's sake. You're looking for a newspaper cutting.'

'I am?'

He nodded. 'That lawyer – Ferid – must have given it to her. I can't see who else it could have been. Pass the brandy, would you?'

SIXTY-FOUR

Could a hallucinated version of my father tell me something I didn't already know? It was probably an interesting philosophical question, but I was far too whacked out on brandy, the anti-epileptic medication and the effects of the concussion to care.

A newspaper cutting ... Something about his words stirred a memory. I went up to the third floor. Everything was still as we'd left it before the wedding – the corridor half painted, the first two bedrooms cleared, the others untouched. Our agroturismo dream, wrecked by my inappropriate behaviour.

I went into my father's painting room, to the chest of drawers where he'd kept his papers. This time, I went through them methodically.

It was gone noon when I found the cutting again. It was quite small, and folded in half, so I almost missed it at first. Then I opened it up, and remembered why I hadn't been able to read it before – at the time, I'd thought it was in Russian.

No, not Russian, I decided, as I looked at it more carefully. I had a vague idea that letter like an M on its side was a sigma.

Greek.

I don't think they realised anyone could understand them. But I'm quite sure they were speaking Greek . . .

Of course, it was perfectly possible that the Greek-speaking part of Albania had a Greek-language newspaper. The cutting could be about anything – a recipe, a record of some sporting event, the weather.

But why would Ferid give Ruensa or Roze an article about any of those?

I turned to the internet, and found a website where I could, laboriously, click on individual Greek letters to make a rough translation.

To begin with, as letters slowly became words and words built up into sentences, I couldn't see how it might be relevant. But then I reached a word – κόρη – that suddenly made sense of it all.

Daughter.

And I felt a cold and murderous rage wash over me as I realised what it meant.

SIXTY-FIVE

There are some women, it seems to me, who exist separately from their own beauty. Their bodies are a gift bestowed on them by genetics, in which they have only a lifetime interest – a kind of *usufructo*. Some of those women understand how lucky they are, and do their best to be careful and generous with their inheritance, but some simply use their occupancy to lord it over others, and debase the very palaces they have been entrusted with. Those are the women who can't always see what's best for them, and sometimes you need to go to extreme measures to teach them.

I thought I knew what had happened now, just as I understood why my father had said I had a greater hold over Roze than I'd ever imagined.

It was time to go and get her back – to assert my inheritance. And, this time around, things were going to be very different.

'Yes, I speak Greek,' Ferid said calmly. 'My family are not from there originally, but, as I think I mentioned, I grew up in Athens.'

'Your parents were migrants?'

He nodded. 'They left Iran in the 1980s, after the revolution. My father believed Greece was the cradle of Western civilisation, so that was where he decided to settle.'

'And do you take a Greek newspaper, by any chance?'

I watched him carefully as he plucked an imaginary piece of lint from his trousers.

'Occasionally,' he replied at last. 'Why do you ask?'

Silently, I took out the cutting and pushed it across his desk.

'Ah, yes,' he said, picking it up and glancing at it. 'This was quite a notorious case, a couple of years back. It concerns a Greek woman who killed her husband. She claimed she'd acted in a justifiable fit of rage – a legitimate defence in Greek law, but one that is used more often by men, when they have killed wives who have been unfaithful or who are trying to leave them. In this case, the woman claimed that she killed her husband because he was violent and controlling towards her. She was granted bail on condition that she surrender her passport, but before the case could come to trial, she vanished, along with her twenty-three-year-old daughter.'

'Whereabouts in Greece did they live?'

'On Lesbos.' His eyes regarded me calmly.

'Where you worked for your humanitarian organisation. An organisation that was censured for crossing the line and actively assisting migrants, rather than simply advising them.'

He nodded. 'And your next question, no doubt, is whether I ever met this woman or her daughter – to which I will give you the same answer I gave your father: I don't believe I did.' He tapped the cutting. 'I'm afraid he didn't believe me. He became quite obsessed with the idea that this Greek woman and Ruensa were the same person, and that I must somehow have had a hand in bringing her here.'

'But you didn't?'

He shook his head, a hint of a smile in his eyes. Did he mean no, he hadn't had a hand in it, or no, he wouldn't answer my question, because it would mean incriminating himself?

'Theirs *was* a marriage of convenience, though?' I pressed. 'A sham to get Ruensa residency, just as mine was?'

His gaze didn't waver. 'I have no reason to think either marriage was a sham. Indeed, I was always struck by just how much both of you adored your wives.'

'So where are Roze and Ruensa now?' I nodded at the cutting. 'You see, unless Roze returns immediately, I'm going to tell Subinspector Parera who she and Ruensa really are. The police might not expend resources tracking down a couple of Albanian migrants who've overstayed their welcome, but I'm guessing that suspected murderers from within the EU would be a completely different matter.'

I remember the pine marten that my father chased out of the house that time, the one I thought I'd tamed. A few weeks later, I was walking back from the fields when I saw it again, gnawing at a fallen orange – it was easily identifiable by its misshapen leg. It was painfully thin by then. They're territorial creatures; it had probably been coming off worst in altercations with other pine martens.

I knelt down and, gently, tried to stroke it. Turning its head, it bit me savagely in the fleshy part of my hand, between my thumb and finger.

I went back to the house, found my father's gun, and shot it. There are limits to even my patience.

Ferid raised his eyebrows. 'She's not at home with you?'

'I think you know she isn't.'

'I'm sorry to hear it. Well, if you do hear from her, let me know. I will have to communicate with her soon – I've already sent her a message of congratulations, of course, but there are still a few details about her residency that will need tying up.'

I frowned at him. 'Congratulations? What for?'

He looked surprised. 'You didn't know? Her appeal has been successful. Two weeks ago, now. The tribunal ultimately accepted the argument that, in certain cases, a victim of human trafficking can fall within the definition of a persecuted person. Once it was clarified that this was indeed the case here, she was granted indefinite leave to remain.' He gestured at the cutting. 'And I think you'll find that a recent asylum tribunal decision trumps a wild theory supported by nothing more than a two-year-old newspaper article.'

'Did either of them ever produce any actual proof Roze had been trafficked into sex work?' I said hotly. 'Or was it all just words – a hint from you that she jumped on, as soon as she realised it was her only chance?'

His eyes were steely. 'I find it is always best to believe what my clients tell me. Otherwise – well, look at your father. That way madness lies, to quote your national poet.'

'No one recognised her photo when I showed it round the clubs.'

He shrugged. 'I'm not surprised. The turnover in those places is brutally quick. Do I take it, then, that you were no longer getting along?'

'She's left me,' I said shortly. 'The two of them are in hiding somewhere, I assume. But now . . .' I stopped as the implications of what he'd just told me became clear, even to my befuddled brain. 'She doesn't need to be married now, does she? She doesn't even need to hide. She's got what she wants.'

Ferid said nothing, just continued to watch me for a moment. Then he sighed. 'Even so, perhaps the two of you can sort things out. Put it this way – I have certainly not been made aware of any instruction to start proceedings for a divorce. And, while there is silence, there is hope, surely?'

Desperately, I tried one last sally. 'If that article isn't about her and Ruensa, why would they keep it?'

Ferid shrugged. 'As I understand it, Ruensa saw it in *Laiko Vima* – the Albanian-Greek newspaper – and, knowing my interest in the many iniquities of the Greek legal system, and that I had lived on Lesbos, cut it out, meaning to show me. However, it slipped her mind, and then your father came across it.'

The words flowed from his lips so reasonably. What could I possibly say to refute them? There was nothing, I realised. I was simply grasping at phantoms.

Or spiders' threads, perhaps. And the more I struggled, the more hopelessly I was enmeshed.

When I didn't reply, he nodded. 'You know, sometimes it really is best to take these things at face value. It is so difficult to be both happy and, at the same time, full of suspicion.'

SIXTY-SIX

So I still had no answers, but somehow, the questions no longer seemed quite so important anymore. She was gone, and I just had to accept that it was up to her whether she ever decided to come back.

Sometimes I wandered the grounds of the finca, hoping to trick my brain into just one more hallucination of her. Sometimes I called to her out loud, the only response the mocking echo of the mountain. And sometimes I spoke to my father, even though I only saw him one more time after I cleared the drawers in his painting room. Whether that was because I had effected some kind of exorcism, or my brain was simply starting to heal, I don't know.

That final time . . . It was a week or so after I'd been to see Ferid. I was sitting at the kitchen table, typing furiously on my laptop, when I happened to glance up. He was sitting at the other end of the table, watching me.

'Oh, hello,' I said.

He grunted. 'Worked out how I died yet, have you?'

'As it happens, I think I have.' I gestured at my screen. 'I've been writing it all down – everything that happened here. And I realised that, even though I can never know the whole truth about Roze, I can guess the truth about *you*. Because I'm your son, and I know how I feel about certain things. And, of all the possible endings to this, there's one that feels more . . . right, somehow, than the others. One that's not quite a reparation, but an apology, of sorts.'

'Sounds suspiciously like hippy bullshit to me.'

'Maybe. But it also fits with what little evidence I do have: the nude sketches of Roze; the painting from them that never happened – which was probably the canvas I found half-destroyed in the painting room, I think; the drinking . . .' I took a deep breath. 'I think you genuinely did try to clean yourself up. It's like what you said about Sandra – how you got excited about her partly because you thought that, with her, things would be different. But they weren't. Same old same old. I think something similar happened with Ruensa – I think you genuinely fell in love with her, before suspicion and paranoia started to eat away at you. I doubt you ever told her about the *usufructo*, though – I think you let her assume the house was yours, rather than confess that the money she was putting into it was effectively being thrown away. Then, at some point, after you were married and drinking again, you made a pass at her daughter. Perhaps it was because you'd told yourself Roze was going to be your muse, or some such bullshit. Or perhaps it was just because you're a vain old bastard who's always done exactly as he pleased. You'd always had open marriages, after all. I even think that text you sent Jess was probably meant for Roze, not her mother. *If you will not be a WIFE to me . . .*

Not *my wife*, you see, just *a*. You'd probably convinced yourself it was all part of some rule-breaking bohemian polyamory that an artistic genius like you was actually entitled to. Anyway, she was having none of it, and you started drinking even more heavily – out of self-disgust, I'd like to think, but with you, who knows? And then it got to the end of the year – the crucial year that Ruensa needed to endure, to get residency on her own account – and you could feel whatever power you still had over them slipping away. That was when you realised you were about to lose them both, forever – that your appalling, toxic, uncontrolled behaviour had sabotaged any chance of happiness you might once have had. Instead, you faced a future of drinking yourself slowly to death.' I was silent a moment. 'I can relate to that.'

'All this talk about feelings,' my father scoffed. 'Such feeble Californian claptrap.'

'So you decided to hasten the process. You were never lacking in physical courage, I'll say that for you. You probably convinced yourself that they'd be better off without you, too – that we all would, that it was the only possible way of indicating the depth of your remorse.

'You knew how dangerous oleander is – of course you did, you've lived here more than thirty years. So you lit the bon-fire, mixed the paracetamol with your brandy, and – well, we know the rest. Roze and Runesa found you, but thought you were simply drunk. Then, after you died and the police started asking questions, they decided to keep quiet about the breakdown in the marriage, in case the police thought it was murder and they got deported.'

'If this is true,' he said, 'and I'm not saying it is, what does it mean for you?'

I didn't answer him for a long time, and when I eventually looked up, he was gone. But I spoke the words anyway – spoke them into the emptiness of Finca Síquia.

'That's what I'm still trying to work out.'

JESS

I was initially alerted to my brother's death by my lawyer, Tomàs Bellot, who in turn had been contacted by Finn's wife. She had returned to Finca Síquia after a long period on the mainland, she told him tearfully, only to find the house empty and Finn's body lying beside the remains of a bonfire – a bonfire, as it turned out, of oleander branches. A brandy bottle was found nearby which contained traces of crushed paracetamol. The parallels with my father's death had been immediately apparent to the police, and a full investigation was already under way.

The death, the medical examiner established, had taken place about a week before the body was found, a period for which Finn's wife and mother-in-law had cast-iron alibis – they were in Madrid, finalising Roze's residency with Spain's cumbersome bureaucracy, and had been in a number of meetings with officials from the Officina de Extranjería, the department of immigration. Together with a lengthy document found on Finn's laptop – a laptop from which he had removed the password shortly before his death, implying that he wanted it to be found – that was enough for the coroner to decide he must have taken his own life. It is, apparently, well established that the risk of suicide more than triples in the months after a traumatic brain injury; paranoia, depression and impulsive but poor decision-making are also common side effects. A simultaneous reinvestigation into the circumstances of my father's death was also opened by the police, but eventually closed again for lack of evidence.

The post-mortem and investigation delayed the funeral by over a month, and it was late October before I finally flew out to Mallorca for the service. By then, I had read my brother's document – the police had sent it to me, along with a request for my comments. I told them what I thought of it, which may have helped to satisfy them that no foul play was involved.

The day after the funeral, Tomàs and I had a meeting, over lunch at Finca Síquia, with Roze and her mother. I had, of course, gone back to the house once already, on my ill-fated attempt to warn Roze that marrying Finn might not be a good idea – at least, not without knowing much more about him. So I'd glimpsed some of the improvements then, although I had been in too much of an emotional state to really take them in. Despite his attempts to paint me in his memoir as a cold-hearted gold-digger, flying to Mallorca that time had been a decision I'd genuinely grappled with, my residual loyalty to my brother conflicting with the certain knowledge that the marriage could only be a disaster for them both; and, of course, I'd been furious with him for trying to cut me out of my inheritance and for blocking me from his phone. It was only on this second trip, therefore, that I was really able to take in just how beautiful they'd made the place. My father's eye, Ruensa's flair and Roze's appetite for hard work had made the finca highly covetable, and – as an assessment by an independent valuer had already established – extremely saleable.

Under Spanish laws regarding intestacy, Roze had automatically inherited Finn's half of the freehold – the 'will' he had left with Tomàs turning out to be, as his memoir had suggested, just a series of wild accusations that she was going to murder him, a possibility the police had already considered and ruled out. Based on his account of how much Roze and Ruensa loved the finca, and that business idea he had become so attached to, I had expected the negotiation over exactly how much she and her mother should be paid in recompense for giving up their portion to be a long and arduous one. Tomàs, too, had warned me it might be difficult: 'Their lawyer's smart, but slippery as hell,' were his exact words. So it had been a pleasant surprise when it actually turned out to be both brisk and reasonable – they hadn't been a pushover, Tomàs reported, far from it, but they had named a fair price and then stuck to it, and by the time we met up, the deal simply required our signatures. That could probably also have been done via our lawyers, but by then I was curious to have a proper conversation with the women whose motives and behaviour my brother had found it so hard to get a fix on.

We had lunch at the tiled table on the veranda that featured so heavily in Finn's account of his summer at the finca. There was still enough warmth in the sun for it to be pleasant outside, particularly after England, but the breeze blowing down the side of Puig de Galatzó definitely had a bite to it, and the food Ruensa served was autumnal – pork casserole with pumpkin pisto, and a large ensaimada for dessert.

We talked about Finn for a while, and then – because there was so much that was better left unsaid – fell silent; I suspect that was partly because they didn't want to put me in the awkward position, as his sister, of having to either defend or condemn him.

'We should probably take care of the formalities,' Tomàs said at last. He produced an envelope. 'This is for you,' he said, handing it to Roze. 'And here are the receipts for you both to sign, saying that this is in full and fair payment of what you are owed. Ferid has looked them through, of course.'

'Of course,' Roze said. 'Do you have a pen?'

I watched as they signed. When Tomàs had checked the signatures and date, I said, 'Thank you. Despite the sad circumstances, it's been a pleasure doing business with you both.'

'We feel the same way.' Roze hesitated. 'And I wanted to thank you, too, for coming out here that time, to warn me. It might not have seemed that way at the time, but I really was grateful.'

I nodded. 'Will you tell me one thing?'

She shrugged. 'Of course. If I can.'

'When you came here and found Finn's body – why had you come back? You didn't need to, after all – you had your residency; you could just have got your lawyer to tell him you were divorcing him. Was it because you felt you owed it to him to say it face to face? Or because it would have given you pleasure to tell him that you weren't in his power anymore?'

Even as I spoke, it occurred to me that there was a third possibility: that it was her friend and confidante, Ferid, who had laced Finn's brandy bottle with toxins, and that she had come back to check that the job she had begun on the mountainside that day really was finished. But I dismissed that as overly fanciful, and certainly not a speculation that it would be helpful to voice out loud just then.

Roze thought for a moment. 'No, neither of those.'

'What, then?'

There was a long silence. 'I . . . liked him. Not the way he liked me, obviously, but enough . . . There had been some good times, along the way. And the business plan . . . We really could have made a go of it, if he'd only been prepared to change.' She shrugged. 'Perhaps he could never have changed that much. But his father managed to – for a time, at least. And I suppose I wanted to give him the chance to say sorry.'

I nodded. 'Will you stay in Mallorca?'

She shook her head. 'We'll start an agroturismo, but somewhere cheaper. The Sierra Nevada, perhaps.' She paused. 'We'll miss him, though. Your father, too.'

I have reflected on those words of hers many times since then, wondering what they tell us about Finn's account and its accuracy. I'd told the police his document was paranoid nonsense, of course – by his own admission, when he came to write it, his head injury was still colouring his recollection of events, let alone his interpretation of them. The only thing it seemed to prove was just how toxic, unhealthy and downright dangerous his own attitude to women had become – a hard discovery for any sister to make about her brother, even if the warning signs had always been there – while the obsessive way he analysed and reanalysed every last gesture or remark that Roze and Ruensa ever made bordered on insanity. But Roze . . . Did she simply think it was easiest to stick to the same story she'd been telling all along? Was it tact, to soften any sisterly grief I might be feeling? Or was she even quietly proud of being Finn's nemesis, and bringing a kind of restitution to the many women over the years whose lives he had affected, not least poor Sophia? To this day, I still can't tell.

People of my generation are sometimes mocked for talking about 'my truth' rather than 'the truth' – an easy habit to criticise, but one which accepts, perhaps, that, in a world where so many different versions of the facts are constantly available, what matters is not so much what actually happened as who one chooses to believe. And that, I suppose, is what one is left with regarding the events at Finca Síquia, now that the house itself is sold and the players dispersed or dead: a choice of narratives, a judgement about character, and – to use Tomàs's phrase – *una zona d'ombres*, a place of shadows. Was Roze a master manipulator, or simply the object of my brother's twisted obsession? It is, quite frankly, a judgement that I do not feel qualified to make. I am simply happy that justice has been done, and content not to speculate too much about the details.

AUTHOR'S NOTE

The New Wife had an unusual gestation. Five years ago, I was discussing with my then US editor, Kate Miciak, the thematic similarities between my book *The Girl Before* and *Rebecca*, by Daphne du Maurier, a writer I've always admired. '*Rebecca*'s a great book,' Kate said. 'But I prefer *My Cousin Rachel*. It's more modern.'

Intrigued by her comment, I went back and reread *My Cousin Rachel* to see what she meant. What I'd taken, when I first devoured it as a teenager, to be a straightforward story of a young man's infatuation with a *femme fatale* was actually anything but. Despite playing with all the conventions of noir fiction, the book was really a subtly drawn portrait of what we might now call toxic masculinity, all the more remarkable for the fact that du Maurier wrote it in a first-person male voice, something that was never remarked on in contemporary reviews but which today would seem brave, almost transgressive. I began to wonder what a great-great-grandchild of *My Cousin Rachel* would look like: a story about inheritance, yes, but also assumption, doubt, obsession; a game of cat-and-mouse in which one is never quite sure who is the cat; or, indeed, whether it really wants to eat the mouse, or if it's actually the other way round . . .

I started playing with some ideas, and wrote a few chapters, but then lockdown happened, and, like many other writers I know, writing anything at all suddenly seemed impossible. I busied myself with the screen adaptation of *The Girl Before* – which was filmed in the partial lockdown of 2021 – then with writing *My Darling Daughter*. It was only after that was completed that I returned to the first chapters of what was to become *The New Wife*.

Du Maurier always maintained that she'd never decided whether Rachel was innocent or duplicitous, the better to keep the ambiguity unresolved in her readers' minds. I tried to do the same with my own lead character, but now, having lived with Roze for so long, I do have a pretty strong feeling about her – a feeling that I won't be sharing with my own readers: this is a story where, as Jess says, the final judgement is left to you. In a way, that seems to me to be the most modern thing of all about du Maurier's novel: it's a narrative about competing truths, prejudice, and uncertainty, and about how we decide who and what we believe. Today, social media has made spin doctors of us all, and often, facts become weapons, to be deployed in support of judgements already made on instinct or tribal grounds. Roze and Rachel are, of course, very different characters, in very different circumstances, but I always loved that sense of ambivalence in du Maurier's creation. Every statement Finn makes about Roze is actually a statement about himself.

Many people helped me with this book. I'd especially like to thank my agents, Caradoc King and Millie Hoskins, both for their initial critique and for their enthusiasm about the reworked pages; Tina Sederholm, for being a great early reader; my publishers, Stef Bierwerth and Jon Butler, for being so open to what might have seemed like a very strange idea, pitched over a memorable publication lunch; Stef again, for her excellent editorial contributions; Mar Janer Campos, for correcting my Mallorquí (any remaining errors are, of course, my own); and my wife, Sara, for acting as my driver on what must surely be the most terrifying coastal road in Europe – and for so much else besides.